"What Are You Going To Make Me Say, Lannie?

"Nothing," she murmured. Then she continued recklessly: "Only I wish things were different between us."

"I do, too," he said almost bitterly, "but they never will be. The sooner we accept our relationship for what it is, the happier we'll be."

"And what is our relationship, exactly?"

"It's very simple, really," he replied, his voice masking his emotions. "We need each other in a very basic way. I want you, and I intend to have you."

ANN MAJOR
is not only a successful author, but she also manages a business and runs a busy household with three small children. Among her many interests, she lists traveling and playing the piano—her favorite composer, quite naturally, is the romantic Chopin.

Dear Reader,

Silhouette Special Editions are an exciting new line of contemporary romances from Silhouette Books. Special Editions are written specifically for our readers who want a story with heightened romantic tension.

Special Editions have all the elements you've enjoyed in Silhouette Romances and *more*. These stories concentrate on romance in a longer, more realistic and sophisticated way, and they feature greater sensual detail.

I hope you enjoy this book and all the wonderful romances from Silhouette. We welcome any suggestions or comments and invite you to write to us at the address below.

Karen Solem
Editor-in-Chief
Silhouette Books
P.O. Box 769
New York, N. Y. 10019

ANN MAJOR
Brand of Diamonds

Silhouette Special Edition
Published by Silhouette Books New York

America's Publisher of Contemporary Romance

Other Silhouette Books by Ann Major

Wild Lady
A Touch of Fire
Dream Come True
Meant to Be

SILHOUETTE BOOKS, a Simon & Schuster Division of
GULF & WESTERN CORPORATION
1230 Avenue of the Americas, New York, N.Y. 10020

Copyright © 1983 by Ann Major

Distributed by Pocket Books

ISBN: 0-671-53583-8

First Silhouette Books printing March, 1983

10 9 8 7 6 5 4 3 2 1

Map by Ray Lundgren

America's Publisher of Contemporary Romance

Printed in the U.S.A.

Brand of
Diamonds

LOUISIANA

Places in _italics_ are fictitious.

ARKANSAS

MISSISSIPPI RIVER

LOUISIANA

MISSISSIPPI

TEXAS

SABINE RIVER

PEARL RIVER

Baton Rouge

Lake Pontchartrain

Gallier's Landing

New Orleans

N
W E
S

Delta of the Mississippi

GULF OF MEXICO

Chapter One

$\mathcal{A}$ cool October breeze gusted across the brown expanse of the Mississippi River and stirred the fringes of Spanish moss that dripped from the gnarled live oaks beside Gallier's Landing. Beneath the oaks a beautiful woman in tightly fitting jeans and a blue turtleneck lazed with her eyes blindfolded while a thirteen-year-old child fished beside her.

Lannie lay drowsily across the coarse planking, enjoying a moment of relaxation after an unusually arduous day in her eighth grade classroom. From behind her she heard Denise's reel spin as Denise cast again. There was a satisfied giggle as the cork hit the water.

Though no one called Lannie by it, Solange Gallier was her full name, and except for her unusual coloring she was as Louisiana-Creole as her name. Her rich black hair fell about her shoulders framing the delicate oval of her face with its soft, lustrous beauty. Slanting dark brows above dark brown eyes gave her an almost

7

exotic appearance. She considered her eyes too large and her lips, which were curving and sensuous, too wide. She would have preferred a pale, Southern-belle complexion like her cousin Velvet's to the rich, olive tones of her own smooth skin. But whatever the imperfection of each feature taken alone, together they blended harmoniously into an arresting whole.

A mosquito buzzed and Lannie slapped at it, missing. She heard nearby branches sigh before the wind touched her cheeks. In the distance the engine of a tug purred. The pungent odor of the sulfur fumes from nearby Brandon Chemicals mingled with other indefinable swamp scents.

Sounds and smells—and darkness. Lannie fingered the navy silk scarf wound tightly around her eyes as a blindfold. This was what it was like for Denise—always. For her it was not possible to rip away the blindfold that concealed the brilliant collage of fall colors, the sweeping expanse of cobalt-blue sky. This was Denise's world.

Of course Lannie knew better than most what it was like not to see; six years before she herself had been blinded for ten months after a car accident. It had been Denise and her unique brand of courage who'd pulled her from the depths of self-pity and despair. They'd met in the hospital. Denise's bright seven-year-old voice had piped through the veil of darkness and touched Lannie's heart. At the time Denise had been recovering from the hit-and-run accident that had left her blind.

It had been a slow process, but Denise had shown Lannie the way to a new life. Before her accident, Lannie had been quite a different person than she was now. In fact Lannie was not at all proud of her past life. *And now,* Lanny thought idly, *it is my turn to help Denise.*

Lannie's thoughts were suddenly interrupted. It was

the oddest of sensations—a strange warmth tracing lightly down the length of her spine causing her drowsiness of a moment before to vanish completely. There was a tingling in the pit of her stomach. Lannie sat up on the coarse plank landing and was instantly alert. Was someone that she could not see because she was blindfolded watching her? The feeling was uncanny, and involuntarily she shivered. The sensation was all the more inexplicable because it was familiar to Lannie.

In her other lifetime—seven years before to be exact—one man had produced that rippling warmth every time he looked at her, every time he touched her. But that man and that time were far away. The instant that Lannie's thoughts touched on Mark Brandon, she tried to banish him from her mind. Nervously she rolled the diamond engagement ring around on her finger as though to remind herself that now another man claimed her love. But as always the memory of Brandon lingered.

She felt strangely excited. Her love affair with Brandon had ended disastrously years before. And she was glad. If the flame of her love for John lacked the intense bright heat of her old love, at least it was sure and steady.

Lannie's fingers pushed against the navy silk scarf covering her eyes and removed it. Quickly she stood up and looked around. Her firm high breasts jutted against her blue sweater; the luscious curve of her hips encased in tight jeans was enticing. Her burnished hair fell about her shoulders in wild disarray. She almost expected to see Brandon step from the dense forest, and when she did not, her heart fluttered jerkily.

Lavender skies, fading colors. The woods surrounding Lannie and Denise were thick and deep, and someone could be watching them even now. It would be dark before too much longer.

"Anything wrong, Lannie?" Denise asked.

"I was just looking. . . ."

"Ah, ha! You cheated!" Denise cried with childlike glee. "You owe me that ice cream cone!"

"I'll know you're truly grown up, Denise, when you lose your enthusiasm for ice cream cones." Lannie sighed. "I never can seem to leave that blindfold on for a whole hour any more."

Denise expertly fingered her special wristwatch that had been a birthday gift from Lannie. "You made it twenty-five minutes tonight."

"Not too good."

"I don't blame you. If I could see again, I wouldn't ever—not for one minute—not look at everything. Why, I'd even sleep with my eyes open."

"Sometimes I need to remind myself what it's like for you, Denise. That's why I like to play our game."

Denise cocked her head to one side. Her black pigtails bobbed. "Someone's at the Sugar Castle. He was in the woods watching us a minute ago."

The Sugar Castle was what Denise called The Shadows, a vast, ruined plantation house that stood between Lannie's own Belle Rose and the more fabulous Brandon House. The Sugar Castle crowned a small rise just beyond the levee.

"What? How do you know?" Lannie's tone was faintly anxious.

"Different sounds," Denise returned calmly. "The birds got quiet for a while when he was in the woods."

"Why didn't you tell me?"

"Because I thought you might make us go home before I catch this old stinker that keeps stealing my worms. And I could tell by the night smells, it's getting dark."

"It is getting late, and John's coming to dinner. But you keep on fishing a minute or two longer. I think I'd better go check and see who's up there. You'll be all right by yourself, won't you?"

"Sure. I'm going to catch this old boy and Mom and Hilary can cook him for dinner."

"Good girl!"

As Lannie trudged over the levee a tumble-down fence overgrown with creepers came into view, and she turned down the lane that wound to Sugar Castle.

Lannie was more curious than worried about who might have been watching them. Nothing ominous ever happened in the rural section of Louisiana where she lived.

It was with some difficulty that she struggled through the tangled overgrowth. The English garden that the original builder had planted over a century before had grown to gigantic proportions. Palms and camphor trees, oriental exotica, gigantic azaleas and camellias all grew in a tangled maze, strangling one another for the occasional rays of light that filtered into the dim green gloom.

From the branches of live oaks and sweet gum trees hung huge wild vines, some of them as thick as Lannie's own forearms. Lannie's sandals crunched into the hundreds of rough little brown gumballs and pine cones that lay scattered about on the ground. There was a lushness, a tropical overgrowth that was indigenous only to Louisiana.

When Lannie reached the Sugar Castle she slowed her pace for a moment and looked around. No one was in sight. Beyond the Sugar Castle she saw the enormous white sprawl of Brandon Chemicals Inc., its smokestacks belching furious white tufts of steam into the blue haze. It seemed to her that every year the enormous plant encroached even further on the old estate. Once the Sugar Castle had belonged to her own family. Now, like so much of the property in the neighboring vicinity, it was Brandon property.

Lannie's eyes ran sadly over the magnificent ruins of the Sugar Castle. Every year destruction loomed a little closer, the inevitable total decay a little nearer. And somehow as always the melancholy of the house imparted itself to her.

Lannie had been coming to The Shadows ever since her childhood, and though she loved the peaceful, brooding solitude, she was always depressed by the sight of the old house. It had come to signify what could very easily happen to Belle Rose, her own home, and other old plantation houses that stood along the river road.

One by one they were gradually disappearing. Some had been lost to fire, others to the river which could change its course in a night, still others to neglect.

Lannie marched resolutely up the crumbling brick stairs in search of whoever might be there.

Once the house had been a fifty-room palace, and its owners princes of the land. Against the soft-pink plaster walls that were still whole in places, delicate filigree shadows danced. Armies of vines attacked in other places, sending tough roots through even the tiniest cracks.

The veranda was still almost whole as it had been constructed of giant cypress trees which were almost immune to rot. As she paused at the gaping door to adjust her vision to the dim light an owl, startled from its nap, hooted as it swooshed past her. Lannie shrieked once and then again and threw her hands in front of her face for protection. Next she thought she felt the flap of a bat's wing against her hair.

As her eyes ran over the plaster medallions on the ceiling of what must have once been a ballroom, she no longer saw the ruin. Instead her imagination painted a magnificent tableau. Brilliantly lit chandeliers hung beneath the medallions. Lannie could almost hear the swish of a silken dress on the curving stairway that had once been dustless. The ballroom was filled with music and soft laughter as Southern belles smiled up into the eyes of their dashing parish swains.

And then the war had come, and with it the collapse of the sugar market.

Lannie was deeply sensitive about the old houses; she cherished a deep determination to save her own.

Sure that the house was as empty as always, she stepped out through the back door, and a green lizard skittered in front of her sandle.

If only she had the money to save the Sugar Castle from its final hour of destruction, but it was almost more than she could do to keep her own Belle Rose up. Thankfully Belle Rose was not nearly so large, so her project, while difficult, was more feasible.

The whir of disturbed wildlife flapping in the garden was the first signal of the man's approach. Lannie was about to descend the stairs when she heard the slam of a car door.

In one paralyzing second she froze, the blood draining from her face. The moment of suspended time seemed to go on and on as she stared mesmerized at the tall, lithe figure alighting from the silvery Mercedes. Then she drew a deep, gasping breath as Mark Brandon stepped into her view. An aura of vital maleness emanated from him.

At the sight of him, Lannie crept back into the long shadows of the veranda. Her pulse was racing with apprehension, and she felt the familiar curling in the pit of her stomach that the mere sight of him could produce even though her heart was filled with dread. The last thing she wanted was to see him! She hated him! And she knew that if he could, he would destroy her.

What was he doing here? Not that he didn't have the right—he owned the place, after all! But for years he had lived in New York where the headquarters of his many businesses were, and she had expected him to go on living in New York. Suddenly she realized how much she'd counted on him doing so.

Brandon strode briskly around the car. In spite of the danger Lannie could not prevent herself from drinking in every detail of his appearance. His ink-black hair shone in the setting gold of the sun. His skin was deeply tanned, the harsh planes of his face were as boldly masculine as ever.

He wore no coat. She remembered how he hated coats. A cream-colored, striped, long-sleeved shirt stretched across the taut muscular expanse of his chest. At his neck was a tie, undoubtably a fine Italian *peau de soie* in wider stripes of navy, camel and taupe. Navy slacks molded his lean hips and thighs.

A white smile slashed his darkly handsome features as he bent his black head to speak to the woman inside the car.

For the first time Lannie registered that he was not alone. Though she felt like a spy, she could not tear her gaze away. A stray breeze gusted across the meadow and rumpled his thick, heavy hair.

Lannie recognized the regal tilt of Genevieve's silver head inside the gray Mercedes. Brandon's grandmother. What was Genevieve doing back in Louisiana? What did it mean?

Lannie didn't dare remain a minute longer for fear of being discovered. Even now Brandon was telling his grandmother to wait for him while he took a look around the house. No doubt he'd heard her own scream when the owl had startled her.

Lannie tiptoed back to the stairs and carefully made her way down them before she darted across the meadow toward the copse of pine to the levee where she'd left Denise.

Five minutes later she saw the glint of silver on the road, and she realized that Brandon had abandoned his search of the house and that, for the moment, she was safe.

Had he been in the forest watching her earlier? A shiver of apprehension raced through her. Brandon's return could mean nothing but trouble.

A large splash from the landing arrested her attention. "Denise!" Suddenly Lannie was flying over the levee. Fear for Denise lashed through her. She should never have left her for so long.

"I'm all right," Denise responded, although her voice was tight with impatience as she floundered in the waist-deep water.

The line of her dainty little mouth was pursed with frustration. The expression was all too familiar to Lannie, and she had to fight back an urge to help Denise as her tiny hands fumbled over a low branch that hung over the water. She was searching for her fishing line that had snagged.

Several minutes passed. Lannie gave a silent prayer of relief when she saw Denise's hand close over the line.

"There!" Denise cried triumphantly, freeing her line and tossing Lannie one of her brilliant smiles.

"Let me help you get back up," Lannie said, extending a hand to Denise. "Move toward me and you'll feel my hand."

Dripping like a wet rag, Denise clambered onto the dock. She was shivering and her teeth were chattering, but she was too thrilled over having managed to free her own line to care.

"Go ahead and reel it in, Denise. We're going to have to save catching that big one for another day. It's almost dark, and when Sherry sees you, I'm going to have a lot of tall explaining to do."

"Lannie, Lannie! He's still on the line." Her face alight with pleasure, Denise reeled in an enormous bass.

The fish slapped against the dock, and Denise, determined to remove the hook from his mouth herself, reached downward. But her hands never reached the hook, for Lannie was pulling the child into her arms and hugging her fiercely.

"You're something else, you know that, don't you?" Lannie murmured. Tears of joy streamed down her cheeks.

Denise gently brushed the tears away, and said softly, "Don't cry, Lannie. Don't ever cry."

Brandon and what he might do was temporarily forgotten, and Lannie savored a precious moment with this child she loved so deeply. Denise, who constantly faced the challenge of her handicap with enthusiasm; Denise, who struggled against incredible odds to lead a normal life had been the one person who'd shown her how to live. Lannie owed her so much, and it was a debt she was determined to repay.

Brandon was not easily forgotten once Lannie returned to Belle Rose. His presence could only mean disaster. Of one thing she was certain, Brandon would not be in favor of her engagement to his stepbrother, John. Though the two men had never been close, long ago Brandon had forbidden her to have anything to do with his family. But it had hardly been her fault when John, overriding all her protests, had started asking her out six months before.

When John had slipped his ring on her finger only a few short days before, she'd begged him to keep their engagement secret for a while. She'd felt she'd needed more time before the world knew their intentions. But John had only laughed at her. And now Brandon was back in Louisiana. She was sure that it was no coincidence.

That night as she went down to dinner with a bright

smile pasted on her wan features, she felt that her new life that she'd worked so hard for, that she prized so dearly was coming to an end.

"Brandon, please," she whispered in the hushed emptiness of the ballroom, "don't, please, don't ruin everything!"

Chapter Two

*H*er lime-green napkin fluttering in her hand, Lannie's heels tapped faintly across gleaming parquet floors as she rushed toward the phone. Her diamond engagement ring twinkled on the slender hand that lifted the receiver abruptly in the middle of its third ring.

"Hello," she murmured almost dreamily into the receiver. The glass of white wine she'd sipped had gone to her head, and John had just paid her an outrageous compliment.

"Hello . . ." The masculine greeting was like a husky caress. Instantly all dreaminess was washed from Lannie's face. Her dark eyes shone with an almost feverish brightness, and her olive skin went unnaturally pale.

The man's voice was smooth and deeply melodious with only the faintest lingering trace of a Southern drawl. Yet the unexpected sound of it jarred through Lannie's nervous system, and she felt doomed. Though she hadn't heard his voice in almost seven years, she immediately recognized it as belonging to Mark Brandon. So he had come back because of her!

Lannie had fought hard to put the past behind her, to forget the old ways, to become a new person . . . and, most of all, to forget *him*. She was a teacher now, no longer the glamour girl he'd once known. She was fighting valiantly to save her plantation home.

The faint creaking of the antique chair as it received her weight told her that her legs had buckled and she was now sitting down.

Because of the hushed stillness of the library, other sounds drifted through the open windows and doors to Lannie's ears—the tinkling of crystal and silver and Hilary's pleasant, earthy laughter from the dining room, the awkward strains of Ralph's latest composition as he banged enthusiastically on his piano in the *garçonnière* where a rapt Denise was doubtlessly listening. Ordinarily Lannie would have said a silent prayer of thanks that she'd had the foresight to establish Ralph and his piano so far from the big house and her other boarders. But tonight Brandon washed her thoughts clean of everything except her achingly painful awareness of him.

The voice, faintly impatient, continued, "I'd like to speak to John Tibodeaux, please. I'm in a hurry."

She longed to cry out, "He's not here!" But what would that accomplish? "Y-yes . . . of course," she stammered. "I'll get him."

"Lannie, is that you?"

Just the way he said her name did something to her. She squeezed her eyes tightly shut against the darkly handsome, rough-cut visage she remembered so well in spite of all her attempts to forget him.

More grimly, Brandon persisted. "Lannie?"

Involuntarily she shuddered at the menace in his cold

tone, and she could not trust herself to speak. Setting the phone down on the library table, she walked heavily toward the dining room.

Beneath the golden glow of the chandelier the three people Lannie loved most in the world were laughing—Hilary, the slim, earthy poetess who looked like a silver-haired flower child who hadn't realized yet that she should have grown up; Sherry, Denise's mother, whose simple, soft brown beauty betrayed her Cajun ancestry; and John, the overlarge, rumpled sandy bear Lannie was engaged to. As usual John's plate was piled high with Cajun delicacies. He was leaning across the table to refill Hilary's goblet with jewel-red wine. Sherry, her brown eyes shining, was animatedly retelling them a favorite Cajun joke about the fertile nutria which inhabited the swamps.

If only she didn't have to tell John that Brandon was on the phone, Lannie thought desperately. Then maybe everything could stay as it was.

John rose to pull out Lannie's chair. His tumbled, sandy hair fell untidily across his freckled brow. His broad, kind face was beaming. "Don't tell me I'm going to have to deliver Tu Tu Brousard's baby before I've gotten a chance to eat!"

"It's . . . Brandon," Lannie replied dully.

"Well, that's a relief!" John was pushing back his own chair. "I wrote him last week to see if he could be my best man, and would you believe it, he said he'd make a special trip home to congratulate me. That's incredible—Brandon finding time for something personal."

Not incredible if one knew the whole story. When she spoke her voice shook slightly. "You wrote him? You didn't tell me," Lannie said defensively.

"I'm sorry, honey. I must've forgotten to mention it, but he's my stepbrother even if we don't see each other very often. Who did you think I'd want as my best man?"

"I hadn't really given it any thought," she replied weakly.

John had a habit of forgetting to tell her things. Lannie had always found it amusing before.

If only he'd told her he was planning to ask Brandon to be in their wedding, she might have thought of some way to prevent it.

Though Lannie strained to hear the low, distant tones of John's voice as he spoke to Brandon, she could make out nothing of their conversation, and her anxiety built with the passing of each minute. What was she going to do?

There was only one thing she could do. She had to tell John everything about her past . . . everything about Brandon . . . before Brandon did.

It wasn't as though Lannie hadn't tried. But in the beginning of their relationship when she'd attempted to explain, John had silenced her, saying, "Honey, no woman reaches the age of twenty-six without having loved a man. I have a past and so do you. But what you did before has no bearing on our relationship. . . . I don't want to know about another man."

Especially not if the other man was his own step-brother, Lannie had thought dismally.

John lumbered dejectedly back to the table and reached for his rumpled blue, seersucker jacket that hung crookedly on the back of his chair. "I'm afraid you all are going to have to excuse me." His blue eyes went regretfully to his bowl of steaming crawfish bisque and heaping plate of spicy butterfly shrimp. "Brandon wants me to drive into Baton Rouge with him on business."

"Can't you eat first?" Hilary queried, crunching into a shrimp.

"No . . . Brandon wants me to come right now."

"So Brandon's really here in Louisiana?" Lannie squeaked aloud, truly comprehending for the first time what her eyes had told her earlier.

"Apparently so, though I haven't had a chance to see him yet. It sounds like he plans to stay for a while. Genevieve is with him, and he said he's going to keep the house open this winter."

Brandon was planning to stay for a while! Inside Lannie felt she was coming to pieces. The palm she inserted into John's large hand was cold with perspiration. But somehow she managed to lead John to the door as though nothing were the matter.

Outside the damp night air was cool with the hint of autumn. The tangy scent of the *batture* and the marshes blended with the sweet night smell of the tall lush sugarcane. In the distance a tugboat's foghorn sounded across the broadly rolling waters of the Mississippi. Silver rays of moonlight slanted through the spreading branches of towering live oak and pecan trees.

Now! She had to tell him, now before he saw Brandon!

John was pulling her into the deep shadows of the veranda and taking her into his arms. His sandy head descended to claim a perfunctory, good-night peck when she stopped him with the softest whisper.

"John, there's something I have to tell you. . . ." Twisting out of his arms, she glided to the wrought-iron balustrade that edged the veranda. A shower of moonlight fell about her, making her cream-colored silk skirt glisten.

"I'll call you from the house . . . as soon as I get back," he said agreeably, briskly descending the swirling staircase. "We can't talk now. Brandon . . ."

Just his name, and she was trembling. Already he was coming between herself and John.

She whirled jerkily. "I-I need to tell you now," Lannie insisted, "before . . ."

He paused. "You sound . . . almost desperate. . . ."

"That's exactly how I feel," she admitted gloomily, clasping her hands together to control their tremor.

"Honey, what is it?" She felt the vibration of his tread as he reluctantly moved back up the stairs toward her. When she felt the warmth of his hands on her shoulders, she almost flinched.

"Suppose you were to find out that I'm not the woman you think I am? Suppose that once I did something that would make you ashamed to be marrying me. . . ."

"That's not possible. You're the dearest, kindest—"

"I'm not!" Her low voice rippled with irritation now, in sharp contrast to his own mild mood. "You never let me tell you about . . ."

"Oh, yes, about that shady past of yours you're always so ready to confess." He laughed easily against her ear. "Why is it people who are eager to confess never have anything really bad on their consciences? What did you do—fail to bake cookies for some sick neighbor?"

"John, I'm serious," she continued, her voice sharpening. "You never listen to me when I try to tell you something that's important to me."

"Honey, I know you. We grew up together." He pulled her against him, failing to notice how wooden she was in his arms. She would have spoken again, but the gentle pressure of his lips on hers silenced her. "You're much too fine to have ever done anything wrong," he said at last, releasing her. There was finality in his tone.

His words, his faith in her, should have made her feel good, but they had the opposite effect. She was seething with frustration as she always was when he wouldn't listen.

"Sometimes it's impossible to talk to you, John," she snapped. "You think you already know everything."

He brushed aside her ill humor. "I'm a doctor, honey," he whispered. "We doctors already know it all." The humor of the familiar joke between them was lost on her. Instead of laughing lightly, she stared out into the lush darkness and fumed with bottled-up frustration.

She was about to try another tack in an effort to communicate with John when her sentence was cut off by Hilary, who burst through the front door holding a foil package that was as bright and shiny as her own face beaming up at John.

Usually Lannie appreciated Hilary's unfailing thoughtfulness where John was concerned, but tonight it only further irritated her.

John's hands dropped away from Lannie's shoulders as he turned to regard the woman silhouetted in the doorway with real interest. Gone was his usual absent mildness, and Lannie observed Hilary more intently herself in an attempt to fathom this change in John. But Hilary was no different than usual. An unfashionably long, unpressed, Indian-print skirt swirled around Hilary's shapely body. Her long silver hair glowed in the soft light of the parlor lamp.

"Why, Hilary, I sure do appreciate this," John responded with genuine warmth, carefully taking the package from her as though it were a rare treasure. "That was very thoughtful of you."

"Yes, Hilary, it certainly was," Lannie mouthed tonelessly, her own mood blackening as she realized the opportunity to tell John about her past had once again eluded her.

Hilary, her face radiant, and Lannie, her own expression one of brooding frustration, watched silently as, package in hand, John leapt down the stairs two at a time and then disappeared into the thick blackness in the direction of his green Volkswagen.

When they returned to the dinner table, conversation flowed on all sides of Lannie, but it was a blurred sound. She caught only snatches of it. Her mind was whirling in turmoil as she desperately tried to think of a way to save herself.

"Lannie . . . Lannie!" Sherry was gently shaking her. "You haven't heard a word we've been saying, you! Is something wrong? You're as white as a sheet! I hope I didn't upset you earlier when I said I thought you should be more careful with Denise." Sherry's soft, faintly accented voice was filled with concern as she broke into Lannie's tumbling thoughts.

Lannie's fork slipped through her trembling fingers and clattered as it hit her untouched china plate. "N-no . . ." she murmured distractedly, thankful that the crystal chandelier only dimly lit the vast dining room. Then more firmly, she continued. "I'm fine. What makes you ask?" Carefully Lannie tried to compose her lovely features into what she hoped was a serene expression. Inside her heart was thumping wildly.

"Ever since John was called out you haven't been yourself, you, " Sherry persisted on a different tack. "If you're going to marry a country doctor, you'll have to get used to—"

"Naturally I was disappointed he couldn't stay, especially when you and Hilary went to so much trouble to cook all this. . . ." Even to Lannie's own ears her voice sounded hollow.

Hilary, who was sitting at the opposite end of the table, carelessly brushed a long strand of pale hair behind her ear so it joined the blond tangle that cascaded down her back. She leaned toward Lannie. "Oh, I wouldn't worry about that. I gave him that shrimp and any leftovers will get eaten when he comes over the next time. Honestly, I think he's more in love with our refrigerator and my cooking than he is with you!" She laughed heartily before picking up another shrimp and biting into it.

"Hilary!" Sherry clucked her tongue in mock disapproval.

Only the faintest smile curved Lannie's own lips. It was a household joke the way John spent most of his evenings rummaging through the refrigerator.

The conversation was changed to another topic, and no one seemed to notice that Lannie did not participate. Lannie could not stop herself from thinking of Brandon and wondering what he was planning to do.

At last dinner was over, and because it was Sherry's night to do the dishes, Lannie could escape to be alone with her thoughts.

Lannie hurried up the gracefully swirling staircase to the landing and then down the wide central hallway to her room. She paced wildly around, her heels making hollow clicks like a tap dancer's on the wooden floor. She paused, chewing a nail until she chided herself to stop. She was much too restless to stay inside with thoughts of Brandon tearing at her peace of mind.

Quickly she unbuttoned her blouse while she simultaneously searched through her armoire for her jeans and emerald-green pullover. She pulled a small flashlight from her dresser drawer.

Then she burst from her room and back down the stairway. "I'm going to ride Sugar," she called toward the kitchen as she grabbed a carrot out of the refrigerator on the side porch. She didn't really care whether anyone heard her or not.

She ignored Hilary's "At this hour?" as she rushed out of the house. All her life Lannie had eased her tension on the backs of horses and tonight would not be the exception.

As Lannie approached the stable her bobbing flashlight triggered a wild neigh, and she let the light roam deliberately about the paddock. This was a nightly ritual.

"It's okay, girl. A little ol' light can't hurt a big girl like you." Lannie shone the light for a few more minutes until Sugar got used to it and calmed. Then she flicked it off.

The bridle and reins jingled faintly as Lannie removed them from the hook on the stable wall. Sugar whinnied softly at Lannie's approach, and then moved warily across the paddock toward her mistress. Though the carrot lying on Lannie's outstretched hand was inviting, the horse was careful to stay just out of reach. The thoroughbred bay mare was not unaccustomed to late-hour rides, but she enjoyed a game of hard-to-get before allowing herself to be caught.

"Not tonight, Sugar," Lannie whispered into the darkness. She knelt down, a signal to the mare that the game—before it had even begun—was over. Obediently Sugar came closer and nuzzled her head into Lannie's hand and chomped into the carrot. Lannie then slipped the bridle over her satiny head.

Deciding against a saddle because she felt so marvelously free when she rode bareback, Lannie guided Sugar over to the fence so that by climbing onto the lower rail she could mount more easily.

Her reddish brown ears laid back, Sugar pranced skittishly at the added weight. Lannie leaned forward to whisper soothingly, and the mare gentled. Then she stroked Sugar's neck.

Sugar represented one of the few extravagances Lannie had allowed herself in the last seven years. Three years ago, for a mere two thousand dollars she'd bought the horse from wealthy Hamlin Trajan, her own cousin Velvet's husband. Hamlin lived nearby and was a breeder of race horses. Though Sugar came from good bloodlines no jockey had ever been able to get much out of her. She'd been easily spooked by lights and unexpected noises. Twice she'd tangled herself up in the starting gate, and Hamlin had given up trying to make a racehorse of her.

"Haven't found a jockey yet who can relate to her," Hamlin had sighed dismally three summers past as he'd allowed Lannie to beat him down to a giveaway price.

It had taken those three years, but with Lannie's consistent gentleness, Sugar was much better. Even though she still occasionally shied at bright lights and sudden sounds, she could now be led up the ramp of a truck without lashing out.

Lannie was walking Sugar slowly to warm her up when Denise emerged from the *garçonnière,* her dark head cocked at an angle which signaled she was listening.

"It's me, honey," Lannie called, knowing only too well from her own painful experience how important it was to identify oneself immediately to the blind child. "On Sugar."

Denise tilted her head in the direction Lannie's voice had come from. Lannie had very carefully taught her to turn toward a person when she was spoken to for this helped seeing people to feel comfortable with her in spite of her handicap.

"Can I go with you?" Denise asked.

Lannie hesitated only briefly. She felt an intense need to be alone, but this was the first time Denise had ever offered to accept the challenge of attempting to ride a horse since her accident. Lannie knew that Sherry, who was very overprotective, would highly disapprove, especially since it was nighttime.

"I'm bareback."

"That's okay."

Lannie detected a quiver of doubt in the child's voice.

Quickly Lannie slid from Sugar's back, and led the mare toward Denise.

Denise, dressed impeccably in a soft-blue pants outfit, looked like a little doll with her black hair pulled neatly into two blue-ribboned pigtails. But the outfit was too immature for Denise. It was as though Sherry was determined to deny that her little girl was growing up.

Denise was holding out her hand, and she squealed with nervous, childish laughter when she felt Sugar snort warmly into it.

"That's her way of making friends with you, honey," Lannie said softly.

"I know . . . but it tickles."

Lannie gave the child and the horse several minutes to get acquainted. "Ready for me to give you a hand up?" Lannie asked after a while.

"I think so."

"What I want you to do is stand right where you are. Feel with your hands for my hands and then place your left foot in them. You need to grab for Sugar's mane and pull yourself onto her back."

Deftly Denise did exactly as she was told.

"I'm going to lead her around for a minute and let you get used to how it feels up there." A short time later Lannie swung up behind her small charge. "You're doing great, honey. Just great!"

Slowly Sugar plodded beneath the double alley of live oaks. Moss swayed eerily from low branches in the silvery moonlight.

"Where do you want to go?" Lannie asked." To the gate and then back again?

"No! I want to really go somewhere! Let's go down to Dr. John's."

The exuberant reply thudded through Lannie. That was where Brandon would be staying. That was the one place Lannie had intended to avoid.

"We can't go on the highway. Sugar doesn't like cars, honey, especially at night."

"We don't have to go on the highway. Why don't we take that old back way—you know, the one that goes past the Sugar Castle."

Carefully Lannie considered Denise's suggestion. Sherry wouldn't like it, but Sherry's overprotection was becoming more of a threat to her child than Denise's actual handicap. And Lannie's own desire to free Denise from Sherry's gentle domination had been the main reason she'd invited Sherry to live with her.

Oh, Lannie had given Sherry other reasons, and because Sherry was a divorcee and burdened with medical debts resulting from Denise's accident, she'd accepted. It wasn't charity. Lannie desperately needed the room and board that Sherry was able to pay.

After she'd left the hospital, Lannie had kept in touch with Sherry and Denise. Over the years she'd visited them, and when she'd regained her own sight, they had been the first she'd shared her news with. But Lannie had grown increasingly concerned about Denise as she witnessed Sherry's determination to protect Denise from everything. Denise was beginning to rebel, and Lannie had hoped that by bringing Denise to Belle Rose she could find a way to make Sherry see that Denise had to be allowed some freedom to make mistakes, to explore her world herself. If a toddler didn't take a few falls, he never learned to walk. So it was with a blind person. It was essential that Denise do things for herself if she were ever to be independent. How well Lannie knew that from her own experience.

Lannie's thoughts returned to the present as Sugar plodded beneath the trees. The twisting old dirt road they were going to take lay forgotten by most motorists, so there was little danger of traffic that might frighten Sugar. It was early, early enough for them to go and return long before Brandon and John would return from Baton Rouge, long before Sherry would have time to grow anxious.

"All right," Lannie agreed uncertainly and dug her heels into Sugar's sides.

Denise gasped as the horse eased into a trot. Her small body was rigid with tension, and she clutched Sugar's mane fiercely. But she managed a brave, "If only Mother could see me now . . ."

"We'd both be in trouble—for sure," Lannie said dryly, pulling against the reins so that Sugar slowed her pace. Fleetingly she realized that no matter how strongly she felt about Sherry's overprotectiveness, she shouldn't have taken Denise on a ride without asking Sherry's permission first.

But we'll be back—long before Sherry realizes Denise has even gone, Lannie told herself quickly.

"Mother doesn't want me to do anything anymore," Denise said, a note of defiance creeping into her voice. "She acts like being blind is the same as being dead."

"She's afraid for you," Lannie said softly. "You'll have to give her time."

"She's had six years. If I'm not afraid, why is she?"

"She's a mother. Some day you'll understand. Besides, not everyone is as brave and strong as you, Denise. I wasn't."

"You weren't?"

"Don't you remember that after *my* accident I lay in bed for a whole month. I was too scared and miserable to even get up. Why it was because of you that I finally did. The doctors kept saying they couldn't find anything the matter with my eyes, and that my vision would probably return. . . ."

"And it did."

"But not for ten whole months, not before you showed me that I'd better get busy living again. I've told you and your mother so many times that my blindness and you, especially you, changed my life for

31

the better. If I hadn't had the wreck and met you, I would have gone on making the same mistakes that blinded me."

"I've never been able to understand why you say that."

"Well, take the night of the wreck. I was driving much too fast, and only because I liked the thrill of driving fast. Velvet was in the car with me, and a child ran out into the road after her dog. I had to swerve into a concrete embankment to keep from hitting her. I very nearly killed that child. Thankfully I was the only one injured."

And how typical that accident had been of her selfishly reckless lifestyle. Of course she had been young, but youth alone was no excuse for her behavior. She'd felt buried in Louisiana; she'd wanted to live. Thus when Genevieve Brandon had asked her to move to New York with her as her companion, she'd agreed even though her mother had been ill.

Velvet already lived in Manhattan and had written Lannie glowing letters of her glamorous life. Lannie had been only too eager to follow Velvet's lead. Like so many other beautiful young girls, she'd hoped of finding fame and wealth in a modeling or acting career. Instead she'd found wealthy men who promised to help her with her career in return for certain favors. Some of them had been content to have an empty-headed beauty clinging to their arm. Others had wanted more, and none of them had seen her as anything more than a pretty face. She hadn't even felt like a person.

Shivering, Lannie remembered those men. They were like wolves ready to prey on the dreams of young innocents, but she'd been smart enough to string them along with no more than a kiss and a promise until . . . Mark Brandon had come into her life.

At just the thought of him, a strange tightness gripped her throat.

Suddenly Lannie was remembering the time, nearly seven years before, after the wreck. She and Velvet had scarcely been pulled out of her car before it had burst into flames. She'd smelled the smoke, felt the heat of the fire against her skin, but she hadn't been able to see. She'd suffered a severe concussion, and her doctors had told her they thought the optical nerve center at the back of her head had been damaged.

Usually in such cases patients regained their sight in a matter of days or weeks. Sometimes it took longer, and sometimes they were permanently blinded.

Lannie had regained her sight, but not before the terrible ordeal had changed life completely—for the better. Blindness had been the first challenge that couldn't be met with the flash of a pretty smile or the coy flutter of an eyelash. For the first time in her life she'd had to work for everything she accomplished, and she'd learned how deep the emotional rewards could be for such efforts.

"Honey, I lay in that bed a month, too scared by what I'd nearly done to get out of it. I didn't know how I was going to manage without my sight."

"It didn't take me nearly that long," Denise was saying proudly. "As soon as my leg was well, I wanted to get out of bed. But Mother wouldn't let me. If you hadn't come along I'd probably still be locked up in a hospital room somewhere. You've done as much for me as you say I've done for you."

Lannie could feel Denise's muscles relaxing as she grew accustomed to the feel of the horse. The child was a natural rider as Lannie herself had been as a child.

The dirt road twisted through an aromatic grove of pines and then through lush tall cane. Narrow misty streamers of ground fog had settled in the low places.

"Everything smells and feels so wonderful!" Denise exclaimed.

"There's the Sugar Castle, gleaming white and ghostly in the moonlight," Lannie said, taking special pains to describe it so Denise could visualize its loveliness. "It must have been a marvelous place over a hundred years ago when it was filled with people," Lannie said. A wisp of ground fog encircled the old house.

Lannie was glad that the subject of their conversation had changed. Just thinking of the past, of the kind of person she'd once been, made her feel ashamed. She was different now, and she didn't like to remember.

"Tell me again about the people who used to live there, Lannie."

Lannie spun the familiar story to Denise, and each of them enjoyed their time together as much as they did the story. It seemed that it took them almost no time to reach their destination.

The pillars of Brandon House gleamed in the moonlight like a Grecian temple nestled in a deep woods. It was brilliantly lit, and Lannie noted several cars in the driveway—one of them a pale gray Mercedes with the swirling emblem of a dragon blazing on one fender.

The sight of it seared through her like lightning, burning her with pain. Brandon . . .

She saw John's Volkswagen parked in front of the guest house out back where he lived—because he said Brandon House was much too large and grand for a bachelor like himself. Her throat constricted. Uneasily she realized that Brandon was already home.

She felt almost panicky as she hastily directed Sugar back in the direction they'd come. Ground fog drifted across the road in dense patches.

Halfway home Denise said, "Let's gallop."

That suited Lannie. The faster she could put distance between herself and Brandon, the better. Lannie's heels dug into Sugar and the horse leapt eagerly forward. The smooth flowing gait made the two riders feel as though they were flying as they raced headlong around several sharp turns in the road. The fog seemed to grow thicker and thicker. But Lannie, flying as though some demon from the past pursued her, paid no attention.

Suddenly from out of nowhere, a brilliant light streamed against the thick cane wall beside the road as a motorist in a silvery car unexpectedly rounded the curve from behind them. Twisting shadows curled against the thick cane.

Instantly spooked, Sugar reared, neighing and snorting, throwing her head wildly. A horn bleeted impatiently. Then Sugar backed into the middle of the road, directly in the path of the oncoming car.

Breaks squealed frantically as the driver swerved to avoid the horse. Denise was screaming. Desperately Lannie fought to regain control of Sugar. In her terror Denise had let go of her hold on Sugar's mane, and her small body was slipping against Lannie's, throwing Lannie off-balance. When Lannie knew they would fall, her only thought was to shield Denise's fall with her own body.

Then all was blackness and silence.

A car door slammed. The beam of a flashlight bobbed like a golden wand as a tall, dark man strode purposely across the road toward the two girls. Denise could feel the vibration of his footsteps and hear the crunch of his shoes as he stepped on a loose pebble.

"Who's there?" she called out uncertainly, looking wildly around.

Brilliant light bathed her face, and Brandon unthinkingly observed that the girl's failure to react to the light was somehow strange. All he consciously understood was her fear. The light flicked to Lannie, and his pace quickened.

"It's me—Brandon," the man answered harshly.

Though Denise had never met Mark Brandon, she'd heard of him. Relief at the familiar name flooded her. "I-I think Lannie's been hurt."

"Lannie . . . Gallier?"

Denise nodded, registering the subtle softening in the man's voice.

"My God!" His utterance was ragged.

The sight of Lannie lying like a broken doll in the road, her face pale, her beautiful hair streaming across the dirt, cut through seven years of careful control with the swift savageness of a knife. He stared down at her in anguished amazement.

For an instant he was stunned by his own powerful reaction. Ten minutes before had he been asked, he would have said he hated her—even though the mere sight of her on the dock this afternoon had made his blood race. He'd thought her wildly beautiful with her rich black hair billowing in the breeze, her breasts outlined by her thin blue sweater. But that was lust, nothing more.

His involuntary response to her loveliness had made him damnably irritable for the rest of the day until even his own kindly grandmother had accused him of being unfit to live with. Ah . . . Lannie . . . Damn her. . . . Why could this one woman arouse him so powerfully when at the same time he disliked her?

The thought of Lannie coldly conniving to marry his stepbrother John had incensed him so much that he'd dropped everything and come directly to Louisiana to stop her. He'd been so angry as he'd driven toward her house he could have gladly shaken her senseless. And now feelings which he hadn't known he possessed were swamping him. Yet no emotion showed on his harshly drawn features.

Quickly he knelt beside Lannie and lifted her limp wrist so that he could feel her pulse. "Who are you?" he asked Denise in a gentler tone.

"Denise Prejean. Mother and I live with Lannie—to help her out with her bills and chores."

"I see." When Brandon felt the steady, sure heartbeat hammering beneath his calloused fingertips, his grim expression relaxed. Expertly his hands went over her body as he felt for broken bones or any sign of hemorrhaging.

"I think she's just stunned," he said at last. "But how about you—are you hurt?"

"Oh, I'm fine." Denise's voice was normally bright once more. "I landed on top of Lannie."

Ink-black lashes fluttered against soft olive skin, and Lannie groaned faintly. Gently Brandon's hand touched her forehead, and he brushed a strand of her black hair aside.

Opening her eyes, Lannie blinked against the harshness of the bright light. When Brandon averted it, she stared questioningly up at the man who knelt beside her.

His face was shadowed, and she could not make out his features. Yet there was something about him that was achingly familiar—the shape of his jet-dark head, the slope and breadth of his massive shoulders.

She felt confused. "What happened?"

"We fell off Sugar because Sugar got scared of the car. You got hurt, but I didn't." Denise stated the facts succinctly.

All of Lannie's attention was focused on the man. Who . . . She felt as though she knew him. Then *his* hands that lingered on her body told her unmistakably who he was.

He had such strong, hard hands, yet when they touched a woman they always felt velvet-soft. How well she remembered their touch.

"Brandon . . ." she murmured, too stunned to be as dismayed as she would be when she recovered from her fall. "You've really come back."

"Yes. I've really come back." His voice was uncustomarily gentle.

"But, Brandon, why?"

For a long moment he hesitated, and when he spoke there was no trace of anger in his voice.

"Because of you," he said at last.

Chapter Three

*B*ecause of you . . ."

The full import of Brandon's words ricocheted through Lannie. She was coming out of her daze and remembering that Brandon was no friend of hers.

"Do you think you can sit up?" Brandon asked in his smooth, deep voice that sent an unwanted, fiery sensation searing through Lannie's arteries.

"Of course I can sit up," Lannie lashed out, angry that any remnant of the old chemical attraction between them still lingered. Mark Brandon's false solicitude was the last thing she wanted. She hated him, and everything he represented, just as much as he hated her. She'd always known he'd come back, if only to deliberately ruin her life.

Brandon ignored her burst of temper. His arms went around her to help her. She felt the hard warmth of his hand curving around her waist and was too acutely aware of him as a man as he pulled her into a sitting position.

She was glad that in the moonlight he could not see the telltale blush suffusing her cheeks. "I can do it without your help," she snapped. "I'm not really hurt at all!"

"I'm not going to let you do it without my help. You might not be as strong as you think." His expression was hard and unyielding.

She attempted to push his hands away, but he merely caught her wrists in his own hands and placed them around his neck where she felt his warm flesh beneath her fingertips and the springy thickness of his black hair curling over her fingers. Her breasts were flattened against his broad chest as he held her closely against him.

"We'll have to crash into one another more often," he whispered, his warm breath so close that it tickled the sensitive flesh of her neck. "I'd forgotten how much fun rescuing a damsel in distress could be."

She was terribly aware of the hard contours of his body pressing close, of her own heart beginning to race with unwanted excitement. She started more from the violence of her response to him as a man than to what he had said.

She longed to slap the bold, slashing grin from his face, but she was virtually imprisoned in his arms. Thus she settled for a verbal insult.

"I'd hardly give you credit for rescuing me. If you hadn't been driving like a maniac—"

"I never drive like a maniac—that's your specialty. If you hadn't been riding a black horse at night and trespassing on my property—"

"Sugar isn't black! And this is the old Gallier road."

"It's Brandon property now. Or have you forgotten I bought this from your father ten years ago?"

"How could I forget?" Her voice broke bitterly. "You Brandons have almost gobbled up the entire

Gallier estate. You won't be satisfied until you own Belle Rose itself and there's not a Gallier left in the parish."

"How right you are." A trace of bitterness edged his own voice. Then abruptly his mood changed. "I never did enjoy arguing as much as you did, especially when I was holding you in my arms."

Again she was aware of the almost electric excitement his embrace aroused, and frantically she tried to twist free. His arms about her tightened to lift her up from the ground.

"Brandon . . ." The feel of his sinewed strength was sweeping the years away as well as her anger, and she was feeling the strange, inexplicable wildness she always felt in his presence.

"You used to like for me to hold you; you used to beg me to." His husky voice was mockingly seductive, reminding her of moments she didn't dare remember.

"Don't say it!" Lannie hissed. "Denise won't understand."

"Ah, yes. Denise . . ."

Denise turned trustingly toward the sound of his voice. "Will Lannie be all right, Mr. Brandon?"

"She seems fine, except for her bad mood. And that's not unusual." Lannie tensed in his arms. "You haven't changed, Lannie," he muttered softly. "Your temper's still as hot as a Louisiana red pepper!"

"That's enough! You have no right coming back into my life . . . and acting like . . . you own me."

"I have every right, as you well know," he answered with renewed grimness.

Ruthlessly Brandon swung Lannie into his arms and strode toward the car. Denise, clutching Lannie for guidance, sprinted rapidly beside Brandon toward the car.

The sight of Denise's fingers groping across gray

metal in search of the door handle arrested Brandon's attention. Slowly his eyes traveled upward to the girl's face, and he saw that she was looking off into space. Then it hit him. The child couldn't see. Without saying anything he waited patiently for her eager little hands to find and snap open the handle.

In the muted, interior light of the car, Brandon examined Lannie more carefully for further injuries, and while he did, Lannie made her own examination of him.

He hadn't changed! Not really. The masculine angles of his features were a little more harshly drawn than she'd remembered, the lines etched beside his lips more deeply carved.

Although his face was too rugged to be classically handsome, there was a certain compelling distinctiveness that was boldly attractive.

His eyes were his most arresting feature. They were intensely black, yet flecked with gold. She had the feeling they missed nothing, and they alone could betray that inner excitement that was so much a part of him. As he looked at Lannie she could almost feel the power surging through him, a power he deliberately sought to curb. All sorts of memories flooded her mind. She remembered him well; he was rarely still, always on the move.

His skin was bronzed from the sun. Lingeringly her gaze touched his mouth that was full and sensual.

With a deliberate effort she forced herself to look away.

"Like what you see? You used to . . ."

The bold confidence of his tone infuriated her once more.

"No, I don't!" she rasped, scarcely able to speak. "You're the most conceited . . . the most . . ."

"Liar!"

He was so near that when he spoke the word, his

warm breath caressed her cheek. She tried to ignore the rush of heat that swept her.

"Why did you ask if you aren't going to believe me?"

"I wanted to hear what you had to say."

"Well, you've heard! Start the car! I want to go home!" He made not the slightest move to obey. "I said—"

"I know what you said, and we'll go when I'm ready."

He was as maddeningly obstinate as ever. She felt the control of her own life slipping into his hands, and the sensation made her begin to panic.

"Well, if you won't go back on my account, the least you could do would be to think of Denise. Her mother will be worried sick."

A long moment of heavy silence filled the car. Then the key clicked in the ignition and the engine purred to life.

"I don't wonder," he said, heavy sarcasm coating his words. "No mother in her right mind would have given you permission to take that child for a bareback ride at night on such an unmanageable horse."

"Sherry didn't give her permission," Lannie admitted weakly. Feelings of guilt were swamping her.

"But you took her anyway. That figures." For the first time his deep tones were accusing. "You're still the same reckless, unthinking little hellion you always were."

"I am not! I took Denise for that ride because I thought it would be good for her!"

"Good for her? She could have been seriously injured! What if I'd hit you?"

"Well, you didn't! And how was I to know you'd be ripping around that curve?"

"You should have foreseen that possibility," he returned gravely. Where were you going anyway?"

Lannie was reluctant to admit what their destination had been for fear he would misconstrue things.

"Brandon House!" Denise chimed in. "We were on our way back home."

Lannie flushed at the quick gleam in his intense dark eyes. Brandon's gaze raked Lannie with unfeigned curiosity. A faint smile danced around the corners of his mouth. "So, my return is of more interest than you're willing to openly admit."

"It was Denise's idea! Not mine—if you're interested in the real truth—which I very much doubt!"

"And you were so eager to oblige her that you didn't even bother to tell her mother where you were going. Lannie . . ."

He twisted everything! "It's not what you think! You don't interest me in the slightest—not in the way you mean, at any rate!"

"Then that's something I'll have to change." Again she felt the mocking glint of his eyes as they slid over her. His hand reached out to cup her chin, and she trembled at his touch. "I don't think it'll be too hard."

The arrogance of the remark inflamed her. But as she folded her shaking fingers together in her lap, she realized there was more truth in it than she would have liked.

The road curved, and he let his hand fall back to the steering wheel.

"You haven't told me what *you* were doing on this road instead of the highway," Lannie said, hoping to put him on the defensive for a change.

"Haven't I?" His sensual mouth curved. "Why, Lannie, I was coming to see you! And this is the short-cut, remember?"

Lannie gasped. He hadn't wasted any time in heading over to see her. But of course, not wasting time was a characteristic of his.

The powerful car moved slowly beneath the alley of oaks that led up to Belle Rose.

"Home again," Brandon gibed as he braked in front of the house.

The thick mockery in Brandon's tone made Lannie's blood bubble heatedly. But she managed to hold her tongue. It was better not to arouse his own deep wrath until she had to. She knew too well how dangerous he could be.

Sherry's slippered feet lightly flew across the veranda and down the steps toward the automobile. Brandon had already negligently removed his lean frame from the car.

Behind Sherry at the top of the stairs stood Ralph, a tall, thin man whose posture was as crookedly awkward as a marsh bird's. Wire-rimmed spectacles were perched precariously on his nose, giving him the look of an absentminded intellectual, which was exactly what he was. But his face was one of kindly concern as he strained to see into the darkness.

Sherry hesitated on the bottom step. "Denise . . ." The name quivered uncertainly on Sherry's lips as her brown eyes met Brandon's questioningly.

"Denise is just fine," Brandon said reassuringly, realizing at once that she was on the verge of hysteria. He moved with swift grace around the car to fold her into his arms. "I'm Mark Brandon and we've got her safe and sound in the car," he began in explanation. "I know how worried you must have been," he continued soothingly as he patted Sherry's back. "Lannie feels terrible that she didn't tell you she and Denise were going riding."

Lannie pushed open the other door, and Denise jumped from the car. "Mother!"

"Over here, *chérie!*"

Sherry would have run to her small daughter to have

saved her the difficulty of finding her own way, but the pressure of Brandon's hands on her shoulders restrained her.

Denise moved confidently to span the brief distance in the direction of her mother's voice, and when she was within reach, Sherry seized her by the hand and clutched her closely.

Ralph called timidly down from the stairs. "Denise, I'm glad you're home."

"Ralph . . ." Denise's voice filled with affection, and she glanced upward toward the sound of his voice.

Denise endured her mother's fervent embrace for almost a minute. Then she wriggled free. "I rode Sugar, Mother." She was still flushed with excitement from the adventure.

"I know, *chérie*. I was so worried."

"Lannie took me. It was wonderful—until we fell off. And then Mr. Brandon came along and brought us back." Denise's bright young voice was full of confidence, in sharp contrast to her mother's own shaky one.

"You and Lannie should have asked me first, darling," Sherry said with attempted lightness.

"But you wouldn't have let me go," Denise stated.

"Then you shouldn't have gone." For the first time, sharpness edged Sherry's normally gentle tone.

"I'm sick and tired of not doing things because you won't let me."

"Denise, it's just because I'm afraid you'll get hurt. And tonight when Sugar came galloping up that drive with her reins dragging in the dirt, I thought you had been."

"So now you'll never let me go anywhere again?" Denise cried, sensing both the determination and terror that lingered in her mother's voice. "Well, if you don't I'm going to run away—somewhere where you'll never find me. And you can be scared all the time!"

With that she pulled away from Sherry and groped her way to the railing of the stairs. Then with the railing to guide her, she fairly flew up the staircase. Once inside the house, she knew her way perfectly.

"Denise! Denise," Sherry cried after her. But there was no response.

"She's never spoken to me like that before," Sherry murmured distractedly to Brandon.

As he leaned casually against the hood of his car, Brandon's dark face was impassive.

Lannie, feeling absolutely wretched, moved slowly toward her friend. "Sherry, I'm sorry. I should never have . . ."

Sherry focused on Lannie for the first time. "How could you do something like this, Lannie? And to think I trusted you. How could you?"

Sherry had never spoken to Lannie in such a hurt tone.

"She wanted to ride Sugar, and I thought it would build her confidence to realize that she could."

"I would have thought you of all people would understand! Why can't you see that Denise is blind? Blind people don't ride horses!"

"What do blind people do, Sherry?" Lannie queried softly. "Sit in dark little rooms where they're physically safe and listen to the radio hour after hour. Maybe she could learn to weave baskets and brooms. Have you any idea what that kind of life will do to Denise?"

"She's my child, not yours! And if you won't promise me that you'll never take her anywhere without asking me first, she and I will be gone in the morning."

Lannie went as white as the gleaming ivory pillars of Belle Rose as the blow wounded her to the heart.

"Sherry!" Ralph reproached in an anguished voice. "You're being unfair to Lannie. She's only trying to help Denise. And she can do it better than you or I could ever hope to."

"Ralph, don't you start trying to tell me how to raise my own child! You're almost as bad as Lannie. Last week you took her off into the swamp in that leaky old pirogue of yours. She could have been bitten by a snake! Not to mention drowned!"

Ralph and Lannie stared at Sherry in amazement; they had never seen their gentle friend even slightly angry. The thought of Sherry and Denise moving away was unbearable.

"You have my word, Sherry," Lannie said in a tear-choked voice. "I won't take Denise anywhere without your permission. I just hope you know what you're doing."

"Then we'll stay," Sherry said quietly, before turning to mount the stairs to join Ralph and go inside the house.

The front door thudded shut. When they were gone Lannie was suddenly aware of Brandon again, who was still lounging indolently against the hood of his car.

Embarrassment and anger trembled through her. She would have given anything if he hadn't been a witness to such a private scene between herself and Sherry.

Anxious to get away from him, she muttered almost inaudibly, "I'd better go see about Sugar. . . ." Briskly she started in the direction of the stable.

From behind her she heard his drawl. "I see you're still capable of causing quite an uproar without even half trying."

Enough was enough! Her frayed nerves snapped. Whirling, she spat, "And you loved every minute of it, didn't you?"

Her angry words seemed to bounce off of him. A smile touched his mouth. "I wouldn't say that. I would have preferred having you all to myself tonight. But it's been a revealing evening, all in all."

She longed to snap his head off so that he would stop

talking. But that, of course, was impossible. "Well, I hope you're happy! This is really all your fault. If you hadn't been on that road—"

"You'd have done the same thing again, perhaps with even more disastrous consequences," he returned evenly.

The logic of his statement only served to further antagonize her.

"Why don't you go home where you belong? Haven't you caused enough trouble for one night?"

"I really think you ought to see a doctor and make sure you're all right," he suggested blandly. "You seem a little overwrought."

"If I'm overwrought, it's because of you."

"I still think you should see a doctor."

Hotly, she retorted, "Thank you for your concern, but my health is my own problem."

His expression grew more implacable, and she knew better than to argue. She would call John. She was about to say so before she realized that might be a very foolish thing to do.

It struck her suddenly that she hadn't once thought of John since her accident with Brandon. But . . . but that was only because too much had happened to distract her, and with the additional burden of Brandon's infuriating presence it wasn't any wonder she hadn't thought of John.

Brandon hadn't budged, and she was sure he had no intention of doing so until she gave into his demand.

"All right, I'll see someone," she agreed. Anything to get rid of him!

He was staring at her intently, and his broad, triumphant smile had its usual devastating impact on her senses. She felt a strange tingling sensation curling in the pit of her stomach as though he had touched her. Exasperated at her own response, she muttered an impatient, "Now, will you go?"

He straightened his lean frame. "I'm going," he stated matter-of-factly. His eyes raked her in a slow stripping gaze that made her feel he still found her to be a very attractive woman. "Because it's late and I have an early appointment."

"Good!" She whirled to go after Sugar when his low, resonant tone vibrated through her.

"But I'll be back. When you're better. You and I need to have a long talk—soon."

Lannie bristled at the implied threat in his tone. He spoke as though it were still his right to come and go at Belle Rose as he pleased. Belle Rose was her home! And he had no right to visit, no matter what their past relationship had been.

The savage desire to put him in his proper place surged through her and triumphed over her rational judgment. She stopped in midstep and blurted defiantly back at him, "Have you forgotten? I'm engaged now, to John. You no longer . . ."

As soon as the words were out of her mouth she knew they were a mistake! Brandon's lazy expression instantly hardened into a black mask of rage. Long, forceful strides carried Brandon to her and she shrank as he seized her and yanked her to him.

As her soft curves were pressed to his towering length, she regretted willfully antagonizing him. His debonair facade had completely vanished. She could almost feel the primitive passion coursing through him. Her own pulse was racing wildly; the sound of it pounded fiercely in her ears.

"No, I haven't forgotten about John," he snarled, his black eyes blazing. "When I come back, you and I are going to have a long talk about him and all the reasons why a marriage between the two of you is out of the question."

"You can't tell me who I can marry!"

"I don't give a damn who you marry, just so long as it isn't John!"

"You can't stop me!" she hurled back, as enraged as he.

"If you really believed that you wouldn't be shaking like a leaf right now! No, my dear one, you're not going to marry John because I've come back to Louisiana to stop you!"

Chapter Four

Sunlight streamed through the french doors and bathed Lannie's bedroom in its golden light. A faint breeze stirred the filmy mosquito bar hanging from the half-tester of the Deep South empire bed.

Lannie, lying listlessly against her plump feather pillows, emitted a small moan as she massaged her temples. Every time she sat up, her entire head seemed to throb. Her hip had an enormous yellowish-purple bruise.

Even though John had given her a sleeping pill, she'd scarcely slept. She'd been too worried about Brandon. Why had she deliberately antagonized him? There was no telling what he might do.

He hadn't even seemed angry at her until she'd lashed out at him. But of course that didn't necessarily mean anything. Brandon was an expert at concealing his true feelings. She knew from experience that he didn't mind stalking his prey and toying with it before

he attacked. He always thought things out very carefully before he made a move.

Lannie was only dimly aware of a man's heavy
footsteps ascending the stairs. At the creak of her door
being opened, Lannie sat up and the sheets fell away,
exposing her naked shoulder. Carelessly she drew them
over her once more as John ambled into the room and
sat down a very proper distance from her at the end of
the great bed. He was dressed in another blue seersucker suit that had narrower stripes than the one of the
night before.

"How're you feeling this morning, honey?" His
gentle smile went over her fondly.

She forced a smile, and squirmed restlessly. For some
reason she felt vaguely annoyed at his presence. But
that was only because she was still so upset from her
encounter with Brandon.

"I have a headache. That's all. I'll be okay as soon as
I take an aspirin."

"You're sure?"

"Yes, John, really," she said in what she hoped was
her sweetest voice. It certainly wouldn't be fair to take
out her frustrations on him. "I don't know why you're
making such a fuss. You didn't have to come by again
this morning. Last night you said I was fine." She
paused, twisting the edge of her sheet as she smiled up
at him. "If I didn't know better, I'd think you were
making sure I was following your orders to stay in bed
and not go on to school."

"Brandon wanted me to check on you before I went
into the office," John said benignly.

Dark slanting brows whipped together into an unbe-
coming frown. This time when the sheet slipped, she
didn't even notice.

Just the mention of Brandon's name was enough to
bring back her driving rage of last night.

"Brandon!" She drew a deep, furious breath. "Hasn't he caused enough trouble without sending you over to see me when I'm perfectly all right?"

"He really is concerned about you, honey. He feels responsible."

The telephone tinkled downstairs.

"I'm surprised he admits I didn't just fall off Sugar all by myself," Lannie said peevishly.

"Well, honey, I wouldn't blame Brandon. I've tried to tell you Sugar can't be depended on. Brandon thinks she's dangerous. And I'd feel a lot safer if you'd get rid of that animal and buy something a bit tamer."

"Brandon . . ." she was sputtering. "Why, he hasn't been home one day and already he's interfering in our lives like some know-it-all busybody. He doesn't know anything about Sugar, and I have no intention of selling her on his say-so!" With each sentence her voice rose to a shriller pitch.

"Now, now, I didn't mean to upset you. Nobody's going to make you sell Sugar until you feel like it's the right thing to do. But I do want you to consider it. And as for Brandon, he's only trying to help. Why only last night he said—"

"John—" Acute exasperation edged her voice. Her head was pounding. "Do we have to talk about Brandon? We've dated each other nearly six months without ever mentioning his name. And now suddenly he's all we can find to talk about!"

"Why, no, honey." John shifted uncomfortably. He was regarding her curiously, as though he didn't understand her at all this morning. "Say, how would you feel about a drive-in movie tonight?"

"That would be nice, John," she mouthed mechanically. Actually she'd hoped to spend a quiet evening at home, alone.

"I'll be over before the sun goes down then

54

. . . whatever time that is. Hey, maybe Hilary would like to come."

"Hilary? On a date to the drive-in?" Lannie's brows drew together in a puzzled frown.

As if on cue Hilary, dressed in tight jeans and a faded madras halter called an airy "Knock . . . knock . . ." before skipping into the room. Her silver hair was twisted into a careless knot on the top of her head, and overlarge, gypsy earrings dangled to her shoulders. As she looked at John, her quick smile illuminated her gamine-like features until she was quite beautiful.

"John," Hilary spoke his name breezily, and her smile brightened as it always did when it was directed at him. "Telephone. It's TuTu Broussard's husband and he said it's urgent."

"I bet I know what he wants," he said, getting up from the edge of the bed and following Hilary to the door before he turned back to Lannie. "I want you to stay in bed today. We've got to have you on your feet again or my medical reputation will be ruined."

"Yes, sir!" Lannie threw a mock salute defiantly at the door he closed behind him as he left with Hilary.

"Bed . . . my foot!" Lannie grumped to herself half-aloud. "There's nothing the matter with me that Brandon couldn't cure by getting on a plane and flying back to wherever he came from."

Lannie could hear Hilary's gay, "John, I scrambled you up some eggs on the off-chance you'd have the time. There's bacon, and grits. . . ."

"Sometimes babies won't wait for breakfast. . . ." was his almost woeful response.

Dutifully Lannie stayed in bed for ten minutes until she heard Hilary's cheery goodbye floating up from the veranda and John's Volkswagen as it roared down the drive. Then Lannie got up gingerly and pulled on her faded housecoat. She swallowed two aspirin and then slowly hobbled downstairs to join the others at breakfast.

Even if she weren't going to teach, there were a million things she needed to do around the house and she was much too restless to stay in bed. She wasn't about to let Brandon use John to order her about.

The dining room was deserted. Only the telltale crumbs on the linen tablecloth told her the others had been there.

"Lannie, what are you doing up?" Hilary cried from the kitchen as she carried a pitcher of orange juice from the sink to the refrigerator.

"I'm starved," Lannie answered, moving a bit more easily as she joined Hilary in the kitchen and took a plate and some silverware from the rubber dishrack on the drainboard.

"I would have brought you. . . ."

"I know, Hilary." Ignoring the grits because she'd never liked that particular Southern dish, Lannie spooned a small helping of eggs, bacon and toast onto her plate. "But I don't feel like staying in bed this morning. My leg already feels a little less sore just from walking on it. Where are the others?"

"They ate with John. The girls are upstairs getting dressed, and Ralph's outside doing a little raking while they get ready. Don't you remember? Today's the day Ralph's driving Sherry and Denise into New Orleans to see that new eye doctor."

Dishes clattered in the sink as Hilary scoured them in her ramshackle fashion, using as little water and soap as she possibly could.

"Oh, yes . . ." Lannie muttered, sitting down at the small breakfast table in the kitchen and pouring herself a cup of tar-black Louisiana coffee.

"I'm going with them—just as soon as I finish the dishes. There's a poetry workshop at Tulane. It's not over until five, and we promised Denise we'd take her

56

out to eat at that restaurant that serves those scrumptious strawberry sundaes she's so crazy about before we drive home. We might even stop off at Sherry's Tante Michelle's. So we'll probably be quite late."

So, she would have the day to herself, Lannie mused. She needed it! Her episode with Brandon the night before had shattered whatever fragile hope she'd had that Brandon might not try to ruin her happiness with John.

An hour later at her desk in the library Lannie stacked the last envelope on the top of the pile of bills she'd paid. Then she pushed the nosepiece of her reading glasses firmly against the slender bridge of her nose.

Her letter opener carefully slashed the last envelope —the estimate the roofer had sent. She'd been putting off the task of opening it, dreading its contents.

Fifteen thousand dollars to reroof Belle Rose! That was even worse than she'd expected! She had only a third of that amount which she'd carefully saved from her own salary, admission charges to the plantation, last year's harvest and the room and board Ralph, Sherry and Hilary paid.

Lannie gasped in despair. With Belle Rose already mortgaged, she was scarcely in a position to borrow more money. Nevertheless, she would have to try.

She scanned the lengthy note at the bottom of the estimate in which Mr. Herbert strongly advised against patching the roof again.

Wearily she looked out onto the grounds where sunlight filtered through the trees, dappling broad banana leaves so they glowed a translucent lime-green.

The upkeep on Belle Rose was staggering, and it wasn't something a schoolteacher could really afford to do. But she was determined to keep her family home from being gobbled up by Brandon Chemicals.

Sighing, Lannie removed her glasses and got up,

stretching her legs. What she needed was some exercise.

Immediately she thought of Sugar. Last night's ride had hardly been a success, but in broad daylight without Denise to worry about, a ride on Sugar would be relaxing. As she moved across the room she realized that her leg was feeling much better.

When Lannie approached the stable, Sugar plodded over to her immediately, for once forsaking her favorite game of hard-to-get. She nuzzled Lannie uncertainly as though to apologize for what had happened the evening before.

"Who says horses don't suffer from guilty consciences, old girl?"

Lannie slipped the bridle on and saddled her. Then she climbed astride and urged Sugar into a slow walk beneath the vaulting branches of the oak alley. As though she wanted to make up for their misadventure, Sugar behaved like a perfect lady, obeying Lannie's lightest suggestion with the reins.

Lannie followed the same twisting road she had the night before. Bordering one side of the road was the distant, green rise of the levee which hid the broad rolling brown river from view. Absently Lannie scanned the other side of the road where flat land blended with the horizon, broken by an occasional stand of pine and oak trees, and the vast stretches of lush cane fields.

All was familiar to her and gave her a sense of peace that she'd craved. Brandon and his threat seemed suddenly very unreal.

Over and over she thought there had to be a way to come up with the money for a new roof, if only she were creative enough to think of it. But fifteen thousand dollars . . . It seemed like a fortune!

Suddenly she dug her heels into Sugar, and the horse sprang into a gallop. The roof was forgotten as an exhilarating wildness pounded through her arteries as she gave herself up to the sheer enjoyment of the ride. Her hair flew behind her, streaming in the wind. Sugar's hooves pounded into the firmly packed earth. Recklessly, Lannie urged the mare to jump a fence, and Sugar flew over the thick marsh grasses.

Thunderheads tinged with pink shot like billowing puffs high into the sky. But Lannie took no notice. Nor did she see the silver car that came to a standstill alongside the road as the driver strained to watch the wildly elemental ride.

After several minutes, Lannie slowed Sugar. All her tension was gone. Slowly she directed the horse back toward Belle Rose. The sun had gone behind a cloud, and the wind whipping her face was cool and smelled faintly of rain.

"No, please don't rain," she prayed silently, remembering again her roof and the much-needed repairs.

Gray skies lingered through the afternoon, and the air was oppressively humid. But no rain fell. Lannie busied herself inside cleaning and vacuuming the downstairs area.

At four o'clock when the doorbell rang, Lannie, dust mop in hand, went to answer it.

"Special delivery."

"Hi, Mr. Avery."

Slender fingers curved with excitement around the cardboard edges of the gilt box the postman handed her. The expensive emerald scrawl was that of the exclusive New Orleans dress shop where last Saturday she'd purchased a new dress for the annual Brandon Chemicals barbeque which would be held soon. Velvet had gone with her and insisted that Lannie buy a new dress for the occasion.

Tissue paper rustled and Lannie caught her breath with feminine excitement as she pulled the cardinal-red gown from the box. The layers of filmy organza flowed through her fingers. She hadn't had a dress so beautiful in seven years, not since Brandon had taken her to Paris and purchased a couturiere's collection for her.

Visions of that wonderful holiday bombarded her— the coffee house in Montmartre where they'd spent a long, cozy afternoon just talking over tea; the excitement of an evening nightclubing at cabarets and the Moulin Rouge; that magic hour just at dusk when a sudden downpour had forced them to huddle in one another's arms beneath a doorway near the quay along the Seine.

Deliberately she pushed Brandon and that other lifetime from her mind. She clasped the dress to her body so that the soft folds floated like a transparent flame. She'd had to leave the gown in New Orleans for alterations.

Suddenly the irrepressable urge to try the dress on at once to make sure it fit seized her, and she dashed upstairs to her bedroom.

But one glance at her face in the long silver oval above her dresser told her that she would have to put on her makeup and brush her hair if she wanted to get the full effect of the gown.

And she wanted the full effect. Half an hour later Lannie smiled her slow, sweet smile as she admired her reflection. The scarlet dress clung provocatively to her slender curves as it flowed over her body in cascading waves of fiery chiffon. With her every movement the material glistened and swirled.

The low-cut neckline set off the creamy texture of her neck and shoulders. Yet something, some adornment was lacking. Hurriedly Lannie tugged the drawer of her bureau open and rifled through her jewelry box, but she wasn't able to find exactly what she wanted. Inadvertently she spied the edge of the long black velvet box peeping from beneath a pile of silk scarves.

Nervously she hesitated for a moment, then she pulled the box out and before she lost her courage snapped open the lid.

In the final, slanting rays of the sun that filtered through the sheer draperies of the long windows, a necklace of diamonds glinted against rose velvet. She forced back the vague stirring of emotion the sight of those diamonds produced.

Defiantly she lifted the necklace from the jewel box and fastened the clasp behind her neck. The circlet of diamonds flashed at her throat, and the effect was dazzling.

But of course. She couldn't wear the necklace in public to the barbeque; long ago Brandon had given it to her.

Outside, leaves rustled as though someone were moving purposely through them toward the house, and she left the mirror and sped to the windows. Peering down through spreading gray branches and tawny leaves, she saw nothing.

The firm tread of a man's footsteps resounding on the veranda was somehow vaguely familiar, and Lannie suddenly remembered that John had said he would be over just before dark so that they could go to the drive-in.

Leaving her filmy chiffon wrap draped across her bed, Lannie rushed out of the bedroom in her stockinged feet to glide down the stairs.

The doorbell buzzed, echoing through the vast rooms. Nervously Lannie smoothed the flowing folds of her scarlet ballgown. She hoped John would approve of her dress for the barbeque.

Through the beveled, leaded-glass window of the door she could see that the man outside was tall and dark. Too tall and too dark to be John. The breadth of the man's shoulders seemed to span the width of the enormous door. A sudden sense of dread gnawed in the pit of her stomach, but she told herself shakily she was being ridiculous.

For an instant her slender fingers that curled around the ornate brass doorknob stiffened, and she hesitated. Then she fought back her fear and pulled with all the strength she had against the heaviness of the door. A lean brown hand on the other side of the door eased her struggle as the man used his superior strength to push it open effortlessly.

The rush of cool, damp evening air that flowed into the room had nothing to do with the goosebumps that pricked the bare flesh of Lannie's arms. The door, continuing to swing open, groaned on its massive hinges in unison with the sigh of horror that escaped from her lips as she stared full into the angry black eyes of Mark Brandon. All her strength seemed to drain from her body. Yet she stared at him, mesmerized.

He'd said he would come back to talk. But she hadn't expected him now! For a long moment he stood in the shimmering half-light outside regarding her.

His eyes bored into her, taking in every detail of her appearance from the unnatural pallor of her olive skin against the inky black of her rippling hair to the bold sophistication of her lowcut and tightly fitting gown. As his gaze roamed suggestively, touching her lips first and lingering before descending slowly to the swelling softness of her breasts, she reddened. She fought against the urge to cross her hands protectively above her revealing gown.

Involuntarily, trembling fingers clutched at her throat and beneath her fingertips she felt the cold stones of the diamond circlet blazing against her warm flesh. She drew her hand instantly away as though she'd touched fire. But the quickness of her movement had caught his attention, and as his eyes rested on her throat, his expression darkened. She knew he was remembering that once his fingers had lifted up her heavy hair and fastened that necklace there, branding her as but another of his possessions.

Elegantly attired in black evening clothes, Brandon stood framed like a massive giant in the doorway. For one long instant the grandfather clock in the foyer seemed to stop ticking. Behind Brandon a gentle breeze wafted, and brown leaves curled and skittered across the gray painted floor of the shaded veranda. Weakly Lannie noticed that the wind had tousled Brandon's thick, black hair rakishly across his brow.

An aura of raw power emanated from him. Involuntarily Lannie's shoulders sagged in defeat as she backed further into the room.

"Hello, Lannie."

When she opened her mouth to reply all that came out was a strange, choking sound.

Taking her incoherent utterance as an invitation to enter, Brandon strode casually into the room with the air of nonchalant mastery. It was as though he knew already that he was in control of both the house and its mistress. She caught the tangy scent of his aftershave, and was at once made treacherously aware of erotic memories she thought she'd locked away forever.

His black glance flicked with sardonic interest over the neat but threadbare furnishings of the mansion and then back to her again. She tilted her head back proudly as he noted the vivid contrast between her lavish attire and her home. At least there was no pity in his ebony eyes, only cool assessment.

A small painted sign beside her caught his attention, and he looked away and focused on the bold black lettering. There was a long pause as he read:

Belle Rose Plantation Home—$5.00 Admission
Plantation Store and Mini-shops

VISITING HOURS: Monday through Friday—10:00 A.M. to 4:00 P.M.
Luncheon served—12:00 P.M. to 1:00 P.M.

A jet-dark eyebrow arched mockingly, and his gaze swept her again.

Suddenly for no reason at all she felt oddly out of place in her own home. She was remembering Newport and New York City and his glittering world that she'd once been a part of.

For an unendurably long instant his black, penetrating gaze continued to hold her own, and she had the strangest sensation that the seven years that had separated them were stripped ruthlessly away and she was again the Dragon's mistress.

The Dragon—the swirling, fiery emblem that stood for Brandon Chemicals Inc., an international company of vast proportions—had come to symbolize the man who owned and ran it as well. It suited Brandon, she thought briefly, for he was a man who took what he wanted no matter who or what opposed him. And once he had wanted her.

Flushing, Lannie looked swiftly away from him, no longer able to meet his unwavering stare. "W-what are you doing here, Brandon?" she managed to ask at last, in a voice that sounded stiff and strained—not in the least like her own.

Though she wasn't looking at him directly, she was keenly aware of his movements, of the easy grace of his tall, muscled frame as he shut the front door behind him. "Isn't that rather obvious," he said at last in a tone that was velvet-soft. "I told you last night I wanted to talk to you."

A strange warmth rushed through her that she didn't understand at all. Wildly she concentrated on the layers of gathered mist at the top of a distant curtain rod in the parlor. How was it possible that she still felt on such intimate terms with him? Aloud she said, "I was hoping you'd change your mind."

"No chance of that." Brutally he snapped out the sentence. For the first time his voice was as bitterly harsh as his demeanor.

Desperately she tried a new tack. "You should have called first. I wasn't expecting you. As a matter of fact I—"

"That's exactly why I didn't. If I had, you would scarcely have been here alone and dressed so . . ." She was crimson as his appreciative gaze slid over her voluptuous curves. His eyes, alight with male interest, finished his sentence far more effectively than any words could have. "Besides," he continued laconically, "I didn't have time to call first. I was busy."

"Busy!" she blurted hotly, suddenly angry. "How could I forget how busy you are with all your conglomerates to manage and board meetings to attend in between juggling all the beautiful females in your life."

He smiled then. His broad white grin and his flashing black eyes made her acutely aware of his more than devastating male charm. She realized uneasily he'd enjoyed her outburst. "I'm glad to see I can still stir your passions, Lannie," he mocked softly.

Her nerve ends went as hot as flame as his remark evoked unwanted memories of the sensuality of their former relationship. It was a purely physical response, she told herself quickly.

"I'd hardly call making me as angry as possible stirring my passions," she snapped.

"Nevertheless, you haven't forgotten me, or my habits, as completely as you would have me believe, and I'm glad."

His statement fanned the flames of her rising fury, but she said nothing. She didn't know what to say or what to do for fear he might further misconstrue her words. There was no defense against his overinflated ego.

Some part of Lannie wanted to deny that this was happening, that he was real. She'd wanted to believe her encounter with him had been a bad dream and nothing more. But here he was, boldly alive, very much a part of the moment.

Chapter Five

Aren't you going to invite me to sit down, or do we stand here and regard one another warily for the rest of the evening?" Brandon's manner was condescending, faintly derogatory. "Surely Southern hospitality isn't a thing of the past at Belle Rose."

"I was hoping you would take the hint and leave," Lannie replied, seething.

"Not until I've said what I came to say," he returned with an almost careless indifference.

She stood still looking at him for a long moment, not inviting him in, yet realizing it was futile to demand that he leave. For the first time she was aware of the autumn chill pervading the house, of the unlit fire in the parlor grate.

A tremor quaked through her, and she rubbed her bare arms to bring warmth back to her numbed flesh. A strip of scarlet organza, her wrap, lay across her bed upstairs, but before she could voice her desire to escape him and rush after it, Brandon was deftly stripping off his black evening coat. She couldn't help noticing how the crisp white cloth of his long-sleeved shirt tugged across the broad expanse of his muscled shoulders. His stomach was flat, his waist narrow, his body lean and powerful. His movements toward her, though swift, were fluidly graceful.

Gently he folded his jacket that was still warm from his body heat around her. He was so tall that he towered over her, reminding her of how very small and feminine she'd always felt in his arms.

The pressure of his fingers seemed to burn through the fabric of his coat and sear her skin with their touch. He curved her body against his own hard warmth, and held her for longer than was necessary as though he enjoyed the feel of her next to him. And strangely she didn't try to stop him. . . .

His eyes lowered, and her own lifted to meet his searching gaze. "Thank you," she murmured, wishing that she wasn't so easily chilled and aware that they were repeating actions which had once been a ritual to them.

"You know how good it always feels to me to get out of that monkey suit," he said at last. "Your thin southern blood to the rescue. . . ." His arms around her had tightened. He laughed easily, and the sound was warmly pleasant to her ears.

"And your *hot* southern blood to my rescue as usual." Why had she said that last quip, as though they still had a relationship? Her own shaky laughter joined his, as, fleetingly, she remembered all the times when he who was so hot-natured had shed jackets or coats to wrap her in them.

His black, intimate gaze seemed to go right through her, caressing her and leaving her breathless.

His arms dropped away, and though his features were no longer so grimly set, the light mood was instantly broken and the barriers between them that had dropped away were all rigidly back in place. *Where they belonged,* she thought hastily.

"Do come into the parlor and make yourself comfortable," she said, trying to assume an appropriately formal tone to dispel the intimacy that had been between them. She sensed his eyes boldly following every feminine movement of her gracefully swaying body as she led the way, and she felt strangely awkward.

"That's easier said than done," he remarked dryly as he scanned the furnishings of the parlor in vain for a comfortable chair.

The antique carved rosewood chairs were far too fragile for so large a man. She rushed toward the large settee upholstered in a soft wool floral pattern faded with age, and she patted it. Then shivering, she clutched his jacket more tightly to her.

"You're still cold. I'll light the fire before we sit down." He strode toward the fireplace and struck a match crisply against the heel of his shoe. A fire leapt up instantly, casting a pale, mellow glow about the room.

Brandon sprawled easily against the settee making it look far more comfortable than it was. When she would have darted to a chair of Louis XIV design a safe distance from him, he seized her left hand and pulled her down beside him. Because of the smallness of the settee she was pressed close against his muscular thighs. The hard feel of his lower body, the warmth of his breath fanning her cheek, the scent of him filled her with disturbing sensations.

"No, I . . ." Her protest died on her lips as she realized by Brandon's determined expression it was useless. He continued to hold her tightly, his strong fingers pleasantly warm against her own cool palm.

Lannie could feel her tension mounting as the silence between them lengthened. She certainly didn't know what to say, and for once Brandon didn't seem to be in a hurry. He acted as if he had the whole night before him.

He was using his keen powers of observation to take in every changed detail of the room—the carefully polished rosewood *étagères,* the marble mantels and brass window cornices. The walls still flocked with the original French paper were now adorned with family portraits and shadow boxes, treasures Lannie had found in the attics and refurbished as much as possible before she brought them down. Rich brass andirons added beauty to the fireplace. There was an abundance of freshly cut flowers—the last of the season—atop several small, carefully waxed tables.

Although there was a certain aura of delapidation in both the house and the furniture owing to the lack of funds required for extensive renovations, the room was still charming.

"You've done wonders with this place," Brandon said. Something about this statement obviously surprised him. She fought against the feeling of pleasure his praise brought her.

"Why?" he continued. "I thought you hated Belle Rose. There was a time that the last place I ever thought I'd find you was here."

The past was dangerous ground, and she had no intention of discussing it.

"I doubt very seriously if you came here to talk about Belle Rose or my feelings about it," she said coolly.

"No, but now that I'm here, I can't help being curious. You were hardly the domestic type, as I remember." His black head was tipped to the side as he studied her with new interest. "You found rural life dull. You craved constant excitement; you lived at a feverish pace. Paris . . . London . . . New York . . . You wanted designer clothes, jewels. And now . . ."

"People change," she retorted curtly.

"Not completely."

She detected the faintest note of cynical mockery in his deep tone, and for some reason, though she knew it was useless, it prompted her to try to explain.

"I have, Brandon. There are things about me, things that happened since . . . us." Why had she said that? The warm, appraising gleam instantly lighting his black eyes heightened her color until her cheeks burned. It was pointless to try to explain anything to him. Suddenly she was furious. He could be insolent without even saying a word. "You don't know me any more," she bit out. "That's all!"

"And I once knew everything about you," he mocked huskily. One of his hands had somehow made its way up to her creamy shoulder, and his fingers played with a dark strand of her hair in a familiar fashion that further irritated her.

She jerked her head away, and a slow, sexy smile curved his lips.

"Tell me then," he said. "I'm intrigued. What happened? Why the interest in Belle Rose? Your mother never cared before, and neither did your father."

"My mother and father are dead."

"So I heard some time back. I'm sorry." He sounded almost sincere.

Lannie stirred restlessly. She had not expected small talk and on such intimate topics. The last thing she needed or desired was Mark Brandon poking around in her life, and she was determined to change the subject at once.

"I thought you lived in New York. I didn't know you came to Louisiana anymore."

"You should know better than that." Again the husky tone shattered the remnants of her composure, sending a wave of heat pulsating through her. "I keep a watchful eye on anything that belongs to me." A certain possessiveness had come into his fathomless black eyes as he regarded her, and she swallowed quickly to mask her nervousness. "I fly in to check on the plant from time to time," he said casually. "And *Grandmère* comes down to check on the house."

"How is Genevieve?" Lannie asked, genuinely concerned. Though talking to Brandon was difficult, Lannie was glad of a safer topic of conversation.

"She's eighty and not as strong as you remember her. In fact she's opening up the Brandon House for the next few months because she didn't think she could endure another northern winter."

The grandfather clock slowly chimed the hour, and as the soft tones echoed through the house, Lannie was reminded of the lateness of the hour. She shivered, remembering that John would be arriving any minute. The thought of him finding Brandon alone with her was distinctly unpleasant. John would be understanding, of course, but she couldn't be sure of how Brandon would react.

"Brandon, we can't talk. Not tonight. I'm expecting someone any minute."

Brandon's intent gaze watched her mouth as nervously she slowly licked the dryness of her lips with her tongue to moisten them. There was an erotic element in his black eyes that she dared not analyze. He didn't touch her or do anything, yet she had the strangest feeling that he was seducing her.

Quivering, she rose and would have rushed toward the door to throw it open, but he moved more quickly and blocked her escape. Careless that he was crushing the soft folds of her dress, his powerful arms pulled her slender curves against his lean hard body. She felt the heat of him burning through the filmy fabric and firing her flesh with a strangely wild warmth.

"I have no intention of leaving."

Something in the tone of his voice sent her pulses racing.

"John . . ." she protested weakly.

". . . won't be coming tonight. I've seen to that."

Just his nearness was doing odd things to her. One of his hands was moving across the bare flesh of her back beneath the rich heaviness of her rich black curls, down the curve of her spine. A thrilling tingle coursed through her. He knew exactly how to touch her, where to touch her.

"You what?" she gasped, desperately trying to struggle free of his embrace.

He held her effortlessly. "There was a convenient emergency at Brandon Chemicals, and so I called the good doctor. When he told me of his plans, which I already knew about, I gallantly offered to stop by and explain."

"You arranged . . ." A tiny pulsebeat was pounding painfully in her head. He was holding her so tightly against his chest she could scarcely get her breath. "You?"

Brandon gave her a slow, considering look. "That's right," he replied, unperturbed.

"Let me go, Brandon! I can't breathe when you hold me like this! I feel like I'm going to faint!"

Abruptly he released her, and she spun free of his reach. Her unexpected freedom emboldened her. "And stay out of my life!" she lashed. "You have no right. . . ." Even to her own ears her voice sounded ineffectual and almost tremulous.

"I have every right! You and I made a bargain once, and you walked out on me before the terms were fulfilled. You disappeared without a trace, remember? I never said you could go."

A shiver of true fear went through her as she backed closer to the warmth of the fireplace. "Brandon, you can't expect to hold me to that now," she began desperately. "You don't intend to ruin my life. . . ."

He was moving slowly toward her. "The last thing

I've ever wanted was to ruin your life. However, there was a second part of our bargain. You promised to stay away from my family."

"But you meant Genevieve, not John! And I did stay away from her. John's not even your real brother."

"He's the only brother I have. And you are the last woman I would choose for his wife."

"Did it ever occur to you that who John marries is John's decision, not yours? He and I *are* engaged! Surely you don't intend to do anything. You don't care about me anymore."

"Wrong on several counts."

"Brandon, no! I love him."

"You couldn't love any man! He thinks you love him. Just as he thinks he's in love with you, the poor deluded fool. But you're the wrong kind of woman for a man like him."

"Brandon, you don't know me any more. I've changed."

"So you've been telling me. But nothing you've said or done convinces me. And now it's my turn to convince you that I know you better than you know yourself."

"Brandon, w-what are you going to do?"

She gasped as her stockinged heel slid off the edge of the carpet and onto slippery, polished oak. The rough texture of the flocked wallpaper touched her shoulderblades, arresting the backward motion of her body.

She realized with a start that she'd backed as far away from him as she could. Yet still Brandon moved toward her. She was trapped, as surely as though he placed his hands on her shoulders and pinned her to the wall.

His smoldering, black gaze burned through her, holding her spellbound, and she was unable to will herself to twist out of his path. It was almost as though she welcomed his deliberate approach for she merely waited until he spanned the distance that separated them. It was almost as though some secret part of her yearned for his touch and even invited it.

He towered over her so that she had to tilt her head to look into his eyes, and she drank deeply of the sight of him. His thick black hair glinted in the golden firelight. His hooded gaze was intent; his sensual lips half-parted. For a breathless instant she felt dizzy and weak in the knees. Her hands groped along the wall so that she could steady herself.

A strange excitement was coursing through her. He hadn't even touched her, yet the languid sensuality of his gaze stirred her senses as no other man had ever come close to doing. Heartbeats fluttered against her ribcage, and involuntarily she swayed toward him.

Slowly he raised his hand, and with a roughened fingertip traced the feathery line of her dark brow. She drew a quick, shallow breath at the electric sensation he could so carelessly evoke. Then the gentle descent of his fingers explored the softness of her cheek before he curved his hand at the base of her neck beneath her spilling black tresses and drew her face more closely to his.

His touch was infinitely gentle, and as always it amazed her that a man of his ruthless nature could be so gentle with a woman. The roughness of his cheek grazed her soft skin, and dreamily she moved her head back and forth against him in a nuzzling motion. She was acutely aware that his lips hovered only a fraction of an inch above hers. She felt his fingertips move beneath her hair, lightly fondling the silky edge of her earlobe.

"Brandon . . ." Though she'd spoken to try to stop him, his name was a husky whisper, betraying the extent of her desire. "B-Brandon . . ."

She felt the warmth and moisture of his mouth as it slowly descended to cover hers, silencing her weak protest. His tongue slid inside her mouth and mated with hers, and suddenly she was lost in a whirlpool of dangerous emotions.

She felt deliciously warm and her warmth had nothing to do with the fiery embers in the nearby grate. A wild recklessness was sweeping her.

Their bodies were not touching, and Brandon pursued his slow method of tantalizing arousal, letting his lips roam slowly over hers until it was Lannie who arched her trembling body to fit the hard contours of his muscled frame. It was Lannie who hungrily reached beneath his waistband and freed his shirt so that she could feel the hard warmth of his flesh beneath her fingertips. Frenzied, awkward movements released the tiny black studs of his dress shirt to reveal a tanned strip of lean, dark flesh. Then her fingers combed through the bristly black hairs matting his chest before her palm crept round his neck and then back down over his broad shoulders. She reveled in the touch and feel of his hard muscles, of the incredible heat of him, and a soft moan escaped her lips. His own deep and haggard breathing told her that he was no more immune to the inferno of desire than she.

Sanity abandoned her as a rush of wildness threatened to engulf her. She was a captive to a force so powerful she could do nothing but surrender. As he rained a burning trail of kisses from her lips to her throat, a sweet, aching torment that only he could quench rippled through her like a painful tide, and her hand slipped beneath the waistband of his trousers to caress the firm flatness of his lower stomach. His clothes and her own softly flowing gown seemed like cumbersome barriers that separated them.

Then his arm came around her and he crushed her against him with a groan. She responded to the hard pressure of his hot mouth on hers with a passion that matched his own. The antique furnishings, the outlines of the room blurred, and she was aware only of him and the haze of passion that fused his lips to hers.

She ached all over. Seven years had passed, and in all that time she'd never felt as she did now—wild, and weak, wanton with flaming desire. She wanted him as she had never wanted him before. She longed for him to undress her and pull her down onto the soft, thick carpet and make love to her while the roaring fire bathed their naked bodies with its golden glow.

As if in a dream she heard the ring of the telephone on the nearby table beside the settee. She would have ignored the jarring sound. And when the pressure of Brandon's lips eased on hers, she clung to him.

"Lannie. Oh, Lannie . . . It's been too long," he muttered hoarsely against her mouth. Then reluctantly in a deep voice only slightly more controlled, he said, "I'd better answer that. I left your number with Brandon Chemicals. It might be important."

Slowly his arms slipped around her waist, and her own remained around his while he led her to the phone. Her head lay against the comforting warmth of his shoulder as he lifted the receiver to his ear. Her eyes wandered downward over the lean expanse of his chest revealed by his unbuttoned shirt.

"Brandon, speaking. Er . . . yes. We'll accept charges." A wry smile touched the edges of his sensual mouth as his eyes lowered to hers. His dark gaze caressed the beautiful woman in his arms while he spoke. "Lannie, it's Hilary," he said, placing the phone into her trembling fingers.

A bit of static crackled and then Hilary's vibrant voice burst into the phone. "Lannie, I-I hate to bother you. . . ."

"Is anything wrong, Hilary?" Lannie asked breathlessly. The disturbing proximity of Brandon's body made normal conversation with a third party difficult. Devilishly Brandon traced a tingling path with his hand across the bare flesh of her back.

"You don't sound like yourself, Lannie. Are you all right?"

"Hilary, don't be ridiculous." Furtively Lannie caught at Brandon's fingers to arrest their disturbing path. His slow, sexual smile mocked her. "Of course I'm all right. But why did you call?"

"To tell you we won't be coming home until the morning, and I didn't want you to worry," Hilary replied. "The doctor Denise saw wants another doctor to look at her in the morning."

The receiver buzzed when the connection was severed several minutes later. For a long, pregnant moment, Brandon, who had overheard everything, stared deeply into her eyes. His grip around her waist tightened so that she could feel the lean hard outline of his male shape burning through the drifting softness of her dress to her own skin. Then he took the phone from her and hung it up.

"Brandon," Lannie began shakily. "I really think you should be going." Even to her own ears her voice lacked conviction.

A calloused finger covered her lips, shushing her, and slowly Brandon traced their pouting fullness before his mouth swooped down and branded her lips with his fierce possession. As his kiss deepened so did her own response, and she felt an almost desperate need. Her arms twined around his neck, and she ached to belong to him.

When he withdrew, she would have clung to him.

"Don't try to pretend you don't want me to stay," he murmured thickly against her lips.

"I really think . . . it would be better . . . if you didn't. . . ." she somehow managed.

"Do you remember the first time I made love to you?

It was a cold winter night in New York. There was a fire like this one. You were so beautiful, Lannie." The dark seductive power of his gaze stripped the seven years away. He knew her so well, he knew exactly what to do, what old memories to stir.

Lean brown fingers played through the streaming length of her hair, and she was searingly aware of every place his body touched hers.

"I remember," she murmured huskily. "You don't know how hard I've tried to forget that night, to forget everything else about you. . . ."

"No harder than I've tried, Lannie," he admitted softly. His hand continued its stroking motion through her long, thick hair. "And until I came back to Louisiana and saw you again, I thought I'd succeeded."

"So did I," she agreed.

"But now I want you more than ever."

"Things aren't that simple now, Brandon. There's John."

"Not anymore!"

The bitter violence in his harsh voice warned her of his abrupt change in mood, and she tried to cringe away. But he bodily pulled her into his arms.

"No," she cried out as his mouth claimed hers in a hard kiss that was both savageness and bliss combined. Even as she struggled, her pulse quickened crazily as his lips ravaged hers with a complete and brutal passion that devastated the remnants of her control. "B-Brandon, don't do this. . . ."

But the man who held her so tightly that it hurt against his hard warmth was not the Brandon she knew and remembered. She felt the mad staccato of his heart hammering beneath her ear, felt the harsh heat of his uneven breathing against her mouth and throat. He was like some fierce dark stranger out of a dream whose lips obliterated everything from her mind but the ruthless swirling blackness of his passion. Never before had he made love to her like this with such wild, alien abandon, and somewhere in the depths of her being she marveled that she ever could have thought she knew him when she really hadn't known him at all. For the first time he was stripped bare of his careful control by the primitive, carnal desire she had unleashed in him.

He was shaking as though a violent tremor shuddered through him, and suddenly so was she. As his hands roamed everywhere over her body, her clothes seemed to melt away. Vaguely she was aware of a soft, scarlet heap beneath a chair as he drew her down onto the carpet beside the fire. With swift, sure movements he stripped out of his own clothes and he tossed them toward hers. Then he covered her with the blistering heat of his body. As his lips plundered the nipple of her breast, the intimate contact of his thighs with hers told her of his complete, masculine arousal.

She felt hot and breathless, as though she were drowning in a burning sea from his drugging kisses, and still he did not stop. His embrace was bittersweet as she ached for the sensation of his flesh inside hers even while she fought to avoid the domination of his desire.

"Brandon, please, let me go. . . ."

"Not until I teach you that I'm the only man you'll ever belong to," he muttered hoarsely.

Then once more his lips sought hers, muffling her cry as he branded her solely his own possession.

Chapter Six

Firelight danced, casting flickering shadows about the room, but the lovers who lay in its golden glow were aware only of the raging fire of their own consuming need, each for the other.

A fine sheen of dampness glistened on their bodies. Slowly Brandon's lips explored every female inch of her, and then he lay back while she did the same to him. It had been so long. . . . A trembling weakness seemed to spread through her body when once more his fevered mouth kissed hers, and her lips quivered beneath his touch.

"Mark." She murmured his name in ecstatic pleasure. She had never called him by his first name before, but she'd never felt so close to him. "Oh, Mark . . ." Her fingers wound themselves through the rich darkness of his hair, and she hugged him fiercely. As she did so, her diamond engagement ring scraped across the flesh of his back.

He caught her hand in his. His black eyes blazed through her. When he spoke his voice was rough. "Do you still intend to marry John?"

"N-no. I couldn't after . . ."

"Then take his ring off," he commanded. He watched her intently as she did so. When her fingers were naked he laced his own through them tightly. "You're no longer officially engaged, and you'll tell John tomorrow."

"Yes."

The vague relief his words produced were overpowered by the raging passion that soon followed as Brandon's lips seared hers again. Her senses reigned supreme as his lovemaking grew more ardent.

"Don't ask me to stop," he said moments later. Then he buried his lips against her throat. "Because I don't think I can."

"I want you so. . . ." she whispered.

His body pressed against hers, molding her softness to himself. And when he entered her, she almost cried out. He paused, holding her tightly; his hands moved over her, stroking her gently. His handsome dark face was grave with silent wonder and a trace of anxiety as he regarded her.

"There . . . there hasn't ever been anyone but you," she admitted in soft explanation.

For a long, timeless moment he didn't move so that her body could grow accustomed to his. "Why not?" he asked huskily at last. "It's been over seven years."

It was a question for which she had no answer, a question she'd asked herself many times.

"Because . . . oh, Mark, I don't know. . . ." she whispered. "It just never seemed right with any other man."

With infinite tenderness his lips found hers again and he kissed her once and then a second time. "Lannie . . . sweetheart . . . We've been such fools. . . ."

Her hands ran lightly over his back, down the length of his spine and only when she moved beneath him and pulled his lower body more tightly against herself did he resume his passionate lovemaking.

His touch, his body was sheer madness splintering a wild thrill such as she had never known before through her. For the first time she surrendered herself completely, body and soul, to this man whose pagan passion carried her to dizzying peaks that whirled away all of her resistance. The pleasurable crests of passion, wave after wave, that followed erased the slight pain she'd felt before.

Then he was shuddering, and she was trembling against him and crying out his name as he drew her ever higher toward flaming fulfillment.

Later, before she drifted off to sleep in his arms, she lay thinking that nothing she'd ever experienced matched the depth of emotion Brandon had evoked within her. It was as though, for the briefest instant, her soul had fused with his, and never again would she be exactly the same as she'd been before this night. A new and disturbing dimension had been added to her life for Brandon was a complex and demanding man.

The fire had dimmed to an orange flicker, and the room was almost totally dark when Lannie awoke to the sound of Brandon's low voice as he spoke to someone over the telephone. A thick afghan throw, covering her naked body to protect her from the chill invading the room, had been thoughtfully tucked about her.

"Something's come up," Brandon was saying casually. "I won't be able to come tonight after all. No . . . I won't be home tonight either. You can expect me in the morning. That's right, same number if you need me."

Plastic clicked lightly against plastic, and Lannie realized Brandon had hung up.

Lannie glanced in Brandon's direction. He wore only

his black slacks. The massive breadth of his chest was exposed. She couldn't stop herself from admiring how potently virile he appeared.

"Who were you talking to?" she whispered across the darkness.

"Genevieve." He raked his fingers through his tousled hair in an attempt to smooth it.

"You gave her my number." Lannie sat up and the afghan fell to her waist revealing the gentle swell of her full breasts to his view. The air against her naked flesh was cool, and she shivered.

"Is there anything wrong with that? You know I can't just disappear as though I have no responsibilities, and I hardly think she'll put two and two together and realize I'm spending the night with you."

"I suppose not." Still it was an indiscretion that made her feel vaguely uncomfortable. People didn't think the same in rural southern Louisiana as they did in cosmopolitan New York.

He was instantly beside her, draping his black coat over her shoulders and cradling her in his arms, dispelling her doubts for the moment.

"My beautiful little hypocrite," he teased gently. "You're a throwback to the Civil War era when a woman's reputation was the most important thing in her life. After a night like tonight you would have been a ruined woman, unless I married you. But that's hardly the case today."

She could not resist the impulse to weave her hand lightly over his flat, hard stomach in a caressing motion.

"And would you have . . . married me?" A certain breathlessness invaded her soft query.

"Who knows," he returned blandly, evading her pointed question. "Fortunately the twentieth century tolerates alternate lifestyles, and as you well know, I'm not suited to marriage. Just as you're not."

She felt strangely hurt by his arrogant statement that she was unsuitable for marriage. "I'm not the same as I used to be, Brandon."

"No, you're better, at least in bed." A low, sexy chuckle traced his deep tone.

"That's not what I meant," she said, feeling on the defensive in spite of his compliment. "I'm more settled. I don't want the same things I used to. Sometimes I wonder if I'm even the same person. Once I craved constant excitement, and now, really, I'm content with teaching and Belle Rose."

"I don't think contentment will satisfy you long, Lannie. You don't belong on a rundown plantation, taking in boarders, planting sugarcane, and teaching school, all in an attempt to save something that doesn't exist anymore just because it's been in your family for a century. You used to know that, Lannie."

"I was mixed up, Brandon. I didn't know what I really wanted, and now I do."

"And I know what I'm going to want," he grinned, as his lips descended to brush her bare breast. "If you don't put some clothes on pretty soon. . . ."

"You haven't heard a thing I've said!" she snapped, twisting away in anger that he refused to take her seriously.

"Oh, yes, I have. It's just that I don't believe you. The wild creature I just made love to would never be satisfied without excitement in her life. You're only fooling yourself, Lannie."

"Brandon." Everything he said was making her angrier and angrier.

"Stop talking, Lannie. Words only get us into trouble, and I don't want to fight with you tonight."

"But . . ."

The thread of her conversation was broken when he pulled her into his arms with bruising force and silenced her with a long, hard kiss. All of her anger drained away as the hard pressure of his lips against her mouth reminded her of the rapture he could give her.

Only when she was breathless did he release her.

Slowly, with the afghan flowing behind her like a purple wave, Brandon led her to the stairs. Leaning against him for support because her knees seemed weak and rubbery, Lannie climbed to the second floor.

The bathroom door was ajar, and a shaft of brilliance flooded the dark hallway. The light had been left on, and the charming room was clearly visible to Brandon, who, as usual, was both curious and keenly observant. He paused and then pulled her inside and closed the door behind them.

Lannie had done the room in soft yellows and greens with a white trellised effect on the ceiling so that the bath looked more like a garden area than a bathroom. A green porcelain tub of gigantic proportions, with claw feet and gilt faucets, stood in the center of a thick yellow wall-to-wall carpet. An abundance of lush green ivy cascaded from hanging baskets.

"This is the only room I could afford to completely redo," Lannie said, shivering in spite of Brandon's coat and the afghan. She flicked the switch that turned on the heater.

"It's very nice." He leaned over the edge of the tub, plugged the drain, and turned on the water.

"I'm sorry I don't have a shower," Lannie said, remembering his preference.

"That's all right. This tub looks big enough for two."

His warm smile caressed her, and a hot flush crept into her cheeks as she caught his meaning. There was something cozily intimate about sharing her bath with this big rugged man.

What had happened downstairs had changed everything between them. It was no use pretending differently. Even though she knew how dangerous resuming any kind of relationship with him could be, she was completely incapable of stopping herself.

She reached for the lilac bath salts and bubble bath and poured them into the water. The aromatic scents wafted to their nostrils as they watched the mound of bubbles rise.

"You shouldn't have done that," he chided with a grin. "Now I'll smell like lilacs, just like you."

"Serves you right," she teased, letting the afghan slide to the floor so that her beautiful, nude female form was totally revealed to him before she slipped into the tub, crushing the bubbles beneath her. "I'm putting my brand on you."

"For some reason I don't mind at all," he returned, his black eyes alight with passion as he removed his trousers and got into the tub with her.

With a soap and sponge he massaged her shoulders. Then his expert hands bathed her all over, slowly arousing her to an awareness only of him. When he lay back she returned the favor, letting her hands move over the bronzed, supple strength of his muscles with languid, teasing motions until he was as wild with desire as she.

It was a dangerous game she was playing, but she couldn't stop herself. She didn't even want to. Every time she surrendered herself to him, she knew that she forfeited a little more of her hard-won independence.

Before his lips closed over hers, she protested, "But Brandon, my hair. You're getting it all wet and soapy."

"I'll wash it for you later," he mumbled. "Much later . . ."

Then he was pulling her beneath him so that his hard body fitted into hers, so that every part of him seemed to touch her, so that she was aware of nothing save the hot liquid passion that consumed both himself and her.

Much later in her vast bed, Lannie lay uneasily awake in Brandon's arms while he slept. Her wet hair was wrapped in a thick turkish towel; her body was curled in an intimate tangle against his own.

Sleep eased the lines of tension in his lean, brown face, but it did not wholly erase the determined set of his sensual mouth or the harshness of his jawline. Even in his sleep, he looked ruthless, and she could not help wondering what the outcome of their lovemaking would be.

Was she anything more than an evening's entertainment to him? Had she been no more than a convenient way to satisfy the demand of a sex drive she knew to be quite high?

Suddenly a terrible coldness invaded her system that not even Brandon's intense body heat could alleviate, as she remembered that Brandon had come over for one reason only—to convince her to break up with John. He'd been very very angry. When talk had failed, had he resorted to the last weapon at his disposal—making love to her? Had he played dirty and used her physical attraction for himself as a means of getting her to do what he wanted?

A terrifying bleakness filled her. The thought of Brandon not wanting her for himself, but merely wanting to destroy her relationship with John, was deadening. She forced herself to think back over the evening. Brandon had been very passionate. None of his actions had seemed coldly premeditated. Surely he felt something for her.

In his sleep, Brandon smiled and called her name, and Lannie clasped his hand tightly in hers. "I'm here, my darling," she murmured, snuggling even closer to him in an attempt to dispel her doubts. At last she fell into a fitful sleep.

The fringes of sky outside were edged with a pink glow when Lannie awakened in bed alone. For a long moment she felt strangely disoriented. Then from downstairs she heard the resonant baritone of a man's voice as he sang a Cajun love song. Other sounds from the kitchen drifted to her ears. The refrigerator door slammed. A kitchen chair was scraped across the floor. Dishes clattered on the wooden table.

The yellow towel had come loose from her hair and lay across her pillow. At the sight of it, she remembered everything. Brandon had come over and spent the night, and she'd given herself to him with a wild abandon she wouldn't have believed possible.

Lannie tugged on a pair of burgundy corduroy slacks that molded her slim hips and a gray turtleneck. She washed her face and ran a brush through the tangled masses of her dark hair and coiled it at the nape of her neck. Then she applied a touch of lipstick before going downstairs.

Nerves made her stomach do a cartwheel as she stood hesitantly in the kitchen doorway. Somehow, this morning, she was almost frightened of seeing Brandon. She felt uncertain because she didn't have the slightest idea what he felt about her after the previous night. It was as though she were afraid to confront the everyday reality of his personality after the dreamlike passion they had shared.

Brandon was pulling a paper plate piled high with steaming, butterfly shrimp from the microwave. Hilary's shrimp, that she'd been saving for John!

He was again wearing his black evening clothes. His shirt was unbuttoned at the throat, revealing a V of bronzed skin. As soon as he saw her his gaze swept her in an intimate, knowing appraisal, and he smiled. Yet, despite his smile, he seemed guarded.

She felt strangely shy and could scarcely think of a word to say to him. "You must be starved," she murmured. "To be eating shrimp in the morning. Would you like me to cook you breakfast?"

"That won't be necessary," he returned smoothly.

"No Louisiana Creole worth his salt would pass up shrimp—even leftovers—no matter what the time of day. I hope you don't mind my helping myself?"

"Not at all."

She was aware of him watching her when he didn't think she noticed as though he too wasn't sure of her reaction to him after the night before.

"Pull up a chair and join me," he offered.

Even though he dished her out several shrimp, she couldn't eat a bite. They'd both skipped dinner, and still she wasn't hungry. Brandon, however, ate as though he were famished.

"You're up early," she said at last, attempting conversation.

"I need to get to the plant first thing and make sure everything's all right."

Why did talking to him seem so difficult all of a sudden? She sensed that he too was under a strain.

"Last night you said something about an emergency. . . ."

"Oh, that was nothing much," he said, waving it off as he dipped a shrimp in red sauce.

She could not stop herself from thinking that it was nothing except a ruse to eliminate John. But before she had a chance to comment the phone rang, and Lannie, seizing the opportunity to escape, rushed from the kitchen to answer it.

"Lannie." At the sound of John's low, measured tone, Lannie drew a swift, nervous breath.

John hesitated, and Lannie heard something in his voice she hadn't heard before—distrust and hurt. "Is Brandon there? He's needed at Brandon Chemicals."

Suddenly the silence between them was as tense as a tightly pulled cord. It wasn't even seven A.M. If she admitted the truth, John would know that Brandon had spent the night with her, that they had slept together. And without knowing of their former relationship, he couldn't possibly understand. The last person she wanted to hurt was John.

"Uh . . . no . . ." she mumbled guiltily.

"He left *your* number with Genevieve last night." Still the reticence was present, the note of lingering doubt and accusal in his voice.

"Well, he did come over. But he left fairly early. He's not here now."

Just as she said those words, Brandon stepped into the room. His dark frame seemed to fill the doorway, and his black eyes blazed with anger as he regarded her. Beneath his condemning gaze she paled.

Relief flooded John's voice, washing away his distrust. "I couldn't believe I'd find him there," he said in a rush. "Listen, Lannie, I've got a surgery case in two minutes. I'll have to let you go."

"John—" Even as she murmured his name she knew it was too late.

Already he had hung up without giving her a chance to say anything. As far as he was concerned they were still engaged.

With one quick movement Brandon ripped the receiver from her trembling grasp.

"John . . ." His deep voice grated like a low roar into the receiver, and when he realized the line had gone dead, he slammed the phone down with a bang. Then he turned on Lannie. "You little liar!"

She shuddered at the raw violence in his tone, at the dark emotion glittering in the depths of his black eyes.

"What did you want me to say?" she asked softly.

"The truth—that you're no longer engaged."

"I . . . I couldn't. . . ." Her voice faltered.

"You sleep with me, and then pretend that nothing happened between us," he accused harshly. The planes of his face looked as hard and cold as a bronze statue's.

"I didn't pretend any such thing! I just couldn't let him find out like that."

"Why not?" His black eyes tore through her, and she flinched.

She saw that Brandon wouldn't even try to understand. "You wouldn't ask that question if you really had any brotherly affection for him," she managed.

"Let's leave my brotherly affection out of this discussion while we examine your motives." He advanced upon her, backing her against the low table beside the wall. He towered over her, his expression ruthless.

"I didn't want to hurt him. Is that a crime? John is a very dear person."

"A very dear person," he sneered disbelievingly. "I think you're hedging your bets."

"What?"

"You heard me! You had a nice little secure life mapped out for yourself as John's wife. Not only is he a doctor, but he inherited a sizable piece of Brandon Chemicals when Dad died. With his money you could do all sorts of things you can't do now, like restoring your precious Belle Rose or buying yourself a good horse instead of that murderous demon you ride. I'm sure I'd be amazed at how elaborate your scheme is."

Her face crumpled with pain at his accusation. "That's not true," she began in a desperate attempt to explain. "I love . . . loved John for himself, not his money! I didn't even know he inherited anything. I wouldn't have cared, even if I had known."

"Love. I wonder what that word means to you. You love him, yet you slept with me last night, and very enthusiastically I might add! May I ask, what grand emotion do you feel for me?" He said the last with biting sarcasm.

"If you really want to know, for seven years I thought I hated you!" she hurled. She wanted to hurt him, to enrage him, to tear away his guarded, statuelike mask.

"My sentiments toward you exactly!" His eyes drifted over her knowingly, stripping her. "And I'll settle for hate instead of love, as long as it'll get me into your bedroom."

"Why of all the coarse, vile things to say."

She felt degraded and hurt by the contemptuous dislike she heard in his tone, and the last shreds of her control snapped. He was blaming her for what had happened between them the night before. Furious, she lashed her palm toward his tanned cheek, but he anticipated her intent. He caught her hand in his, and gave her wrist a savage twist as he pulled her tightly against him.

The thick length of her glowing black hair came loose and cascaded to her shoulders. The hard warmth of his chest crushed her breasts painfully; she could almost feel his heart pounding against her flesh. One of his hands slid around her waist so that her hips were held to his.

"I wouldn't try to hit someone twice my size if I were you," he warned. "Especially when you've made him mad enough to hit you back."

"If you're mad, it's your own fault! You won't even try to understand!"

"I understand well enough. You were eager enough for me last night. But this morning it's obvious you're more than ready to string both John and me along until you decide which relationship is more profitable." He paused. "I was wrong about you, Lannie. You have changed! At least seven years ago you only took one man on at a time!"

Tears streamed from the corners of her eyes, and she struggled violently in his arms, stopping only when she realized the movement of her hips against his was producing a searing fire in her loins despite her anger, and that he too was sexually aroused by her actions.

"Brandon! That isn't so! What can I do to make you believe me?"

"Nothing. Remember, you and I go back a long way."

Shame washed through her as she realized how difficult, perhaps impossible, it would be for her to live down her past. He thought she cared nothing for any man, other than what he could do for her. And that had never been true, not even in the past. It had only seemed that way.

"I thought I was in love with John, until last night. Now I'm so confused I don't know what I feel." As her eyes lifted and met his angry dark gaze, it was terribly clear that whatever tenuous bond had been between them only a few hours before was now completely shattered. "Oh, why did you have to come back and turn my life upside-down?"

"I told you before. I came back to destroy your relationship with John." The coldness in his low tone chilled her.

If only she could have derived the female satisfaction of believing he was jealous of John. But she knew his determination to break up her relationship with his stepbrother stemmed from his desire to protect John from a woman he considered unfit to be his brother's wife. She knew too well his feelings along that subject. For the briefest instant she remembered the past.

"And that's the only reason you came over last night . . . and . . . and made love to me. You spent the night hoping he would call and find out. . . . You . . . you used me! That's all last night meant to you. Just a means to get your way!" With each word her voice sounded more shrilly hysterical.

The long, hard sweep of his body fitted against hers, his very closeness that seemed to burn her skin made her treacherously aware of his power over her. And he was the only man who could make her feel this way.

When he made no denial, she twisted and spun free of him. An unbearable hurt seemed to expand and tighten in her chest, and she emitted a strange, animal cry of pain before she cupped shaking fingers over her lips to stifle the sound.

"Lannie." The sight of her so distraught drained his anger from him, and his low voice offered a comfort that was strangely more hurtful than his rage. His dark face was ashen.

"Don't say anything!" she cried desperately. "Just go to Brandon Chemicals or to whatever woman you're currently involved with! Wherever it is you really want to be! And don't ever come back!" With that her pain-glazed eyes locked with his for what seemed an eternity before she raced from the room and fled upstairs to the privacy of her bedroom.

Why had he come back and deliberately destroyed the fragile tranquility of her life, when he felt nothing but utter contempt for her?

For the first time in seven years she fell across her bed and sobbed as though her heart were broken.

"Women!" Several muttered expletives coupled with this word were inaudible downstairs as Brandon stalked heatedly toward the front door, determined to leave exactly as Lannie had bid him. When he went out, he didn't even bother to shut the door. But with every step he took toward his car, he moved more slowly. In spite of the fierce anger she'd roused in him, a vision of her lovely, stricken face rose to haunt him.

Pausing in midstride, he mentally went over what had happened. In the cold light of reason everything he'd said was logical. His rage had been more than justified, and yet. . . .

He pivoted. He needed to get on with his day. He had time if he left at once to stop by at Brandon Chemicals before he drove into Baton Rouge for an important appointment with his banker. Then later there was lunch with the plant manager.

It wasn't like him to hesitate. His black eyes ran upward over the softly lit columns of Belle Rose trailing with lush, English ivy to the darkened window which he knew to be that of Lannie's room. At the thought of leaving her crying as helplessly as a child, a powerful emotion he didn't attempt to analyze surged through him. And the next step he took was quicker than his last as he moved once more back toward the house, to her.

Chapter Seven

*B*ecause of her own choking sobs, Lannie did not hear Brandon's almost silent tread as he strode into her room. For a long moment he stood beside her, looking down at her slim, graceful form heaving as though she were tortured. Then she felt the exquisite gentleness of his large hands slowly caress her back.

Instantly she recoiled as though an electric shock jolted through her. She tried to pull away from his touch, but the firm pressure of his hands on her back prevented it.

"Lannie . . ."

She ignored his low, resonant tone and buried her face even more deeply into her pillow.

But Brandon refused to be ignored. "Lannie, listen to me."

His hand moved upward through her thick, tumbling hair, and he turned her body so that she faced him. Her face was red and puffy from crying, but even thus ravaged, he thought it the most beautiful of faces. He

97

brushed aside the loose strands of her hair that stuck to her damp forehead and cheeks.

"I told you to get out," she ordered brutally.

"I never was any good at taking orders," he mocked gently. "Giving them is more my style."

The mattress sagged as he sat down beside her and pulled her shaking body into his arms. Her head was cradled against his shoulder; her hair streamed over his chest.

"Why did you come up here anyway?" she cried. "Brandon Chemicals is looking for you. I know how busy, how important—"

"Brandon Chemicals can go to hell," he muttered savagely in a burst of impatience because he was getting nowhere with her.

"You're not making any sense." She tilted her head back so that she could see the dark handsomeness of his face. She felt the steady beat of his heart.

"Lannie, I can't leave you like this." His voice vibrated with emotion, and she wondered at its cause.

"Why not? You've got what you wanted. You've destroyed whatever chance I might have had of finding happiness with John. You . . ."

As always at the mention of John a tightness came into Brandon's voice. She felt the muscles of his chest and stomach tense. "Let's leave John out of this."

"How can we?"

"I came up here to say I'm sorry."

"For what?" she asked cuttingly. "At least you were honest."

"I'm not sure I was—entirely."

"What do you mean?"

His hands continued their slow, stroking motion along her neck and through her hair. "Last night I did come over to talk you out of marrying John. And maybe that was part of the reason I made love to you, but it wasn't all of it. I wanted you for myself. Lannie, you've always been like a fever infecting my blood ever since you were a young kid. Why, do you remember that time I nearly made love to you over at the Sugar Castle when I was home from college on spring break? You couldn't have been a day over fourteen."

She didn't like the comparison of his desire for her to an illness, and that long-ago frenzied necking session had taught her she'd been playing with fire to tease and flirt with him. She'd been so terrified of him after that, that for years she'd avoided him.

"Why did you leave my number with Genevieve last night?" she demanded.

"I had to leave her a number where I could be reached. But I suppose part of the reason was that I wanted John to find out," he admitted.

At those words, she tensed all over. "Okay, Brandon. You've said what you came to say, and I'm in control of my emotions again. See, I'm not crying anymore. You can go and get on with what I'm sure will be a busy day." Her voice was stone cold.

"Lannie, what I'm trying to say is that I don't know what last night meant to me." The warmth of his ebony gaze sent a trace of shivery fire racing through her nervous system. "I only know I want to see you again."

"To be some convenient plaything while you're here in Louisiana. No . . ."

"Lannie, that's not what it would be. When I leave, you could come with me."

"So you can discard me when you're tired of me. No, Brandon, I'm past the age of thinking a no-commitment relationship would ever satisfy me. I don't want to go with you and make the same mistakes all over again."

"What mistakes? And why do you think I would discard you? You were the one who walked out on me, remember?" His lips twisted cynically at the unpleasant memory.

"Yes, I remember. I walked out because it was hell living with a man who never trusted me, who held me in contempt, who'd blackmailed me into the relationship in the first place."

She sank wearily against his rippling muscles as she remembered. Their relationship had been hopeless from the beginning.

"If I wasn't perfect, neither were you," he stated harshly because her accusations were putting him on the defensive. "You used your position as my grandmother's trusted companion to steal from her. If I hadn't caught you that night in her townhouse taking her diamond bracelet who knows what else you would have stolen."

"I didn't steal that bracelet! I was returning it!" And Brandon had been there in the darkened shadows of Genevieve's bedroom, waiting for her.

"Returning it! What's the difference really? If you hadn't stolen it in the first place, you wouldn't have had to return it! Who knows when you would have succumbed to temptation and stolen again."

"I never stole anything in my life! I . . ." Her anger drove her to twist free of his comforting embrace, but she was keenly aware of the proximity of his lean, hard body.

She couldn't explain now, even as she hadn't been able to explain then. Her cousin Velvet had taken the bracelet, and she'd been returning it to protect Velvet. Only she'd been caught.

Late one long-ago Friday afternoon Lannie had let herself into Velvet's Manhattan apartment in the East Eighties only to find her cousin unconscious from an overdose of medically prescribed pills for her nerves, mixed with alcohol. When she'd managed to revive her, Velvet had confided to Lannie that her boyfriend had jilted her, that she wasn't getting the modeling jobs she needed to support herself, and that in a weak moment when she'd visited Lannie at Genevieve's townhouse she'd stolen Genevieve's diamond bracelet. But Velvet had become too terrified by the enormity of what she'd done to pawn the bracelet for the money she needed. Velvet had felt so pressured by the New York pace and her own inability to cope that she was actually afraid she was going to kill herself.

Velvet had always been the type of person who needed someone to take care of her. She'd sobbed into Lannie's arms until Lannie had taken sufficient pity on her to agree to make everything all right again. Lannie had purchased a one-way ticket to New Orleans for Velvet and had promised to take care of her moving expenses. In the end Lannie had even agreed to replace the bracelet. But when she had done so, Brandon had caught her and accused her of stealing it.

Still, there was no way Lannie could have told Brandon the truth. Velvet had been too weak to face the consequences of what she'd done. It might have driven her to take her life.

Even now if Lannie told him the truth, he might do or say something very destructive to Velvet. Velvet was happily married to Hamlin, and Lannie had no intention of allowing that past mistake to jeopardize her cousin's present contentment.

Brandon was staring at her quizzically as if something about her puzzled him. He reached up and gently cupped her chin. "You've the face of an innocent," he said at last as though this fact always surprised him.

Just his touch and a tingle started in the pit of her stomach. She tossed her head, and his hand dropped away.

"I am innocent, Brandon, but I can't ever tell you the truth about that bracelet." That was more than she'd ever said before in her own defense. As she stared deeply into his eyes, her liquid brown gaze never wavered.

Staring at her keenly, Brandon frowned slightly. In the day-to-day operation of his businesses he had had to deal with all kinds of people, and he'd developed an uncanny sense for knowing when someone was lying. But even though he felt she was telling the truth, she was the one person he didn't trust his feelings with.

"Are you protecting someone?" he finally asked.

He saw the fear momentarily flicker in the depths of her dark brown eyes and wondered what it meant.

"I can't tell you," she said.

"Well, even if you are protecting someone, you can't deny that you were constantly in the company of wealthy men."

Shame fleetingly tinted her cheeks crimson. Yes, that was all too true. She'd craved Velvet's admiration and approval so much that for a time she'd copied her older, more glamorous cousin's lifestyle until she'd learned to think for herself and discovered it wasn't for her.

Brandon continued speaking. "So I decided to have you for myself, but you refused me. And when I caught you with that bracelet, I used it to get what I'd wanted for a very long time—you. Looking back, I don't feel very proud of myself."

How well she remembered his utter ruthlessness. "You blackmailed me into cutting all ties with your family and becoming your mistress instead of sending me to prison."

In the mildest of tones he said, "I wouldn't . . . I couldn't have sent you to prison."

"But I didn't know that." But she knew it now as she stared up into his serious face.

"I can't excuse myself for doing what I did," he said gravely. "But remember, I thought you had been sleeping with all those men when I demanded that you move in with me. I never forced you into a physical relationship with me. You came willingly."

"You made me live with you. After several months of being around you constantly . . ."

"You inevitably came to want me as much as I wanted you. If it hadn't been me it would have been one of those other men. A girl of your passionate nature was bound to sleep with someone," he stated with a chauvinistic matter-of-factness that infuriated her.

He'd never really realized how special he'd been to her, and that hurt. Her thickly fringed dark eyes flashed up at him and her full lips rounded into a becoming pout. At the same time a warm rush of color flooded her cheeks, but her fury only enhanced the voluptuous quality of her loveliness until she was breathtakingly beautiful.

"How dare you. . . ." she cried and as she leaned forward, her breast touched his shoulder.

Sexual desire shot through him like a bolt and he felt himself losing interest in their conversation. "It's the truth," he nevertheless stated baldly. "Someone else would have come along just as incapable as I was of passing up such a tantalizing and willing piece of female flesh."

Erotic memories of just how willing she had been in his bed flooded his mind. She was so near he caught the sweet, fresh, natural scent of her mingling with the lilac fragrance of her perfume. He scarcely thought about what he said. He was too acutely aware of her physically, of the swelling softness of her breasts beneath her sweater, of her generous hips, of the stretch of thigh lying hotly against his knee.

"I think you'd better go," she snapped waspishly, concealing her hurt with anger, "before we get into another argument."

"Not now." His voice held a strange huskiness that she didn't at first comprehend. "And I haven't the slightest intention of getting into an argument." An amused half-smile curved his lips as his black eyes ran over her body suggestively.

When she at last registered his meaning she would have twisted out of his reach had he not caught her arms and dragged her to him.

Incensed, she fought with all the power in her to evade the deliberate descent of his mouth to hers. But every movement of her body only brought her in closer contact with him. She felt herself responding even though it was against her will to do so. A spreading fire coursed through her lower body.

"No . . . Brandon . . . No," she cried out, dismayed at the treachery of her senses. "This . . . we . . . are wrong for each other."

"Not in bed," he said roughly. Was he insane to contemplate taking her again? Vaguely he remembered his nine o'clock appointment in Baton Rouge with his banker. But the ripe lushness of her beauty acted on him like a narcotic that he could not do without, and he thought briefly that his banker and Genevieve and whatever else stood in his way could go to hell.

Stubbornly he gathered her into his arms and laid her onto the center of the bed and followed her down. When his lips touched hers, he thrust his tongue deep into her mouth.

She lay passively beneath him in a vain attempt to deny her own aroused state. But he knew her too well to be fooled. He felt her lips trembling beneath the violent onslaught of his kisses; he felt the involuntary quivering in her muscles even though she lay inert beneath him.

A furious hunger drove him to make her want him as crazily as he wanted her. His hands roamed over her, loosening the fastenings of her clothes and removing them. He cupped her breasts. Then his mouth and tongue teased her nipples into rigid peaks. Unable to restrain her passion any longer, she moaned softly, arching herself closer to the warm, pleasurable moisture of his tongue.

His hands and mouth sought out all the erogenous places of her soft body. Deliberately restraining himself, he made love to her slowly until she was as wild for him as he was for her. Then, though it tested his almost superhuman control, he drew away from her as though he meant to stop, having thus roused her.

A terrible emptiness engulfed her. "Brandon . . ." she sighed. "Don't . . ."

She felt the harshness of his rapid, uneven breaths stir through her hair.

"Don't what?" he demanded roughly.

"Don't . . . go . . . away," she pleaded shakily.

A triumphant smile parted his sensual lips as he bent his head to kiss her once more. Then his own need overcame him, and he took her with the shattering force of colliding stars. It was like a spray of fire against an ink black sky as their mutual passion eclipsed in a shuddering surrender.

Much later Lannie raised her love-soft face from the hard warmth of his furred chest and gazed drowsily down at him. His heavy dark hair lay in a matted tumble across his brow. His black eyes that met hers were indolently shuttered so that it was impossible for her to fathom what he was thinking or feeling.

She felt limp all over, drained. Brandon tensed, stretching his lean frame and then relaxing again. The sheet rustled as his powerful arm moved beneath it and circled her waist so that he could draw her body closer to his. Even now with his passion spent, he liked the silken feel of her against him. He enjoyed thoroughly this moment of shared, warm closeness. The long nights in lonely hotels in faraway places seemed very remote with her in his arms. He experienced the deepest contentment, a refreshing sense of inner fulfillment, as though he'd come home after a long and tedious journey.

Her breasts were mashed flat against his chest, and as his eyes ran over her he took great pleasure in her beauty. She had the look of a woman sated with pleasure, the female mirror-image of his own emotion.

He reached up and pushed back a tangled strand of ebony hair. "What are you thinking, love?" he asked huskily at last.

"I was wondering the same thing about you," she murmured uncertainly.

"That's no answer."

A long but contented silence ensued.

Her impassive face told him no more than his told her. Her lovely dark eyes, so exotically gorgeous, held his without revealing her secrets. Her eyes reminded him of the rich brown darkness of the bayous he'd roamed as a boy. Her creamy olive skin betrayed her French ancestry. She was as much a part of his heritage as Brandon House or as Louisiana itself.

At twenty-six she suited him much better than she had seven years ago, he thought idly. Her beauty had deepened with her maturity. Even her passionate response to him was greater.

When she'd walked out on him, he'd thought it for the best, and that was one of the reasons he had not gone after her. The other had been his stubborn pride. She'd run out on him because he'd made her unhappy, and he'd been too afraid of her rejection to let her know how much he needed her. Even then she'd made him feel uncomfortably vulnerable.

With her awakened, voluptuous nature, he'd naturally assumed she would allow herself to be passed from one man to the next. The fact that she had not had at first amazed and pleased him. It still did even though he'd begun to cynically wonder if she'd really changed at all.

She was smart. Had she only opted to bide her time until she could find a wealthy husband? Then John, who hadn't the slightest idea she was a thief (or if she hadn't actually taken the piece herself she'd been involved nevertheless), and his own brother's former mistress had fallen into her carefully laid trap.

What was the difference, really—marrying for money or being kept by a wealthy man? The shackles of marriage and children only provided a more permanent sense of security, Brandon thought cynically, and even at twenty-six a girl wasn't so young that she didn't realize she had to look to the future.

In spite of what she said, her true character was no different than it had been seven years ago. Not for a minute did he believe she'd ever cared anything for John. Else why had she fallen into bed immediately with himself? When Brandon remembered how eager she'd been in the past for jewels and clothes and furs, he knew that this simple life she was affecting was no more than an act to make her attractive to just such a gullible soul as John.

No, though she suited Brandon well, her type was not for John, and in that instant Brandon determined to have her back. After all, he could afford her, and he was used to women like her. He preferred them, for he never entertained any illusions about them that might lead him into marriage. Thus, his prized independence was never threatened. Besides it was really what was best for her. Marriage to a man like John with all its mundane realities would have her dying of boredom in six months.

As he looked up at her lovely face he smiled benignly, self-confident that once he made it very clear to her how much more profitable being his mistress would be rather than being someone else's wife, she would instantly choose him. For all he cared she could raze Belle Rose to the ground and build herself an entirely new mansion from scratch, as long as she warmed his bed at night. Money was no object, and of one thing he was sure—all things had their price, especially women. It was only a matter of settling on it.

He thought briefly of his own mother, Celia, the first woman in a long line of equally grasping women who'd taught him so painfully this fundamental lesson about feminine nature. Fleetingly he remembered that first torturing rejection. He'd been nine years old. A deep frown furrowed his dark brow.

Then as always when Celia entered his thoughts, however briefly, he swept her abruptly from his mind and forced his concentration back to the pleasant contemplation of the lush beauty who lay pressed closely against himself. He reached out and idly caressed the darkened nipple of Lannie's soft breast, and watched as it grew taut.

"I want you back," he stated simply, staring so deeply into the exquisite darkness of her eyes that he nearly lost himself.

Very softly she replied, and he caught the faint note of regret in her voice. "It's over between us."

"No, love," he returned affably. Having anticipated her initial negative reaction, he was still certain that victory would very easily be his. "It's just beginning."

Chapter Eight

A breeze wafted through golden leaves, showering them downward as Brandon stood on the bottom step of Belle Rose and stared up toward the shaded veranda at Lannie. A fat, brown squirrel fluffed his tail several times and then scampered across the green lawn before he raced up a tree.

Brandon's calm expression and the pleasant scenery were in sharp contrast to the volatile emotions surging through the young woman on the porch.

"I do hate you! Oh, I do!" Lannie hurled the words brokenly down at Brandon. A black brow arched quizzically as he regarded her. He really didn't understand, she thought wildly. He was incapable of it. She felt like something pure and fragile inside her heart was shattering forever. With the sunlight glinting in his jet-dark hair, with memories of their recent lovemaking still languorously fresh on her mind, she was left achingly aware of his virile magnetism. Why, oh why, was he so damnably handsome? Why did she have to be vulnerable to only his appeal? Why couldn't she have met some other man who could make her feel so rapturously alive as he?

"I . . . I can't believe . . ." she quavered. She was trembling so she could scarcely speak. "But then I was a fool to expect anything else. You think you can buy me like . . . like some piece of equipment for one of your factories. Why I'm no more to you than some barge you'd casually make a deal to purchase for Brandon Chemicals."

"Surely not a barge, love," he drawled in that pleasant tone that grated her nerves raw. "You're much too lovely to compare yourself—"

Oh! He dared to joke! She longed to coil herself into a ball of fury and spring from the porch and attack him like some fierce, gigantic cat. His cocky white smile was driving her mad!

Her dark glare did nothing to ruffle Brandon's calm. He was convinced her display of affronted dignity was no more than a feminine ruse to drive the eventual price up. He even admired her the more for it. "If you'd think rationally for one minute you'd see you have as much to gain from this relationship as I," he began once more with what he considered infinite patience. "You could have anything you want, fix up Belle Rose exactly as you please. Fill your stables with good horseflesh instead of that monstrous abomination you're going to kill yourself on. . . ."

"Stop!" she cried. "Don't say another word!"

He did not heed her command. Instead he reached into his coat and pulled out the narrow strand of diamonds she'd furiously stuffed into his pocket upstairs when he'd first broached his idea. The necklace gleamed like a narrow rope of fire as he dangled it before her.

"Jewelry," the low drawl persisted, "diamonds, furs,

clothes, money . . . I'll teach you to make the proper sort of investments so you'll never have to worry about money again."

Was that what he really thought she wanted? Brown eyes sparked, and he thought her expression even more willfully stubborn than before.

"Put that necklace back!" she cried. "I told you I don't ever want to see it again, to be reminded of you again! Give it to some other woman for all I care, but you can't buy me with baubles! Why can't you understand? I want to fix Belle Rose up, yes. But I want to do it myself—not with your money. If I can't do it myself, then I don't even want to, because it would destroy something that's far more valuable."

"And what may I ask is that?" he asked.

"My pride, my independence."

"Lofty sentiments, my dear, but you're hardly in a position to afford them." Nor did he believe they held any real value for her.

"You really think that, don't you?"

"Of course. Your desire for independence is very admirable. And if you agree to become my . . . protégée, shall we call it, you will most certainly achieve it more quickly than following some stupid, outdated, moral inanity that you never believed in in the first place!"

"I detest you, and all men like you who think there is nothing on this earth without a pricetag."

"Very few things, my dear. But where's the rub? Wipe that look of shocked indignation from your face. The sooner you accept this bald truth, the better off you'll be. And so what—I want you. You want me. We've already been to bed. So what's the fuss? Why shouldn't you live with me? And why shouldn't I help you financially? Any other arrangement would be stupid for you to make."

"You think you're so clever, so superior. Just be-

111

cause you have money, you can corrupt anyone you want."

"I'm in no way superior to you," he returned, still in that same bland tone that so infuriated her though she noted his lips thinned as though his own temper were beginning to flare. "I'm merely richer. If the situation were reversed, and I were you, I'd seize this opportunity and run with it. After all, it's obvious that as much as you claim to detest me, sometimes you enjoy my company immensely. Why, only this morning you were begging me to stay and . . ." He flashed her a broad white grin, as if the memory pleased him greatly.

The reminder of her passionate bondage to him frightened her; that was the one temptation she was afraid she couldn't resist. "Stop that!" she whispered wildly. "I don't want to hear another word!" She fiercely resented the sensation that her physical need for him was like a silken chain from which there was no chance of freeing herself. Even now his virile handsomeness was having its effect on her traitorous senses.

Some part of her actually wanted to do what he asked. For the first time in seven years she again felt alive and excited. Just his touch evoked an undeniable and passionate response in her, and no other man had ever come close to producing the same depth of attraction. He made her feel like a woman; he alone could carry her to dizzying heights of rapture. The thought of losing him was both bewildering and frightening. Suppose she never fell in love again. She didn't want to give up this man who could so easily give her so much pleasure. Yet with every word that he uttered he proved how wrong he was for her in all other ways.

An inner voice asked if she wasn't a fool to deny the only man she'd ever really wanted.

She couldn't live as he asked. It would destroy the integrity of everything that she believed in. From the depths of her being she had to summon the courage to say no to this man. And from those ten months of blindness when she'd been challenged to the ultimate she'd developed the courage and strength of character to do anything once she set her mind to it. What he didn't know was that she was no longer the shallow, weak-willed creature he'd so easily overridden in the past.

One thing she knew for sure—it was dangerous for her to linger in Brandon's charismatic presence a moment longer. Her will to do the right thing was wavering. She had to get away from him at once, from the house where they'd so recently made love, from anything that could remind her of him.

"Brandon," she began coolly, descending the steps. "I think we've both said what we felt and there's really not much point in arguing any longer. Besides I have to feed Sugar and run several errands. And I'm sure you have a busy agenda yourself."

"You're probably right," he agreed, ignoring her curt tone and letting his eyes lazily follow the swaying motion of her hips as she moved. "We can resume this discussion later. As I said before, call me when you change your mind."

"Oooooh!" She expelled the sound in a deep, angry breath as she paused when she came to stand so close to him she could have touched him. "You can't take no for an answer, can you?"

In the sunlight the golden flecks in his eyes seemed to glitter against the ink-black depths. "Not when I want something as much as I want you," he murmured softly. The fluid sound of his voice washed hotly through her, and Lannie's desperate urge to escape the compelling force of his presence heightened.

"I-I have to go," she said weakly.

"Where?" The lift of his thick black brow mocked her.

Anywhere!—she wanted to scream—*that takes me*

away from you! "I-I'm going to the stables," she managed quietly.

"If you don't move in with me, you'll be doing a lot more of that," his low drawl taunted after her, "taking out your frustrations on the back of that animal instead of—"

She whirled, hissing, "Don't say it." Then she was running lightly across the thick lawn, the sound of his rich, deep laughter following her.

Minutes later Lannie's anger still had not lessened.

No one could drive her so mad as he! she fumed silently to herself as she placed the bridle on the recalcitrant Sugar. Then she heaved herself in an ungraceful lunge onto the mare's bare back. Lannie flinched at the unexpected pain in her thighs this action produced. It was then that she had her first qualms about the wisdom of this ride. Her fall and lovemaking had left her quite sore. Still she prodded Sugar toward the gate in the paddock.

Suddenly she saw Brandon leaning with negligent grace against the gate. His expression was grim. "You're not going to ride this morning or any other morning without a saddle," he warned in a coldly determined tone. "That horse is too unmanageable."

Even as he said those words Sugar shied at the unexpected sound, bruising Lannie's leg when she struck the fence. What he said was very true; she was taking a risk. But it was a risk she *felt* like taking, and it was *his* fault that she felt like it. "I'll do as I please," she shouted recklessly. "It's my neck, and I can break it if I want to."

"If that's your desire, let me be the one to accommodate you!" With the swift grace that was a characteristic of his, he climbed lightly over the fence and began to walk toward the horse and the woman with the tumbling, glossy hair. "Get off that horse before I drag you off it!" he commanded.

"You'll do nothing of the sort!" As he reached up to grab the reins from her, instinctively her hand flashed at him to ward him off and the ends of the reins snapped across his right cheek, marring the smooth, tanned surface with two ugly red marks.

Even as she gasped in horror at what she'd done and the words, "Oh, Brandon . . . I'm so sorry," were slipping from her lips, his temper ignited and he lunged for her.

She jerked the reins defiantly to one side and prodded Sugar into a turn and then into a furious gallop down the length of the paddock before horse and woman moved like dancers in slow motion into a reckless leap over the fence. The jump was executed with matchless grace. For an instant Lannie felt as though she were flying, as though time slid backward and she was again in the midst of her exuberantly untamed childhood. It was a fleeting moment. Then she felt the harsh jolt of the earth once more and her fingers clenched into Sugar's mane as she held onto the horse for dear life. It would never do to be thrown again, with Brandon watching.

A mixture of curious emotions—anger, disappointment, regret and that strange excitement only an encounter with Brandon could produce—pounded through Lannie as fiercely as Sugar's hooves pounded into the soft earth beneath the thick green grasses. They sped beneath vaulting canopies of live oaks, their branches trailing with strands of wispy moss.

Lannie felt wild with exhilaration, and she gave Sugar her head. The horse ran as she'd never run before; her thundering tread falling into the dirt road with a shattering force. Then Lannie guided Sugar from the road across a stretch of meadow. A twinge of regret stabbed her conscience, and she drew in on the reins. She should never have run Sugar like that, using the mare as a means of ridding herself of her own pent-up emotions without first warming her up.

A horn tooted several times from the nearby road, and thinking it was Brandon, Lannie's first instinct was to ignore it and race toward the levee. In his car he would not be able to follow her. But the bright red pickup belonged to Hamlin Trajan. His jaunty wave signaled to her to come over. Briefly Lannie wondered what he was doing in this neck of the woods.

As she neared the truck, Hamlin killed the motor and stepped from the pickup. He removed his Stetson and swiped a shirtsleeve across his brow. Sunlight gleamed in his hair so that it shone like pale gold. His wide smile stretched his handsome, tanned face, crinkling the corners of his eyes. "Is that Sugar?"

Sugar snorted as though she sensed she were being discussed.

"None other."

He smiled up at Lannie benevolently, and she felt gladdened by the warmth of his friendship. Her anger was for the moment forgotten. She'd often found comfort in his quiet strength in her turbulent, younger years. Hamlin was an extremely attractive man, but not one shred of physical chemistry drew them to one another in a man-woman way. Hamlin loved Velvet. He had for as long as Lannie could remember, and when Velvet had settled down, Hamlin had been there waiting. Lannie was so glad her cousin had found happiness with this man.

"I can't believe that's the same unmanageable piece of horseflesh I sold you three years ago." With the acumen of a true horse-breeder, Hamlin's gray eyes were alight with interest as they traveled over the animal. "Why, Lannie, it isn't often I'm bested in a horse trade, and to think a mere slip of a girl, and one I helped raise . . ." His voice trailed off as he reached up and stroked his hand lightly over the contours of the mare's muscles. "Don't you let it out, mind you. Why, I practically gave you this animal!"

Sugar pranced as though she were quite proud of herself, and Lannie couldn't stop herself from smiling.

"I wouldn't say that, Hamlin. At the time Sugar was so high-strung not one of those big hulks you had working for you could handle her."

"And then you, a raven-haired woman who scarcely came up to their shoulders, walked up and put them all to shame when you gentled this demon."

"It was about time! Why, I'll never forget the way Pete was screaming at her." Lannie leaned forward and stroked Sugar. "The poor darling was practically scared out of her wits."

"The poor darling had just splintered two boards in the wall of her stable. Because of her I could have kept a carpenter on salary full-time."

Lannie laughed. "And you just said you practically gave her to me."

The distant roar of a silvery sports car arrested Lannie's attention and she gazed wildly away from Hamlin toward the speeding car that was rapidly approaching. Her instinct was to run, but there was certainly no way she could rip the reins from Hamlin's fingers and bolt away. Not only would he not understand, but the Southern gentleman in him would be deeply offended by such rudeness.

Only Hamlin's steady hand on the reins and her own soothing voice kept Sugar from rearing as Brandon braked the car less than ten feet from them. Brandon unfolded his lean, powerful frame with negligent grace and got out, slamming the door. There was suppressed violence in this gesture as well as in the carefully controlled expression on his darkly handsome face. Her gaze went at once to the angry, purple marks on his tanned cheek, and she winced.

"Hello, Hamlin." Brandon's measured tone was

cool, his smile forced. Never once did he glance toward Lannie though she knew he was as deeply aware of her presence as she was of his. The sheer intensity of his anger seemed to reach out and coil around her, and she wondered if Hamlin felt it.

But if Hamlin thought Brandon's greeting lacked warmth he gave no indication. And he was too well-mannered to comment on the curious red marks blazing against Brandon's dark cheek.

Lannie flushed with keen embarrassment as her eyes went over Brandon's elegant evening attire. Surely it must be horribly obvious to Hamlin that Brandon hadn't slept in his own bed last night. And Brandon was so furious at her, it would soon be all too apparent who the woman was.

Hamlin released his hold on Sugar and shook Brandon's hand. "It's good to see you, Brandon. I'm glad you're back." A brilliant smile of welcome lit his suntanned face. "Will you be staying for the company barbeque in two weeks?"

The two men had been boyhood friends, and theirs was a deep friendship that had endured long separations and the passing of many years.

"Yes." The one word answer was terse and faintly hostile, though Brandon's anger was in no way directed toward his old friend.

Again Hamlin seemed not to notice there was anything wrong. But Lannie was sure that he was too astute and he knew Brandon too well to have been unaware of Brandon's mood.

"Well, I'll see you then, if not before," Hamlin was saying genially, intuitively understanding that Brandon had not stopped to talk to him and that he wanted him to go.

"I'll look forward to it," Brandon drawled. Hamlin was climbing into his truck. "And I'll give you a call later in the week and invite you and Velvet over to the

house one night so we can catch up on old times."
Brandon smiled for the first time. "It really is good to
see you, Hamlin. It's good to be back."

Casually Brandon's lean brown fingers reached up
and seized Sugar's reins as though he meant to steady
the animal while Hamlin started the truck. But Lannie
realized he had more than one motive, and a faint
tremor of apprehension shivered through her.

When Hamlin had gone, Brandon unleashed the full
force of his wrath. His eyes, black and yet fiery at the
same time, burned through her. His lips curled with
contempt. Then he reached up, and with one deft
motion, his heavy arm circled her waist and he scooped
her easily from the horse in spite of her efforts to
remain astride.

Lannie kicked at him and squirmed wildly, but
Brandon subdued her easily, pulling her close against
himself so that she was intimately conscious of the hard
male contours of his body.

In the process of their struggles the reins slipped
through Brandon's fingers, and Sugar moved spiritedly
away from them as though the animal sensed her
mistress' agitation. Then a luscious tuft of grasses
peeping from beneath a tumble-down fence tempted
the mare, and shaking her mane, she lowered her
glossy head and began to nibble at them.

"Brandon, don't," Lannie hissed. "Let me go!
You're being a bully and a—" She was panting, gasping
for breath as he crushed her even closer against himself.

"You reckless little fool! What were you trying to
prove?"

"That—that—" She spluttered like a boiling teaket-
tle. "I wasn't trying to prove anything! I just wanted to
get away from you, to wash you out of my mind. I-I
wanted to forget that you think I'm no different than
any other property you might want to bargain for."

Suddenly for no reason at all her eyes filled with tears, but proudly she struggled to hold them back. Oh, why couldn't she be indifferent to him? She didn't want to care so much what he thought of her. She'd thought that during their long separation she'd achieved a certain independence, but that illusion had been cruelly shattered.

Long ago he'd possessed her body as well as her heart, but all he'd wanted was her body. He'd despised her as a person, and it was obvious he still did.

He stared down at her into the shimmering liquid darkness of her eyes. He saw her pain, and oddly he felt pain himself. His hands about her gentled, and he had the strangest urge to hold her against him, to comfort her, to say the words she longed to hear.

He continued to gaze down at her. The intensity of his own response to her distress baffled him. Why should this particular woman affect him more deeply than any other, especially when he knew her so well and entertained no illusions about her character? Was it only the aura of angelic innocence that concealed her true nature?

Her exquisite loveliness melted his anger; her passionate sincerity reached some part of him which he sought to deny. His hard expression changed subtly, and for an instant she thought she glimpsed brief bewilderment, as though he almost believed her. But then as always he recalled the past, and his old doubts prevailed.

Time flew backward, and Brandon remembered that night when after hearing a sound in Genevieve's bedroom he'd discovered Lannie. At first he'd been surprised—shocked. He'd read the guilt and shame and terror on her incredibly young and lovely face. She'd tried to run from him, but he'd caught her easily and the diamond bracelet had spilled onto the carpet at her feet, incriminating her.

Lannie was no different than all the other women he'd known—beginning with his own mother—all the other women who eagerly wanted to use him because he was rich. She wanted beautiful things, and he was willing to give her whatever she wanted. But he owed her nothing else, nothing of himself. She was a pleasure he was ready to buy. But she could never be anything more.

When she'd been younger, she'd taken everything he had to offer and then she'd left him. Last night she'd said she'd changed, but he didn't believe her. People didn't change, not really. They only became less direct. They only grew to want more. What she was really angling for now was the ultimate commitment, that ultimate security—marriage—so desired by all females. And that he had no intention of giving her. Then why did he hesitate?

His eyes ran over her flashing brown eyes, the dark curving brows against the olive satin of her skin, the cascading richness of her hair, the lush softness of her lips, the ripe voluptuous curves of her pliant body. He thought her unutterably lovely. She was a sensual wanton, and she aroused him physically. That was all.

He told himself he was a fool where she was concerned. He distrusted this new softness in himself. He wanted her, and she wanted him. It was a simple matter. Physical need in no way presaged marriage. She was throwing ridiculous obstacles in his path!

Of course he could buy her, as she so bluntly put it. He had once before. Suddenly he was supremely confident he could have her on any terms he chose, and he smiled benignly down at her, purposely baiting her.

"You're certainly an unusually attractive property," came his deep, mocking drawl. A wicked light danced in his black eyes as he allowed his gaze to roam over her hungrily. He was being deliberately insolent.

A hot flush stained her cheeks, and her eyes darkened. His own anger was gone, for it was impossible for him to stay angry at a woman whose mere closeness, whose voluptuous body warm against his own, aroused other, more pleasant emotions. He remembered the erotic delights of the morning and smiled so broadly down at her she longed to slap him, for something in his expression rekindled the same wanton memories in her own mind, making her aware of his intense and very masculine sexuality and her own feminine vulnerability to it.

A tiny pulsebeat thudded dully where her heart was. She felt helpless to fight against the power he held over her, and this very helplessness frustrated her. Everything he did, everything he said heightened her own rage. He refused to take what she said seriously. He was making light of her deepest feelings. He didn't believe her. He refused to trust her. And yet, he was able to give her pleasures she'd almost forgotten existed.

As though he sensed her weakening, he continued. "I think the . . . er . . . lady protests too much," he murmured silkily into the thickly flowing midnight fire of her hair. Her soft curves were molded against his granite length.

"You've jumbled the quote *badly,*" she snapped, squirming angrily against him. Still, he did not release her.

The motion of her breasts against his muscled chest and that of her hips against his own tantalized him, causing his blood to race as though he had a fever. Her every movement was provocative as she, doubtless, knew. What was the matter with him that she could make him feel starved for her even when he was satiated? Ignoring the shaft of uneasiness this thought produced, his low voice taunted, "Nevertheless, you catch my meaning. I want you, Lannie. And I intend to get you back."

"And you always get what you want!" she flared.

"Usually," he drawled in that maddeningly calm tone. "However, occasionally a barge or two does slip through my fingers." There was laughter in his rich, dark eyes; her own flashed with the brilliant intensity of sparking fireworks. As she drew a quick, infuriated breath, his bland voice continued the soft yet husky flow of sound. "But I have no intention of letting you go, my dear. You are a rare prize." His pirate-black eyes gleamed as they stripped away her clothes and considered the lush, opulent female form beneath them as though he were indeed a buccaneer who intended to ravish her. "But go ahead and fight me. I think I'll actually enjoy it. You, of all people, should understand that I find challenges almost as irresistible as I do you."

Chapter Nine

*B*randon's throaty chuckle was in sharp contrast to the low, strangling sound—almost an animal growl—Lannie emitted. Then she forced herself to calm down. This was exactly what he wanted to do to her! He was enjoying her burst of temper, deliberately seeking to provoke it. He found her passionate nature amusing, out of bed as well as in it.

As she stared up at the bold arrogance of his handsome face, she despised herself for feeling anything for him, for wanting him as she did. Even through his evening clothes she felt the heat of him, the strength of his powerful body. He was a magnificent specimen of a man, his hard body that of an athlete.

Every fiber of her being clamored for his touch, even while she realized that he was offering her a lifestyle that was no longer compatible with her values.

Wearily she sighed. "Brandon, I really do think we've thoroughly covered this subject. Would you let me go now. . . . I have things I need to do today."

For a long moment his eyes held hers, and she thought he saw every emotion in her heart. Then his hands fell away. "So do I," he murmured dryly, remembering he would be damnably late for his appointment with his banker. "But they won't be nearly as much fun as igniting that hot-pepper temper of yours."

"I'm no more than a new toy to you."

"Not a new toy, my dear, but . . . an old favorite."

Hot emotion surged through her, but as she drew back her hand with the intent of slapping him as he so richly deserved, the malicious sparkle in his devilish black eyes defused her anger. He was a charming rake; his appeal for her was irresistible. And, unfortunately, he was well aware of it.

When her fingers reached up and touched his roughened cheek, her touch was featherlight instead of violent and she gently traced the ugly marks she'd inflicted earlier.

He winced slightly as though in pain.

Softly she murmured, "Brandon, I'm sorry I hit you. I-I didn't think. It happened so fast. . . . I didn't really want to hurt you."

"I know." The velvet sound of his deep voice enveloped her.

"But you made me so mad, as only you can do." She hesitated. "I-I . . ."

"You always were a little hellion," he said, fondly remembering the black-haired demon she'd been as a child. "You'd follow me around like a mischievous shadow, pestering me. Maybe turnabout is fair play." Once he'd viewed her as the brat-kid with the freckled nose who lived on the neighboring plantation until that summer he'd come home from law school and he'd discovered she was a child no longer, but a lush beauty, *sans* freckles, whose untamed wildness he'd found as tantalizing as every other youth in the parish had. Since that time he'd never gotten her out of his system.

Lazily his hooded gaze drifted over her fiery loveliness, assessing her appeal. It was almost as though she were a part of himself, he thought idly, a part that he could not do without. Hastily he amended his last thought—a part that he no longer *intended* to do without.

"I'll drive you home," he said casually.

"I can ride Sugar." This statement was a feeble attempt on her part to assert her independence.

"No, you can't!" The old harshness was back in his tone as well as a new element of command. "And if I catch you bareback on that unmanageable devil, I'll come over and personally shoot that animal myself."

"You wouldn't dare!" Brown eyes snapped with anger. But even as she defied him, she knew that he would do exactly as he said. "You have no right!" she protested weakly, glaring up at him.

"Perhaps not," he agreed, his expression dark. "But I'll do it anyway if you push me to it."

"I'll have you thrown in jail."

His lips quirked as though she were a child whose threats were more diverting than frightening. The fact that he found her amusing only heightened her anger.

"I doubt it," he returned confidently. "Or have you forgotten that favorite old insult of yours that I own everything and everyone in this parish?" His glittering eyes seemed as cold and hard as his voice.

She swallowed. "You always denied it," she said at last.

"But you never believed that for a minute, did you?" As he looked down at her intently and read her stormy expression, his lips curved as though he were cynically amused. "Don't tell me your opinion of me has actually improved with the years?" he mocked. Though her flushed face told him that the opposite was true, he pursued the topic. "And just when I was beginning to enjoy my . . . er . . . black reputation."

"It hasn't!" she declared hotly. "I know that underneath that handsome . . ."

"Well, at least you'll admit you find me attractive, which is more than you were willing to do the other night." The husky undertone in his deep voice was seductive. "I'm definitely making progress." He chuckled, and it was a pleasant rippling sound. "And I've only been home two days." His black eyes sparkled. "If your attitude toward me continues to improve at this rate, I shall be quite conceited before two weeks have passed."

"You missed the point!" she hissed. "I was going to say that beneath your handsome facade, you're vile and . . ."

"There's no need for you to continue," he murmured. "I get the picture. However, a few more nights in your bed, and you'll sheath your tiger claws and purr as docilely as a kitten. Why only this morning you were begging me—"

In her present mood the last thing she wanted to remember was that morning. "I was going to say that you're vile and nasty and . . ."

She would have said more, but he good-humoredly interrupted her heated catalogue of insults, flashing her a white smile.

"You're dangerously near profanity, my pet." Again there was that lazy glint in the depths of his black eyes that so riled her. Pleasantly he suggested, "Let's get this discussion back on the right track. It's your horse that's nasty, not me. Don't ride bareback."

"Brandon—"

He cut her off. "There's no point in our arguing about it further. I won't have my favorite toy trampled. And that's that!" His bold black gaze danced across her features, warming her. "She's much too much fun to play with, that is . . . when she's in an amorous mood instead of a cantankerous one." He grinned broadly down at her.

Cantankerous! She fumed over this last comment! If she were as disagreeable as an old grouch, it was his fault, not hers! His highhanded tactics were unendurable! Her brows narrowed slightly. Hot words rushed to her lips.

But her upturned, pouting lips were too tempting for him to resist. The angry retort she would have uttered was crushed into silence as his mouth claimed hers in a violent kiss, obliterating her rage.

Balling her hands into fists, she made a feeble attempt to resist him, beating against his chest. But he was far stronger than she and far more determined. Ruthlessly he held her against himself, forcing her to yield, needing to show her that she was his to dominate, to conquer and to love.

The strength to deny him drained out of her, and in its place was a strange, inexplicable longing he alone could arouse so effortlessly.

Her hands reached around his neck; her fingers twined through the thick waves of his black-satin hair. Her shaking fingertips felt his heated heartbeats beneath the warm flesh of his throat.

There was a volcanic wildness in his erupting passion that ignited an answering storm of emotions in herself. Her rage of anger was turned into a hotly flowing torrent of desire.

His arms slid tightly around her delicate, female form, his large hands gently exploring her curves and molding her to him. Her body went limp beneath his expert touch and she trembled against the powerful hardness of his male frame.

This was madness! She hated him! And she loved him! And where these two powerful emotions collided, she felt with a flaming intensity she'd never felt for anyone or anything before. Mindlessly she gave herself up to the powerful tide that was washing over her.

Slowly, deliberately, his mouth plundered her shaking lips with devastating completeness, forcing them open so that his tongue could intimately explore the moistened depths within. A molten tingle sizzled through her, and stretching onto her tiptoes, she reached upward and clung to him.

A gentle wind stirred through the moss draperies of the distant cypress trees in the wildly brooding swamp. A river tug's whistle sounded, but neither Brandon nor Lannie heard it for they were aware only of each other. A stray gust swirled around them, whipping Lannie's hair so that it whirled over his shoulders in a fiery spray of glimmering strands. Gently he brushed her hair aside, mussing it.

He was man and she was woman, and the passion that consumed them was as wild and elemental as the primeval land in which they lived.

She was his, and he had only to touch her to prove that this was so.

As abruptly as he'd taken her in his arms, he released her. "Get in the car, Lannie," he commanded hoarsely, moving swiftly to open the door for her.

This time she did not argue but instead slipped into the plush black leather interior of his silver Mercedes. She cast a lingering gaze in Sugar's direction. The mare was still nibbling grass beside the road. Lannie was not worried about her horse; Sugar knew her way home and always returned to her paddock before dark.

As Brandon and Lannie sped in silence back to Belle Rose, she continued to tremble from his embrace. Even though an element of her fury had returned, she still felt weak from the raw, whirling passion that Brandon had so effortlessly aroused. She glanced toward him and wondered what he was feeling. His dark profile was etched against the bright background of the window so that his face appeared shadowed. If he were experiencing the same tumultuous emotions as she was, his smooth, bland expression gave no sign of it.

Continuing her study of him, she saw strength in the hard line of his jaw, rugged determination in his expression and sensuality about his mouth. He was a complex man, brilliant in his field, dynamic in the jet-set social whirl his work forced him into for the purpose of making advantageous business contacts. But was there no tenderness in him? Was he incapable of love? Did he really intend to enjoy a string of women physically and never to marry?

A tiny pain shot through her. He was dominating and arrogant, opinionated and stubborn. He would be a difficult husband, but she was beginning to realize she didn't want anyone else. He would make an excellent father, of that she was sure; he had a rare gift where children were concerned. He liked them, and they instinctively liked him.

As a child she herself had been drawn to him and had followed him about when he was home from school, plaguing him perpetually, and he'd endured her company with infinite patience. It was only when she was no longer a child and he'd begun to arouse dangerous feelings in her that she hadn't understood that she'd turned away from him. It was then he who had pursued her.

Was Brandon capable of settling down to marriage and a family? Or did she desire the impossible? Hadn't he always declared that he wasn't a marrying man? She turned away and stared out her own window as the tires crunched onto the gravel drive that wound beneath an arbor of soft, thick greenery.

When Brandon braked in front of the ancient temple

nestled beneath the flowing live oaks that was Lannie's home, his hand closed over her door handle so that she could not get out of the car.

"Lannie . . ." He paused and for the first time his eyes sought hers so that she would grasp the full import of his words. "Tell John you're breaking the engagement. Tell him today." As always when he spoke of John, his tone was harsh.

"I-I . . ."

"If you don't, I'll tell him about us myself."

She read his cold, determined expression and became alarmed as she realized he would carry out his threat if she didn't do what he said. Her throat felt dry.

"Sometimes I can't always reach him," she murmured, tracing the edge of her lips with the tip of her pink tongue.

Brandon's gaze followed the movement. "This better not be one of those times," he warned. "Because I can assure you, I won't have that problem."

First Sugar and now John! She started to say something, and then thought better of it. What was the use of arguing when he would eventually get his way?

He gave her a long, considering look, smiling slowly as though he could read her mind and all the hot arguments raging there. Softly he said, "Lannie, when you cool down maybe you'll realize that the two things I've asked of you are really quite reasonable. I don't want you to break your neck on that horse of yours, nor does it make sense for you to remain engaged to one man when you're sleeping with his brother. The sooner you break up with John, the easier it will be for all of us."

Lannie was in no mood to think reasonably. Nothing about this whole situation was reasonable. Brandon belonged in her past. That's where she'd left him seven years ago! But he wasn't. He was back, and in the space of a few hours he was as much a part of her life as ever. Now when she thought of hurting John, she realized how difficult breaking her engagement would be.

Brandon flicked the door handle and flung the door open for her. She stepped from the car and then slammed the door shut. As she watched him drive away, she hated the feeling that she was his to command.

Sherry and Denise accompanied by Hilary and Ralph arrived home late that afternoon. Lannie was grading papers in the parlor. The spicy scent of her rich shrimp gumbo simmering on the stove wafted through the open rooms. She'd also cleaned house and made a fresh salad that was cooling in the refrigerator.

Earlier she'd taken a long bath and donned a pair of old jeans and a faded plaid blouse. Her hair was parted down the middle and drawn severely back in a ponytail that swung loosely over her shoulders. She was wearing her overlarge reading glasses which made her look like the primmest of women. Even the keenest observer would never have suspected this demure creature of wildly participating in a passionate interlude during her friends' brief absence.

She was the picture of innocence and schoolmarm efficiency when Hilary burst through the french doors and into the parlor, laughter bubbling in her throat because of something Denise had said.

"Well, aren't you too virtuous to be true?" Hilary mocked gaily, little appreciating the irony of her question. "The house positively sparkles. And you're even grading papers, instead of putting them off as you usually do." She paused, lifting her pert nose teasingly and sniffing the air. "And isn't that dinner I smell?" At Lannie's quick nod, she asked, "Lannie, what's gotten into you? If I didn't know better I'd think you were up to something. You never cook! Not when you know I'll be home to do it!"

With an effort Lannie suppressed a giggle; it would never do for Hilary to realize how close to the truth she was. "Don't act so surprised!" Lannie retorted sweetly. "There's a first time for everything!" Lannie beamed across the room at her friend. How Brandon would have laughed at her if he could have seen how Lannie mused, her lips curving gently in a slow, secret smile. He would have taunted her unmercifully, teasing her that she was his little hypocrite.

He would have been right, and yet she saw nothing wrong in being discreet, in not wanting everyone to know the intimate details of her private life. She thought of her engagement ring lying upstairs in her bureau drawer. Besides, technically, she was still engaged to John and it would needlessly hurt him if others, even Hilary and Sherry, learned of her relationship with his stepbrother before she broke their engagement.

The day had passed without her being able to contact John. Though she left word with his answering service for him to return her call, he never did, which was quite irregular. Usually on Saturdays John was easy to locate, and she wondered where he was.

Lannie spent the remainder of the day puttering outside, first sweeping the veranda until not a single gossamer strand of cobweb remained tucked in the corners nor a stray leaf on the gray-painted board floor. Then she and Hilary raked leaves and bagged them while Denise lay playfully buried in the tall piles of crisp leaves.

But in spite of her physical activity, Lannie felt strangely restless. The thought of breaking up with John hung over her head, and no matter how busy she was she couldn't stop thinking of it. Then her thoughts would return to Brandon and the feelings he aroused in her, and she felt more mixed up than ever.

She was giving up a stable man who would make an ideal husband, a man who wanted to live the kind of life she now wanted to live. And for what? She wanted Brandon physically; she even loved him. But in the cold light of reality she was increasingly sure that a relationship with him could never mature into marriage.

Still, it would hardly be fair to a man like John to marry him when she couldn't love him in the deepest sense of the word.

That evening Sherry and Lannie were alone in the kitchen washing the dinner dishes. John still hadn't called, and Lannie was beginning to wonder anxiously if Brandon had cornered John and told him about their interlude himself. If Brandon did that, why, she'd never forgive him. Never. At this thought Lannie fumed inside and wiped the soup bowl she was drying with new vengeance.

Suddenly the rose-colored china tureen that Sherry was rinsing slipped through her shaking fingers and splattered, shattering into the porcelain sink.

"Lannie," Sherry gasped, wide-eyed. "I'm sorry. I-I didn't mean . . . that was your mother's."

Lannie began collecting the broken fragments. "It doesn't matter, Sherry," she said softly, dropping a sprinkle of pink chips into a nearby grocery bag they were using for garbage. "I have a lot of other old things to remember Mother by, and I know you didn't do it on purpose. It could just as easily have been me."

Lannie's eyes met Sherry's and held them. Sherry's expression was wretched.

"N-no . . ." Sherry wailed. "I should have been more careful. I wasn't thinking, at least not about what I was doing."

Sherry's face was pale; her luminous dark eyes looked stricken. For the first time Lannie realized that

Sherry had been strangely withdrawn all day. She'd scarcely spoken through dinner. But Lannie hadn't noticed because she'd been too upset by her own problems.

Suddenly Lannie wondered if the doctor had said something that had upset Sherry. Alarm thudded through Lannie. Was there some new, worsening development in Denise's condition?

When Lannie had asked Sherry about Denise's visit to the doctor, Sherry's replies had been mechanical. But at the time Lannie hadn't considered that Sherry might not be telling everything. Suddenly Lannie wanted to get Sherry alone outside and find out what was troubling her.

"There's a full moon coming up over the Mississippi," Lannie invited Sherry. "Why don't we go for a walk to the levee and leave the rest of the dishes until we get back? I'd like to talk to you about your trip to New Orleans without the others around."

Sherry snapped eagerly at the suggestion. "I've been wanting to talk to you all day, but you seemed so far away."

"I suppose I'm still a little shaken up from that fall Thursday night," Lannie evaded.

Golden moonlight sifted through the spreading branches of the live oaks and cast eerie patterns of light upon the ground beneath, turning familiar surroundings into a magical wonderland. As Lannie and Sherry walked toward the levee, leaves crunched beneath their shoes. The air that was crisply cool was redolent with the sweet night scents of sugarcane mixing with the tangy damp marsh odors of the Mississippi. Ralph was playing his piano in his *garçonnière* and a dramatic tinkling of Liszt followed the women.

"Ralph sounds more inspired than usual," Lannie said.

"I don't think so. When he plays Liszt, it usually

means he's hit a snag in his own composing and he's playing the master to vent his own frustration," Sherry replied fondly, her gentle face glowing. Lannie had noted that delicate softening of Sherry's features more and more often of late when she spoke of Ralph.

"You and Ralph seem to be spending quite a lot of time together," Lannie said gently.

"I've never met anyone quite like him before. He's nothing like Dan." For a fleeting moment Sherry's face twisted with pain.

Lannie had never met Dan, Sherry's first husband, because he'd left Sherry, divorcing her and taking an overseas job in the Middle East oil fields when Denise's blindness had been confirmed as a permanent condition. But Lannie had seen pictures of him, and she remembered him as a deeply tanned, rugged outdoors-type, the antithesis of Ralph.

"Of course, most people would probably think Ralph's a little eccentric, but then creative people usually are. And he's not really what you'd call handsome, although really he's quite nice-looking. But I've come to discover that beneath that absentminded, intellectual exterior of his, Ralph is one of the most sensitive and compassionate people I've ever known. You know how he is with Denise. He accepts her as she is. He takes her anywhere with him, even places I don't think he should, like fishing in the swamp in a *pirogue* that anything could topple. It's as if he's totally unaware of her handicap. When they're together I almost have the feeling that for him she's a normal little girl. Sometimes when I'm with them, I can almost forget myself, which is pleasant even if it's unrealistic."

"Maybe that's what you should do more often, Sherry. Forget. Treat Denise as though she's normal. You might be surprised how that could change things."

"You think just like Ralph! I'm not capable of

pretending something's true when it isn't. How could that change anything? Denise is blind, and people will never accept her like they would if she were normal. Why, her own father couldn't."

"And neither can her mother," Lannie said quietly.

"How can I? She'll never be able to do all the things normal people take for granted."

"Don't set limits on her, Sherry. Let her set them."

"I just hate to see her want things she can't have. It tears me apart inside when she fails. That night when she fell off Sugar, I nearly died. She has no business riding a horse. Why can't she just be happy doing what she can already do?"

"Because she feels locked in." Lannie remembered her own experience. How could she explain that terrifying feeling of wanting to reach out and not knowing how. The crushing darkness had seemed like walls encircling her worse than a prison cell because the walls had seemed to press against her own body. The rest of the world had been beyond herself, and not being able to see it, she hadn't been able to relate to it.

Lannie continued, "Blindness is like a prison, and everything Denise learns to do for herself opens an avenue of escape. If she learns to do enough things, she will be independent to lead her own life. Sherry, don't you see she needs your support, not your constant fear that she might get hurt if she accepts a new challenge. You're holding her back, and it's making her increasingly resentful. She's growing up, which is tough even for *normal* kids. It's twice as tough for her."

"You're not telling me anything I don't already know. I just feel that she needs to accept that she's different and not try to do things she can't."

"She won't know if she can or not if she doesn't get the chance to try."

"Lannie," Sherry began wearily, "I know you mean

well, but I've given this a lot of thought. I've stayed up night after night, thinking of nothing else, and nothing you can say will change my mind."

As always they reached the same point in their argument, each feeling frustrated by the other's point of view.

For a time they walked in silence, and then Lannie asked, "What did the doctors say, Sherry, about Denise?"

"Well, the first man said what everyone else has been saying since her last operation—that there was nothing he could do. But he did want us to stay over and see his partner who was arriving back in town this morning."

"And . . ."

"Dr. Ludkee examined Denise this morning, and he said that there's a possibility that something might be done for her right eye. There's a new operation, and if it were successful there's a five percent chance she might regain partial sight in it."

"Five percent. That's an even worse percentage than the last operation she had, and it failed." Both Sherry and Denise had been devastated, for they'd both still believed in the doctor's ability to bring forth a miracle.

"Yes, but if Denise could be helped . . ."

Lannie heard the desperate tone in her friend's voice and thought back over all the operations and hospital stays Denise had endured. None of them had helped, and each one had produced nothing but pain and ultimate disappointment. Furthermore, Sherry had long since exhausted her medical insurance and was ineligible for more.

"What does the operation cost?" Lannie asked softly, fearing the answer.

"Several thousand dollars—which I don't have. I'm still paying for the last operation, and Dan refuses to help."

"Well, if you decide the operation is the answer, I'll loan you the money," Lannie offered.

"Oh, Lannie . . ." Sherry's eyes were shining; gently she gripped her friend's arm. "You don't know what your saying that means to me. You've been the dearest of friends, but I couldn't impose on you like that when I know you've been saving for a new roof for ages. And look at that old battered heap you drive. You're barely making it yourself."

"Old battered heap!" Lannie cried in mock indignation. "I guess it takes a crisis to learn your friend's true opinion of one's most cherished possessions, like old Bessie." She chuckled softly. "Old heap indeed!"

"I didn't mean to insult you," Sherry apologized gravely.

"I know that, silly. But Bessie's not in as bad a shape as she looks. And I want to help you. I don't have a child to support and medical bills to pay like you do. I could borrow money if I had to," Lannie lied, knowing full well she was already as deeply in debt as she dared go. "Besides, Denise is far more important than anything else I could spend my money on. Sherry, if you need it, the money's yours."

"If I need it?" Sherry's gentle laughter had a hysterical quality to it. "If only I didn't."

They continued their walk, speaking of other things, but each was really thinking of Denise.

After their walk Lannie left Sherry at the steps to the veranda and went herself to check on Sugar. The mare had returned home at dusk exactly as Lannie had known she would. As Lannie approached the paddock, she whistled and Sugar cavorted toward her, careful to stay coyly just out of her mistress' reach.

Lannie spoke to the mare affectionately. "I sure had you figured, didn't I? You may be a big girl, but you're still a baby when it comes to staying out after dark."

Sugar tossed her head, neighing in agreement, and a throaty chuckle bubbled in Lannie's throat.

At least an hour passed while she cleaned out Sugar's stall and before she was ready to return to the house. When Lannie did, she went directly to her room.

The room was pitch black, the heavy curtains drawn against the windows, shutting out the moonlight that would have otherwise flooded the room. It was odd that the curtains were closed, since Lannie never drew them. She was about to flick on the light when a sound near the bed caught her attention.

"Lannie . . ." Denise's low voice was strangely tear-muffled. "Don't turn on the light. I don't want you to see me like this."

"All right, dearest." It was a custom of theirs to communicate in total darkness on occasion.

Moving slowly but with a sureness most seeing people could never attain in darkness, Lannie went to the child at once. Denise was huddled in the big rocker at the foot of the bed, and when Lannie approached, she threw herself into Lannie's outstretched arms. Her small tormented body shuddered with long wracking sobs.

"What is it, Denise?"

"The operation. Mother wants me to go through another operation." Even through the tears a faint note of defiance was creeping into her voice.

"She told me that Dr. Ludkee said there was a chance."

"I'm sick and tired of chances. They've broken our hearts over and over again. I can't stand it anymore! I've given up that I'll ever see again! Why can't Mother?"

"Because she loves you and she wants the very best for you. You know that."

"Because she can't accept me the way I am. She thinks I'm a freak!" Denise's voice rang wildly.

"Denise, that isn't true!"

"Even my daddy ran away! Oh, I know Mother always says they would have divorced even if I hadn't been in that accident. Maybe once I believed it, but I know now that isn't true. He left because of me."

For a hushed moment, Lannie could think of no response other than to hold Denise more closely against herself.

"Your father wasn't strong enough to face the challenge of your handicap, honey. Maybe it's best he left, if he couldn't have supported you."

"It wasn't best for Mother. I've ruined her life, and until she accepts me, I'll keep on ruining it. She has all these false hopes and dreams. Sometimes I think I should run away."

The magnitude of this statement swept Lannie; this was not the first time Denise had mentioned the prospect of running away. It was becoming a familiar theme, and for that reason Lannie was beginning to take it seriously. The thought of running away would terrify most seeing children, but for Denise to cherish this as a dream only underscored how unhappy and guilty she must feel.

"You haven't ruined anybody's life, honey. You mustn't think like that. Why, you know you've made my life. And as for your mother, she loves you more than anything in the world. She only wants . . ."

Again there was a note of defiance in Denise's voice, only stronger. "I don't care if she loves me anymore. Sometimes it hurts to love the wrong person."

For a minute Lannie didn't answer. There was a profound truth in Denise's last statement. Suddenly Lannie was thinking of Brandon and her own foolish love for him. He was the wrong person, not someone like Denise."

"Oh, honey, how can I make you understand. Sherry loves you as you are, and so do I. But we wouldn't be human if we didn't want to help you. You're not the wrong person for Sherry to love. You're her child."

"Maybe not for long."

The words hung in the thick darkness, and all Lannie's soothing phrases of comfort that followed could not dispel them.

Denise's relationship with her mother was building to a crisis, and Lannie only hoped that she would somehow find a way to help them.

Chapter Ten

It was scarcely eight o'clock Sunday morning when the phone on Lannie's bedside table rang. Drowsily she lay back and suppressed a yawn, hoping that someone was awake downstairs who would answer it.

No such luck! The instrument jangled fiercely two more times, and reluctantly Lannie lifted the receiver from the hook and tucked it beneath the thick tangling masses of her coal black hair.

"Hello," she murmured sleepily, little realizing how huskily inviting she sounded.

"Hello." The deep masculine voice pulsated through every nerve in her body, causing her to awaken instantly.

She sat up in bed, unconsciously drawing the sheets over her lacy nightgown that revealed more than it concealed. There was a sexy quality in his tone that unnerved her. For no reason at all a strange, rippling excitement coursed through her, and she gasped.

"Brandon," she whispered against the cool plastic mouthpiece.

"Were you expecting someone else?" his low voice taunted.

"Not at this hour," she retorted waspishly. "Everyone else I know is too courteous to call before eight on Sunday morning."

"What a commendable set of friends," he murmured dryly. "But then maybe we're giving them credit where none is due. Perhaps, like yourself, they're just late sleepers."

"For your information if they did arise at the break of dawn they'd never dream of calling."

"And for your information, it's ten past eight which is hardly the break of dawn," he corrected her. "I've been up since five and have been impatiently watching the clock ever since—waiting to call you. Since you don't think I'm capable of courtesy anyway, next Sunday I'll just call you at five when I feel like it." There was a playful note in his voice.

"No, I . . . I take back what I said," she replied through gritted teeth.

"Are you still in bed?" he teased.

"Yes."

"Alone?" There was something hot and intense in his voice.

"Of course I'm alone!" she snapped.

"What a waste," he murmured suggestively.

She caught the genuine regret in his tone and something electric pulsed through her. To her horror she found that she actually agreed with him! This very minute she longed to snuggle against his hard warm body. In fact, at the thought, she suddenly felt as hot as flame.

His next question thudded through her with startling violence.

"Have you talked to John yet?"

"I haven't been able to reach him. I tried all day long yesterday!"

"Reach him today because if you don't I'll talk to him tonight."

"But . . ."

"No 'buts'! Just do it!"

Brandon was not the kind of man who sympathized with excuses. He bade her a terse goodbye, and then the dial tone buzzed in her ear.

After that conversation sleep was impossible. Wearily Lannie got out of bed, slipped into her tattered corduroy robe, and went downstairs to the kitchen where she put on a kettle to make tea. Her head was throbbing.

She had no doubt Brandon would do exactly as he said; thus, it was imperative that she locate John sometime today. But how? When she dialed John's number there was no answer. Nor was he at the hospital.

Then to her surprise around ten o'clock in the morning John turned up unannounced at Belle Rose. Still in her blue robe, Lannie was outside on the second-floor veranda cautiously sipping a cup of scalding jasmine tea when she saw his small, apple-green Volkswagen zooming up the drive. Her heart began to pound with dread as she scurried inside at once to run a brush through her hair and slip into a pair of jeans and a long-sleeved cotton blouse.

Pocketing John's engagement ring, Lannie stepped outside onto the balcony once more. She didn't want to go down. Her fingers slid into her pocket and curled tightly around the ring. But she had no choice. She was engaged to the wrong man, and the longer she procrastinated setting things straight, the more difficult it would become.

A brilliant flash below caught Lannie's eye, and suddenly she was smiling as she went to the railing and looked down. Hilary, dressed in a billowing, flame-colored Hawaiian gown was running beneath the trees to greet John. Golden bangles jingled at her throat and on her slender arms. Her pale hair tumbled down her back in charming disarray. In her wild costume Hilary looked exactly like a bright, excited parrot fluttering down from a branch. When she reached John her eyes were shining, her face strangely illuminated, and Lannie realized that never—in spite of her unconventional garb, which, of course, for Hilary was the norm—had Hilary looked lovelier.

Suddenly it occurred to Lannie how strange it was that Hilary never dated any of the men who asked her out. Instead she spent her time writing her poetry, cooking the delicious meals John so enjoyed, and devoting herself to her friends. Hilary passed many evenings with John and herself, and thinking back, it had never seemed that Hilary missed having a man of her own. Neither had Lannie and John for they both enjoyed Hilary's company immensely.

At just that moment John looked up and saw Lannie. After the briefest hesitation both he and Hilary smiled and waved up at her, calling to her to come down.

A nervous tremor raced through Lannie as she descended the stairs. She forced a smile of greeting as John stepped through the front door. As always he wore his favorite blue seersucker suit.

"Long time no see," he said gently, his blue eyes gazing deeply up into her own as he released Hilary and took Lannie's hand in his. He seemed strangely uneasy in her presence.

Lannie felt the light pressure of his lips against her cheek for a fleeting instant as he bent his fair head to her own.

A lifetime . . . Lannie thought ruefully. And it had

only been since Friday morning. Suddenly she felt guilty and awkward.

"John," Hilary began, distracting him. "Since I thought you might drop by, I baked some sweet rolls for breakfast. They've just come out of the oven if you'd like some."

"If?" Blue eyes twinkled as he looked down at the appealing golden waif at his side. "You must be joking. Have I ever turned a meal down? Hasn't it been two days since that last delicious breakfast you cooked me? If you want to know the truth part of the reason I came by this morning . . ."

He didn't finish his sentence, but he didn't have to since the women mentally finished it for him. Hilary's smile was brighter than usual, and she flushed prettily up at him. "Well, you two go out and sit on the porch. I'll bring some coffee and the rolls out a little later. It'll take me a while because I need to brew a fresh pot of coffee," Hilary said.

Lannie was about to protest, but John shushed her, saying to Hilary, "That's the best idea I've heard in two days."

When Hilary had disappeared in a swirl of brilliance in the direction of the kitchen, Lannie spoke, reprimanding him softly. "John, Hilary isn't our servant. We could have easily gone to the kitchen ourselves and—"

"I know. But let her. You know she likes to do it. Besides I've been wanting to talk to you alone." Again he appeared oddly ill at ease.

He wanted to talk to her alone! Had Brandon already called him? John seemed vaguely agitated as he removed his seersucker jacket and hung it on the back of his chair. A large freckled hand reached up and loosened his tie and then unbuttoned the top button of his pale-blue dress shirt.

"Suits," John muttered irritably as he sat down,

stretching his long legs out in front of him in an attempt to relax. "If I could find the man who invented them, I'd personally ring his neck."

"You don't have to wear one, you know," she murmured.

"That's where you're wrong. If I didn't, I'd look more like a hillbilly farmer than a doctor. There's more hocus-pocus in my profession than most of us like to admit. Doctors need to look like doctors or their patients won't have faith in them. If you don't think I look like a farmer you should see me in a straw hat."

"I never have," she smiled.

"And there's a good reason." He was chuckling, and she thought she'd only imagined that he'd seemed uneasy in her presence earlier.

"John . . ."

"Lannie . . ."

They both spoke at the same moment. When their eyes met, each looked quickly away. Then nervously each begged the other to speak first, as though each dreaded to speak himself. John managed to prevail on Lannie to start off.

"John, I thought you were going to call me yesterday afternoon. When you didn't I tried to call you, but you never returned my calls. Where were you?"

He shifted uncomfortably, looking more guilty than ever. Nervously he ran his hand through his rumpled sandy hair. "I should have called you back," he said quietly. "There's no excuse for not doing so, but I was feeling . . . cowardly."

Cowardly? Lannie was more perplexed than ever.

John continued, "But after I talked to you yesterday morning—you remember I told you Brandon had left your telephone number if I needed to reach him?"

Weakly she replied, "Yes, I remember."

"Well, after I talked to you yesterday I got to

thinking. At first I'd thought that Brandon and you might have something going on even though you'd been so negative about him that morning. You see, I remembered suddenly that he'd been attracted to you when he was in law school. So I called you to find out. But as soon as I talked to you and realized how ridiculous that idea was, I was astounded by my reaction."

John failed to notice the telltale flush scalding Lannie's cheeks as she lowered her long lashes to conceal her eyes. "What do you mean?" she managed in what she hoped was a normal tone.

"I . . . I was disappointed. I mean I'd almost hoped that you were involved with someone else. That's why I had to get off by myself yesterday, don't you see? If a man's engaged to be married to a girl, he shouldn't wish she'd suddenly develop an interest in his own brother!"

"John, what are you saying?"

"This isn't easy for me, Lannie." His voice was gentle; his eyes met hers and needlessly implored her to understand. "But I see now that I made a mistake when I asked you to marry me. I love you as a sister, but it's Hilary I'm in love with."

A mixture of relief and joy surged through her. "John." Lannie seized his hand. "I'm so happy for you." Blue eyes widened with astonishment, and the expression on his broad face was one of shock. But she continued, "Because I'd just realized the same thing— that I could never marry you."

If only all problems could be so easily and happily resolved, Lannie thought later. She'd returned John's ring, and when Hilary had come out with her steaming-hot rolls and coffee, Lannie had chatted with them for several minutes. Then after an appropriate interval of time had elapsed, Lannie had left them alone together so John could tell Hilary the news himself.

That evening it had been heartwarming to see them

strolling together beneath the golden and scarlet trees, arm in arm. Hilary was still in her parrot-red gown, beaming shyly up at John, as she revealed freely for the first time the extent of her love for him.

Curled against her stiff settee, Lannie found herself waiting expectantly for Brandon's call that night. Even from the parlor she could hear the incessant ticking of the grandfather clock in the foyer as she attempted to concentrate on the blurred page of one of her students' themes. Two hours had passed and so far she'd graded only three. Wearily she placed the stack of themes into her briefcase and pulled the golden chain that dangled beneath the silk lampshade, turning out the light. Brandon wasn't going to call, she realized unhappily. She might as well go up to bed.

That night a norther gusted down, and as Lannie lay awake in the early hours of the morning listening to the cold winds blasting around the house, a terrible thought recurred to her. Perhaps Brandon had come home for one reason only—to break off her engagement with his stepbrother. Perhaps he'd slept with her with only that purpose in mind and having accomplished that, hadn't the slightest intention of ever calling her again.

A wild throbbing pain slowly dulled into an ache, and she buried her face in the stifling depths of her pillow in a vain attempt to blot out visions of Brandon's bold handsomeness.

The next morning she rose white-faced, with shadows etched beneath her dark eyes. Deciding the only remedy for her pain was to distract herself by keeping busy, she made up her mind to throw herself with a vengeance into her work.

Fortunately the cold spell was a mild one, but that morning before she went to school Lannie talked to the farmer who saw after the sugarcane on her lands. They agreed to begin cutting the crop at once.

The next two weeks were a frenzy of activity, the theme of every waking hour being "to get the cane to the mill before the freeze." Harvesters filled the cane-choked fields, mowing down the green waves of cane, leaving the coarse cane stubble to turn brown in the fields. Every year this same race against the weather was run.

The nearby sugar mill worked twenty-four-hour shifts, chopping and crushing the stalks to extract juice; clarifying and evaporating the juices to produce syrup; then whirling the syrup with centrifugal force to separate it into raw sugar and molasses. The fibrous residue, called bagasse, would be used to make fiberboard, paper and other products.

The thick sweetly pungent scent of the sugar mill permeated the atmosphere with its familiar autumn smell. In spite of the fact that she was so busy, Lannie continued to be very depressed that she heard nothing from Brandon. Every time the phone rang, she had to stop herself from racing to answer it. Each day she went through the motions of leading her life normally when inside she felt that her life was shattered.

She cared for her house, took an intense interest in the sugarcane, worked at her job, helped Sherry with Denise, and tended Sugar. Five days a week she faced five classrooms brimming with energetic eighth graders, a task not made easier by sleepless nights. But strangely she was happiest at school, for only when she was at work surrounded by boisterous children and coping with their mischievous pranks could she distract herself from the intense pain of Brandon's rejection.

Two weekends later the sugar crop was safely in, and after paying his share to the farmer who worked for her, Lannie had a small profit which she desperately needed left over for herself. It was Saturday night, the night of the Brandon Chemicals barbeque, and Lannie found herself alone at Belle Rose with nothing she had to do, a first in the two weeks since Brandon had left.

Ralph, Sherry and Denise had driven to Brandon House together. Hilary had spent the day at Brandon House helping John cook and get ready for the party.

Everyone had asked Lannie to come, but she'd begged off, pleading a headache. Sherry had looked at her oddly and entreated her to come, saying that she hadn't gone out once in two weeks.

Since no one knew of her relationship with Brandon, they secretly suspected her headache was caused by John having broken the engagement, and there was no way that Lannie could explain the truth. She couldn't go alone to a party at Brandon's house where she would be constantly reminded of his absence.

Fortunately the weather had warmed up again and was now a perfect, crisp autumn night for the outdoor affair that would be held on the grounds near the pool and cabana behind Brandon House.

Lannie had learned through Hilary that Brandon had returned to New York the Monday morning after Lannie and John had broken their engagement. Thus, it seemed that her worst fears were true: that Brandon had cared nothing about her. She'd felt numb on first learning he'd gone. Every time she thought of him, she deliberately struggled to put him out of her mind for she was determined to forget him. But no matter how hard she tried, it was impossible for her to forget a man like Brandon. Memories of the time she'd spent with him, of his ardent lovemaking and her own rapturous response to him would assail her.

She was most vulnerable when she was tired or found herself alone with time on her hands. Thus, with everyone gone to the barbeque, the house seemed to press close around her and she could not stop herself from longing for the one man she couldn't bear to think of. In desperation she decided to go outside and try to do a few chores before it got dark.

As she moved slowly across the lower gallery and down the stairs her gaze drifted over the wild lushness of the lawns sweeping to meet the dense woods that edged the plantation. The air was pungent with the thick sweetness of freshly cut cane. Evening shadows were long and deep, the slanting rays of sunlight golden where they fell upon the columns of Belle Rose. It was her favorite time of day; there was an artist's clarity of color at this hour that was lacking in the middle of the afternoon. She was glad suddenly of her decision to leave the house that had seemed oppressive.

Immediately she saw a million things that she could do. Fallen branches littered the lawn and needed to be carried to the back and chopped into firewood. Leaves needed to be raked. The cape-jasmine hedges that were like verdant sculptures hugging the sides of the house were overgrown and needed a thorough clipping. But in her present mood, she felt too lethargic to embark on any constructive task. So instead of heading to the utility room for a pair of hedgeclippers or a rake she walked toward the levee that had been a favorite childhood haunt of hers.

The Belle Rose landing was an ancient affair that had had a tumble-down look even when Lannie had been a child. It was nestled beneath a magnificent cypress tree with great branches swathed in veils of swaying moss and giant knees submerged in the river. Lannie stepped cautiously over the loose planks and sank down, not caring that the boards were dirty and that she might soil her jeans.

With her rich hair spilling over her shoulders, she lay back, leaning on her elbows, her mind a confused tumble of emotions as she gazed upward above the river at the sky that was seared with blazing oranges, lavenders and reds. Yet her thoughts were not on the wildly primitive setting but on Brandon.

Plucking a piece of grass to chew on, she scarcely noted the blue heron skimming low over the broad expanse of sparkling river that curled slowly by on its way to the Gulf, nor the turtle splashing from a low branch into the water.

She knew that she was behaving foolishly. Hadn't she told Brandon she wasn't interested in the only kind of relationship he was willing to offer her? Shouldn't she be happy that he'd taken her at her word and left? And yet her treacherous pulse hammered as she dreamily considered the thought of a second, irresponsible love affair with Brandon. It had been nearly two weeks since he'd reawakened her need for him, and she couldn't stop herself from aching physically for him. But it was more than that. She breathed deeply, feeling tormented. Perhaps he hadn't given her another thought once he'd accomplished his purpose and she'd broken her engagement. In frustration she kicked at a loose board until it fell into the water and floated away. She sighed. If she were so much better off without that charming rogue, why did she feel so rotten?

The last of the season's cicadas buzzed as though in chorus, pausing only occasionally in their boisterous chirrups. On both sides of the river a tangle of semi-tropical plants grew as close as a jungle, but somehow the brooding sounds and silences of this familiar setting were comforting to Lannie. A tug that was pushing a barge chugged into view, and when she waved to the driver, a brawny paw extended from the cabin and fluttered jauntily back. Then for a while there was no river traffic, and her mood darkened once more as she thought of the hopelessness of loving the wrong man.

Suddenly she sensed a subtle difference in the atmosphere. The cicadas had stopped their singing. The only sounds were that of the river gently lapping against the pilings of the dock and the rustle of the willows as a stray breeze wafted through them. A strange stillness had fallen over the woods.

A warm prickle that was oddly familiar traveled the length of Lannie's spine, and nervously she whirled around. Quickly she clamped her fingers over her mouth to stifle a little startled cry. She was no longer alone!

In the evening shadows a tall dark man stood with his back to a wall of sweetly smelling pine trees, their blackened shapes silhouetted against the fiery red sunset. Her eyes traveled up the expensive black cloth covering two masculine legs that were planted widely apart in the deep grass, upward over a pale beige silk dress-shirt that stretched over a lean muscular torso and broad expanse of chest, further upward until her eyes met the deep dark gaze of the very man she'd been thinking of.

"Brandon?" His name was a throaty whisper emitted through tremulous lips. Her liquid dark eyes were shining.

"Admiring the view?" He chuckled, his abominable self-confidence surfacing as usual. Then he strode rapidly toward her, his polished boots crushing the thick grasses in his path.

Her heart leapt with the keenest of wild, pulsating joys, and she couldn't wholly suppress a smile though she struggled mightily to do so. "What are you doing back?" she murmured, pride forcing with much effort the involuntary lilt from her voice.

His black eyes flashed as they roved hungrily over her. "Did you miss me?"

Terribly . . . But she had no intention of admitting it. After all she hadn't the vaguest reason as to why he was here and such an admission would only add to his overabundant conceit. She lowered her lashes demurely over her dark eyes so that it would be more difficult for him to read her expression.

"Not in the least," she finally managed indifferently.

Shaking the dust from her jeans, she stood up, rising to her full height which scarcely brought her to the level of his shoulders. She hadn't liked the feeling of him towering over her, dominating her, for it had made her feel vaguely uneasy.

In spite of his elegant attire his eyes that roamed over her generous curves gleamed with a careless recklessness that made him seem dangerous and primitive, and she was acutely conscious of his masculinity and that she was very much alone with him. She fought against this fancy, telling herself they were two civilized human beings. But her heart was pounding with unaccustomed ferocity, and somewhere in the depths of her being she knew that the emotions they stirred within each other were not at all civilized. They were as anciently old as time itself. She forced her features into a harsh expression.

Frowning, he gave her a quick assessing glance, and not seeing one shred of welcome in her lovely tense face, he said, "You've got the hardest heart in three parishes, and if you weren't so damnably beautiful, I wouldn't have come back."

Had he really come back because of her? A little of her anxiety drained away.

But he gave her no time to dwell on this question. He was reaching for her, his hands sliding to her wrists and pulling her against his hard body. She tried to resist, but his strength easily overpowered her. At last she gave up, and stood still, participating in the intimate moment in spite of herself.

The clean masculine scent of him was like an aphrodisiac. She felt the velvet touch of his hard hands pressing her very close against him. The wild pagan rhythm of his heart thudded as rapidly as her own. His hands fondled the flowing masses of her hair and then moved over her body, molding her softness to himself. Everywhere he touched her, sensuous ripples of response were ignited, and at last she could not stop herself from moaning. She lifted her gaze to meet his own that was fierce molten blackness.

For a long time he held her to him in silence as though she were very precious. It was a magic moment.

"Brandon . . ." A tide of intense feeling flooded her. She whispered his name wonderingly, lovingly. Tentatively her hands reached up to caress his face. Beneath her fingertips she felt the coarse texture of his skin, the heat of him.

"Kiss me, Lannie," he demanded in a passion-roughened tone, "and show me you're as glad to see me as I am to see you."

She stretched upward, lifting her softly parted lips to his and kissing him gently but with the deepest of emotions. When flesh touched flesh, a fierce, consuming hunger surged through them, igniting a wild, erotic fire that raced out of control.

They stood, their lips and bodies fused, their passion as bright and flaming as the sweeping scarlet sunset that inflamed both river and sky.

At last Brandon drew away, and Lannie's lashes fluttered open in surprise and disappointment, her wide, startled gaze lifting to his. The passion he'd stirred made her feel limp and she clung to him.

"Did you miss me?" he demanded. She felt the heat of his breath against her forehead. His black eyes were intense.

"Y-yes," she murmured, wanting only for him to go on holding her and kissing her and thereby drive away the numbed empty feeling that she'd felt without him.

"Why wouldn't you admit it when I asked you a while ago?" he persisted.

Dazedly her mind spun. Why did he keep asking questions when all she wanted. . . . "I-I don't know," she murmured. She tilted her face toward his, longing for his mouth to claim hers again.

But he didn't kiss her. "You won't give me one scrap of affection, unless I force you," he said, his voice tight and strange.

Did he care? She was staring deeply into his eyes, wondering for the first time. But as always, his cool expression was unreadable, and she couldn't believe that he did.

"You don't trust me, do you?" he demanded.

"How could I?" she admitted.

"I'll have to work on that then." He drew a ragged breath, ignoring the upturned lure of her provocative mouth. "But if we're going to the barbeque, we'd better hurry. You still have to get dressed."

"The barbeque . . ." She stared up at him in confusion and dismay. For the first time she remembered the social function that had been the talk of the parish for months.

His sensual mouth quirked in amusement as he read her mind. "I want you, Lannie, now." His deep voice wrapped her with its silken sound. "It's a shame to waste this opportunity when I know everyone's at the barbeque, and we're alone at Belle Rose." Suddenly they were both remembering that other time two weeks ago when they'd unexpectedly found themselves alone.

Desire and need and wild joy banished all of Lannie's carefully thought-out decisions that she must not pursue a relationship with Brandon. All she could think of was that he had come back to her and she wanted to be with him.

"You want me too," he said, and when she did not reply, he pressed on. "Don't you?" His question was a command.

"Y-yes." The one word was dragged from the depths of a despairing soul. Why did she have to find him so irresistible? She should be giddy that he wanted to take her to the barbeque instead of to bed.

"Do you have to look so unhappy when you say it?" he muttered, a look of obvious hurt darkening his features.

"I just wish I didn't feel that you're the wrong man for me."

"But you can't help yourself." There was an edge of bitter sarcasm in his deep tone. "I know the feeling, but, nevertheless, your candor is . . . er . . . far from heartwarming. Really, darling, I would think a girl with your Southern-belle heritage would make the effort to flatter a man more than you do."

She smiled up at him, lightly tracing the bridge of his nose in a teasing fashion. "You're hardly the kind of man who needs to be flattered. Your ego is already much too inflated."

"Is it?" he murmured dryly, kissing her exploring fingers that were now sensuously brushing his lips.

"You know I'm right."

"I believe in thinking positively," he admitted. "Especially when it comes to myself. But that's only because I've found it helps me to get what I want in business as well as in my personal life."

He stared meaningfully down at her, his roughened fingertip reaching out to touch the pouting line of her full mouth with genuine regret while she continued her own tactile exploration of his jawline. Then she kissed his palm fervently, her warm breath stirring between his fingers. After a long moment he drew his hand away, sighing in frustration as he took her own palm in his and slowly removed it from his face. "If we keep this up, we'll never make it to the barbeque."

The intense urge to touch him overwhelmed her, and

her hand moved beneath his shirt and across the furred warm flatness of his stomach in a caressing motion.

"Exactly . . ." she replied, her low voice husky with a silkily seductive invitation she could no more stop herself from making than he could stop himself from accepting.

Chapter Eleven

*B*edsheets rustled. A gentle breeze stirred through the long open windows of Lannie's bedroom. She was giggling with a total lighthearted abandon. She hadn't been so happy—ever.

"You are an irresistible wanton," Brandon murmured.

"Are you complaining?" she whispered pertly.

In answer Brandon crushed her beneath the heated length of his body and kissed her fiercely on the mouth. Everywhere he touched her, her skin tingled in response.

He dragged his lips from hers. "No, I'm not complaining. That's a large part of your charm."

"I'm glad you find me charming," she purred.

"You were most charming, too charming for your own good. Or mine either for that matter. I'm sorry that it didn't last longer, but two weeks without a woman . . . without you," he quickly amended. She moved beneath him, and a hot current jolted through him.

"No need to explain," she murmured, smiling ecstatically up at him as the pleasant thought that he hadn't gone to bed with anyone else since she'd last seen him registered in her female mind. And he hadn't! She knew him too well physically to doubt it. The raw urgency of their desire had demanded immediate assuagement, and their mutual satisfaction had been intense.

"Do you realize," he was smiling down at her, "that we still have time to make it to the barbeque?"

"I was hoping that we wouldn't." Again she moved beneath him so that he could feel her hips against his and the ripe lushness of her full breasts thrusting softly against his chest.

"That's not going to work again," he said dryly. "Now that I've had you once. Besides after the barbeque we have the rest of the night."

"Where? Everyone will be home then."

"You didn't used to be so unimaginative," he teased gently.

"I can't spend the whole night away. What will Hilary and Sherry think?"

"Whatever they want," he returned with the bland indifference of someone who hadn't given other people's opinions about such matters serious consideration in years.

"Brandon!"

"Ever the little hypocrite?" he mocked, smiling down at her earnest, upturned face. "But to safeguard your precious reputation—half the night," he compromised good-naturedly. "Then they can wonder—did she or didn't she—to their heart's content."

"How kind and gallant of you," she teased.

"I thought so." Deliberately he misinterpreted the soft irony of her statement. He was grinning broadly down at her with the bold self-confidence she normally found so infuriating. To his surprise she burst out laughing. "At last we agree on something," he quipped. "Didn't I tell you if I took you to bed again, you'd sheath your claws and purr as docilely as a kitten. You see, you're already complimenting me. And you know how much I love compliments."

When she playfully lunged out at him with a pillow, he caught her wrists, easily overpowering her. The sheet was ripped away so that her lush olive flesh was exposed to his male view. Her body glowed in the soft golden light. His gaze roamed over her full round breasts, her slim, female form, and a fierce male need rose up in him. Suddenly he had to have her again.

Her own heart raged as turbulently as his as Brandon's brown fingers caressed the delicate firmness of her chin, holding her face still so that she could not resist his kiss. His parted lips moved over her velvety soft mouth. She felt the heated moisture of his tongue inside her mouth. Then his arms moved around her like bands of iron, pressing her small soft body against his own hard and muscular one. The strength to resist him drained from her hands that had automatically pushed against the wall of his chest. His slow, burning kiss seemed to go on and on before he dragged his lips from her trembling mouth to explore the satiny texture of her earlobe.

Exquisite ripples stirred through her love-ravaged senses, and she moaned his name, the husky whisper of her voice caressing him, inflaming him. His embrace was wild and passionate, demanding a response.

He drew her with him slowly, his hands wandering over her gently, expertly titillating her, touching all the most sensitive places that he alone knew, blazing a trail of passion that left her quivering from his touch. His mouth lightly teased the rosy crests of her breasts, causing them to grow taut and temptingly erect before his mouth moved away in intimate exploration. She felt on fire with need for him.

"Oh, Brandon . . . Brandon," she sighed in a dreamy haze of exquisite sensations. Everything he was doing to her felt delicious. His black head was in her lap, his lips moving over her soft skin gently, slowly, languorously, teasing her sensitive tissues until she was aching with desire. She wanted him to go on and on, to never stop. Yet she yearned for him to bring this building emotion to its fulfillment, and she stirred restlessly beneath him.

He adjusted her beneath the muscular contours of his body. Then his mouth swooped down hard on hers, gentle no longer, forcing her lips apart, and thrusting his tongue deep within. Primitive hot longings spread like a white-hot fire through her loins and she arched her lower body against his. As she moved her hips against him with deliberate wanton intimacy, his blood pounded through his veins in a violent surge. He paused, his muscular chest heaving, as he inhaled a deep labored breath.

For a long moment he stopped making love to her in an effort to control his passion. His black gaze swept downward like a passionate caress, lingering as he filled his eyes with the vision of her lush glowing beauty. Her hair was like their passion—wild and untamed, spilling over the stark-white pillow in a black blaze.

How lovely she was with her nipples taut with desire, her breasts softly swollen from his love play. The softly delectable mounds of flesh rose and fell tantalizingly with her every breath. The texture of her skin that covered every part of her body was smooth and flawless. His gaze roamed over the gentle swell of her stomach and over her hips, to the perfection of a curving thigh.

The faintest of smiles curved his sensual mouth. She belonged to him; she'd never been with any other man.

Odd that he should care. He was a modern man and in these modern times that shouldn't mean anything. But for some reason that he didn't analyze, it did. A fierce possessiveness such as he'd never known with any other woman shot through him.

She was his alone! And she would remain so! The mere thought of another man ignited a murderous feeling, and his mood of tenderness changed. His handsome features grew sharp, hardening at this unpleasant thought.

Suddenly there was in him the fierce need to dominate her, to reaffirm that she was his, and his alone. He bent his hard mouth to her lips, and ravaged their exquisite softness with unaccustomed violence. She shuddered, her own passion as great as his own, and when he felt her response, his brutal caress gentled. But he wanted to prolong their time of love, and he deliberately fought for control. Even when she cried out his name again and again in ecstasy, begging him to gratify her and give her the sensual release she craved, he made her wait, teasing her, arousing her further. He needed to know that she wanted him as hopelessly and shamelessly as he desired her.

Again she moved beneath him. The swaying movement of her curvaceous hips against his lower body was almost more than he could endure. And she, sensing her power over him, tentatively reached up and touched him in an intimate caress. He groaned aloud and looked deeply into her eyes, drawing out the moment before he took her, prolonging their mutual need until she thought she would faint from the sheer exquisite bliss of knowing the intensity of his desire for her.

When she first touched him, his hoarse voice against her ear muttered love words that he'd never said before to any woman, his warm breaths tingling against her satin skin.

For an endless instant, he rested against her while he held her, looking tenderly down into the beautiful innocence of her face, savoring that first precious moment when their mutual desire fused them spiritually and physically into one being.

A faint sheen of perspiration glimmered on his bronzed skin. His black hair tumbled over his brow. The exquisite intensity of his gaze at last was more than she could bear. Her dark lashes fluttered dreamily downward, and she closed her eyes against the compelling vision of his pagan virility, surrendering to the wave of warm feeling that swept over her.

Gathering her into his arms, he took her, no longer gentle, but with a shattering force that carried them both to new peaks of shuddering ecstasy.

The night was velvet darkness. Over the twang of violins, the throbbing masculine voice sang the traditional French folk song with husky softness, *"Jole blon . . ."* Below the bandstand, dancers twirled on the glossy dancefloor that had been erected on the lawn beneath the age-old oaks and magnolias.

Brandon alighted from his silver car, striding around the front of it to help Lannie out. His large hand folded over her tiny one. As she stepped from the car, her dark eyes shining in her lovely face, her hair tumbling waves of black satin, she was a vision in flowing red organza.

"I never thought we'd make it to the barbeque," she murmured, smiling up at him.

"Neither did I," he countered dryly. "We're a little late and more than a little the worse for wear. I'm afraid I haven't the energy for a polka, but we're here. And that Cajun food smells delicious, even from this distance."

"Don't underestimate yourself, Brandon, when it

comes to your energy level. You're a man of amazing stamina." She was smiling saucily up at him, both her look and tone suggestive. "And I of all people should know."

He bent his lips to her forehead and gently kissed her, causing a strange warmness to flow through her. His tanned palm cupped her chin and turned her face up to his so he could stare deeply into her eyes. Then he flashed her a jaunty smile.

"Another compliment, my pet? I don't know how my . . . how did you put it . . . overinflated ego is going to survive if we spend much more time in the bedroom. Abundant sex certainly sweetens your disposition."

She was in too good a mood to be ruffled by anything he said. Taking his arm, she simply smiled up at him, her beautiful face aglow. "Where do you suppose that food is? I didn't realize until we got here how hungry I am."

Again he smiled. "No, you were too busy satisfying another quite voracious appetite."

A brick path beside a thick azalea hedge curved toward the back of Brandon House where torch lights flickered. Magnificent magnolias towered darkly over them as Brandon escorted Lannie to the barbeque.

A dragon motif had been used to decorate the semitropical grounds. An enormous paper dragon suspended from the tree branches soared above the party-goers.

"How lovely," Lannie exclaimed, her eyes wandering from the enormous flying dragon to the brightly decorated tables scattered about the lawn, each graced with its own replica of the giant dragon.

"Watch this," Brandon said, pulling a small cord beside a tree.

The flying dragon made a low gutteral sound and

belched steam. A gasp went through the crowd that was quickly followed by laughter as Brandon pulled the cord again and the dragon again let out a puff of steam.

"I really wanted fire," Brandon whispered, "but the fellow who put this creation together advised against it."

As Lannie and Brandon stepped into view she was suddenly aware that all eyes seemed to turn to them.

"What a stunning couple. . . ." This whisper floated to Lannie's ears. "Who are they?"

"Why, Maybelle Louise, you mean you don't know. . . ."

Lannie imagined there was a faint lull in the conversation and that more than a few matronly eyebrows lifted in surprise and speculation. Though Brandon was a most eligible bachelor, all the dowagers knew that Genevieve had despaired for years that he would never marry.

Brandon bent his head over Lannie's, whispering into her ear. "We've given the gossips something to wag their tongues about, haven't we, by appearing together at such a public function? I'm going to have to flirt with every beautiful woman here tonight or they'll be marrying us off and naming our children within the week."

Lannie giggled. "I knew you'd think up some clever excuse to abandon me and do exactly as you please."

"Did I detect a note of regret in your voice?" Black eyes snapped as they beheld her. "Would you prefer me to play the host with you clinging possessively at my side?"

Shyly, she replied, "Yes."

"Are you admitting that you're actually enjoying my company?"

She nodded.

"Another compliment." He chuckled. "I really am going to be impossible."

As Brandon moved through the crowd greeting his guests and introducing Lannie to those who did not know her or did not recognize her at once, she was aware of veiled curious glances cast in her direction. Suddenly she realized that this was the first time Brandon had ever publicly displayed her as a woman he was interested in. In the past their relationship had been very private, and she'd been introduced only to a few of his close friends. She could not stop her mind from wandering along the same path as that of the local gossips. What did it mean—Brandon openly displaying his interest in her and in front of Genevieve?

John and Hilary came over. "You're quite beautiful tonight, Lannie," John said, observing the special glow that illuminated her features. "What changed your mind about coming?" Blue eyes, frankly curious, rested lingeringly on Lannie's blushing features.

"I talked her into it," Brandon said, answering the question himself. There was an undeniable possessive element in his deep tone that aroused more curiosity than it satisfied, and Lannie's coloring deepened as John looked at his brother oddly and then back at her.

"Have you all eaten?" Brandon asked, deliberately changing the topic.

"Not enough," John replied.

Everyone laughed.

"Really, John, sometimes it amazes me that you're not as round as you are tall," Lannie said affectionately.

John patted his waistline which did protrude a little over his narrow black belt. "Give me time. I'm still working on it."

Together they walked toward the gay party tents scattered about the lawn beneath which stood yellow-clothed tables piled high with Cajun food.

Boiled crawfish were steaming pink mountains in silver bowls. Thick broiled steaks, and *boudin,* a spicy

French sausage, were being served as main entrees as well as many delectable varieties of fried seafood: shrimp, soft-shelled crabs, oysters, scallops, crab claws and redfish. John served himself jambalaya and bouillabaisse, each fragrantly spiced to perfection with piquant combinations of herbs and spices. There were soups, bisques and elaborate casseroles. Delicious scents mingled and wafted in the cool night air.

Lannie didn't know where to begin, but soon her plate was piled with far more food than she could possibly eat, and the two couples headed toward one of the banquet tables set up on the lawn. As they ate beneath towering pecan and magnolia trees, Lannie marveled that though it was quite late, the party was in full swing.

It was deeply imbedded in the French nature to love festivity, to prolong any excuse to have a good time, she thought fondly as she watched the dancers sway in rhythmic unison with the French music and listened to the animated sound of conversation flowing on all sides of her.

Ultimately Brandon's duties as host forced him from Lannie's side, but she didn't mind. She was having too much fun herself. When he reluctantly left her she was visiting with her cousin Velvet.

As always Velvet was stunningly beautiful in her deliberately dramatic style. She'd cut her thick black hair short in the six weeks since Lannie had last seen her. Dark glossy ringlets now fell in flattering disarray about Velvet's exquisite face. She wore a floor-length Mexican dress made of coarse cotton that was the loveliest shade of lavender, the very color of her eyes.

"I like your hair that way," Lannie said.

"Tell Hamlin. When I came home from the beauty parlor I thought he was going to divorce me." Velvet laughed lightly, making it obvious she wasn't too worried.

As if on cue Hamlin strode up and joined them. He draped his arm around his wife affectionately and entered the conversation, admitting that he hadn't liked her hair at first but that he did now; that she would look beautiful to him no matter what she did.

His eyes glowed when he spoke of his wife, and Velvet's deep contentment was just as obvious. Always it gave Lannie the greatest happiness that her cousin had given up her wild ways and straightened out her life and was now so happily married.

When Velvet and Hamlin glided away to dance, Lannie easily found other people to talk to.

Having grown up in the parish and lived there most of her life, Lannie knew a great many of the guests herself. Her heritage was French, and it never took her long to get into the mood of a party. She was soon surrounded by a throng of admirers, most of them men, who asked her to dance again and again.

She was whirling in a breathless polka when Louis, Hamlin Trajan's younger brother, cut in.

"How does it feel to be the belle of the ball? If I waited my turn, I wouldn't ever get to dance with you," Louis said gallantly, smoothly pulling her into his arms and guiding her across the dancefloor. She laughed.

Like Hamlin, Louis was tall and golden and very handsome. He and she had grown up together. He was now a talented New Orleans entrepreneur, who was even richer than his brother Hamlin. Recently he'd obtained a divorce from his childhood sweetheart and was single once again.

"You can dance with me anytime, Louis. I didn't know you were here."

"Brandon called me about a business deal, and I came down for the weekend."

"Oh."

"I've been wanting to talk to you ever since I saw you come in," he said.

"What about?"

"Sugar." When Lannie arched her eyebrows in surprise, Louis continued. "Hamlin said he had a stopwatch on you the other day when you and Sugar sailed out of her paddock and raced to the road. He judged the distance right at a quarter of a mile, and he said Sugar's time was spectacular. In fact he couldn't stop talking about it at lunch that afternoon."

"Then why didn't he tell me that at the time?" Lannie wondered aloud.

"I think he said something about Brandon coming up and he didn't have a chance."

Lannie flushed and hoped Louis wouldn't pursue that topic.

"I want to buy Sugar," he continued, "for breeding purposes. I'd been trying to talk Hamlin out of her even before he sold her to you. As you know I raise horses. I wouldn't attempt to race her again because Hamlin assures me she's still too easily spooked."

"Louis, I can't sell Sugar. She's like a member of the family."

"Lannie, it's no secret you need money to keep Belle Rose up. Won't you even consider my offer?" They had stopped dancing. When she nodded reasonably at last, he named a figure that was higher than her take-home pay from her teaching job for a year.

She almost gasped. Why, that would be more than enough to pay for Denise's operation, and Lannie would have money left over to spend on Belle Rose.

"I never dreamed . . . anyone would be willing to pay so much for her," Lannie said. "Why I only gave . . ."

"I know what you paid for her, but you've done a lot with her. And because of what you did, Hamlin finally realized her potential."

172

"But you haven't even seen Sugar. And to pay so much . . ."

"Hamlin knows horses. Besides I know her bloodline is impeccable."

Suddenly Lannie knew she had no choice. "I- I'll sell Sugar to you, Louis," she said thickly, fighting back the intense feeling of sadness that was swamping her. Sugar was very very dear to her, but Denise was even more precious.

"For someone not willing to sell, you certainly made up your mind in a hurry. Do you need money that badly?" There was a note of sympathy in his deep voice.

The last thing she wanted was Louis prying into her financial affairs as though she had no pride.

"I thought you wanted to buy a horse," she said roughly.

"I do."

"Then come over with your trailer sometime next week and pick her up."

"All right."

She attempted a smile, and he flashed her one of his dazzling ones and said, "Now that we've got business out of the way, what do you say we concentrate on dancing?"

Her heart wasn't in dancing any longer, but he whirled her slowly across the dancefloor, pressing her close to his own body, moving with an undulating dancestep that was peculiarly French.

"Tell me, Lannie, what does a beautiful girl like yourself find to do buried in the country? You're the last person I expected to stay in the parish. You were always so . . ." He paused, gallantly searching for a euphemism. "So adventuresome."

"That's putting it mildly," she said with a weak smile. "But I grew up, Louis, and I'm quite content with my life."

"Really? And is there room in it for a newly divorced Frenchman?" he whispered seductively against her ear, holding her even closer.

Coming from Louis who was her same age and whom she'd known since her toddler days, this loverlike pose seemed ludicrous and Lannie's depression evaporated. She burst into laughter. Instantly Louis looked hurt.

Sensing that she'd wounded his vanity, she said gently, "Louis, you and Hamlin are like brothers to me."

Louis was not altogether mollified, and as Lannie attempted to soothingly make him see things her way, over his shoulder her brown eyes locked with Brandon's glittering black gaze. Lovely and regal in a shimmering blue gown, Genevieve stood at his side, smiling proudly up at her tall grandson. Her silver hair shone in the soft light.

Other dancers blocked Brandon and his grandmother from Lannie's view, but in spite of the fact that she had barely glimpsed Brandon, Lannie knew him well enough to realize he was very angry. Then Louis began flirting with her outrageously again, and for a time she was too busy defending herself against his courtly attack to think of Brandon.

Lannie was unaware of how beautiful she looked, her organza gown floating like a cloud as she danced. her hair catching the light of the flames as it rippled over her shoulders. As Brandon continued to observe her from afar in the arms of a man who was not only exceedingly rich but whose reputation with women was anything but that of a saint, Brandon's expression grew increasingly more grim. It was obvious to him even from a distance that Louis was intent on conquest. And Lannie's expression was so animated he could not help pondering the purity of her own motives. Cynically he wondered if it were the man or his money she found so attractive that she blushed every time he bent his lips and whispered into her ear.

A low murderous rage burned through Brandon, its intensity shocking him. Jealous—at his age! The emotion was so ridiculous he would have laughed—if he'd been in the mood to laugh. As it was he felt almost malignant.

The music ended and the band took a break. Louis escorted Lannie from the dancefloor to a table where Velvet and Hamlin were sitting with other friends. Then Louis went after drinks.

Wispy tendrils stirred faintly against her forehead and temples as Lannie fanned herself with an unused paper plate. She felt too hot and tired to attempt to take part in the conversation.

Suddenly an electric sensation sizzled through Lannie as she felt Brandon's hand passionately touch the naked flesh of her shoulder.

"Lannie . . ." There was controlled anger in his deep tone.

She glanced questioningly up into the handsome darkness of his unsmiling face, having no clue as to the reason for his change in mood.

"Have you finished playing host?" she asked, hoping that he had. Louis could be quite determined, and she was weary from fighting him off.

"Where's Louis?" Brandon asked, his voice still harsh.

"He went to the bar," she replied easily. "He ought to be back in a minute."

"Then let's get the hell out of here before he returns."

"Brandon! I thought you two were friends."

"Forget Louis . . . if you can. I'm not feeling particularly friendly toward him at the moment."

Again he spoke brusquely as though he were angry. But there was a new element in his voice that made her wonder if he were jealous, but she dismissed this preposterous idea at once because he was usually so cavalier where women were concerned. No, it must be something else that had nothing to do with her.

"Genevieve asked me to bring you over," he said at length as if this somehow explained his strange behavior.

"Oh, Brandon . . ." As she looked up at him her eyes were shining. She couldn't believe that he was actually offering to let her resume her relationship with his grandmother. Could this be the beginning of trust?

"Don't think this is my idea," he snapped curtly, obliterating her happiness in an instant. "Genevieve saw you and asked me to bring you over."

"Oh."

At his words her expression crumpled, and he felt an odd pang of conscience that he'd deliberately caused her unhappiness. Still, it was her own fault he was in this cursed black humor. She shouldn't have let Louis fall all over her for the past hour. It was damnably obvious she couldn't be trusted, and he didn't want her around Genevieve.

As he led her toward his grandmother, Lannie's stiff movements told him she was hurt, but he didn't apologize. He was too angry himself.

Genevieve's face lit with the kindest of smiles as she clasped Lannie's hand tightly in her own. Lannie's own smile was brilliant, and so artlessly genuine that even Brandon was almost convinced that she felt sincere affection for his grandmother. Genevieve asked Brandon to leave them for a moment so they could visit alone, and against his better judgment he obliged, promising himself he would give Lannie no more than fifteen minutes in his grandmother's company.

Still clutching Lannie's hand, Genevieve drew her toward an ornate wrought-iron sofa freshly painted white. Together they sank down into plump, floral cushions.

"I can't stand for too long anymore," Genevieve admitted. "The arthritis in my knees, but never mind that. How have you been, child?" the elderly lady asked anxiously, her bright dark eyes drinking in the sight of Lannie. "I used to worry about you so, when you were younger. Then I heard through Brandon that you'd come home and settled down to teach school."

Genevieve had heard from Brandon. So he had known all along where she'd gone and what she was doing.

"I've changed, Genevieve."

"I can see that, child. You've matured. Tell me. Do you like teaching?"

"Yes."

"I was a teacher once myself . . ."

Fifteen minutes passed all too quickly as they shared amusing anecdotes about their teaching careers. Brandon reappeared, putting an end to their carefree conversation before it scarcely seemed to have begun. Lannie looked up into his darkly grim features and felt disappointed that he was determined to cut the visit so short. She'd always loved Genevieve dearly, and she wished there was some way she could convince Brandon of her feelings.

"The time passed so quickly—our talking together," Genevieve said graciously, rising. She winked, her black eyes sparkling. "I'll only give you up to Brandon if you promise to come see me next week, one afternoon after school. We'll sit out by the pond and watch the swans and catch up on old times."

Genevieve spoke with such wistful eagerness that Lannie could think of no way to refuse. Besides she wanted to see Genevieve as much as Genevieve wanted to see her.

Recklessly ignoring Brandon's glare, Lannie accepted. "I'd love that too, Genevieve. I'll stop by Thursday afternoon, if you'll be home."

"I'm always home. I can't get around as much as I used to."

As Brandon led Lannie away he spoke in a cold flat tone that she hated. "You shouldn't have accepted her invitation."

"Why not?"

"We both know the reason for that. Because I won't have you using Genevieve again."

"I have no intention of using her," Lannie cried, stung. "Why can't you believe I care about her? It's obvious she's very lonely. You heard her yourself. She doesn't feel well enough to get out."

"Spare me your concern for my grandmother."

Her heart contracted with an odd little pain. She felt desperate that he didn't believe her, and without realizing it she raised her voice in an attempt to convince him. "Brandon . . ."

Several guests turned to openly stare in their direction.

"Lower your voice," he warned. "And smile. People are watching us."

With an effort, she did as he commanded; she was no more anxious to make a scene than he.

"Shall we dance?" he invited, forcing a stiff smile.

"I'd rather not," she demured.

"So would I," he returned cuttingly, his black gaze as cruelly slicing as his words. "But it's the only way we can talk without being interrupted."

His arms slid around her and moving with fluid ease, they swirled out onto the dancefloor.

"In your present mood, I'd rather not talk to you," she retorted hotly.

"No, you prefer Louis."

"Louis . . ." She uttered his name in absolute shock. "Why, Brandon, you're not jealous, are you?"

178

She tilted her lovely face up at his in time to see his jawline tighten perceptibly at this question.

"Not in the conventional sense," he responded, his tone deliberately insulting. "I have no doubt you're only interested in his money."

"I'm not interested in him at all!" she snapped, suddenly as angry as he that he would think that of her.

In vain she tried to wrench free, but he folded her even more tightly against himself and effortlessly guided her into the deeply shadowed fringe of the dancefloor.

"Then why did you let him drool over you for more than an hour?"

"Louis is an old and dear friend, in case you have forgotten. He's very despondent about his divorce."

"Despondent like hell! He's on the make."

"You have such a low opinion of me I'm surprised you care."

"Well, I do," he retorted gruffly.

There was something intense in his voice that she'd never heard before. Her heart fluttered jerkily with a wild pulsating joy.

"I wish you could believe me, Brandon," she said softly, breathlessly aware of every place his hard body came in contact with hers. "I don't care about Louis, or his money."

Brandon's lips were crushed into the perfumed, thickly flowing waves of her hair. His strong hands pressed her slim body so that it closely fitted his. "I wish I could too," he muttered savagely, his lingering doubt plunging him into a private hell all his own.

Chapter Twelve

Clutching Brandon's coat more tightly around her in protection against the chill autumn air, Lannie stared up through the thick pines and saw that a sprinkle of stars pierced the ink velvet sky. Brandon had left her for a moment so that he could say goodbye to the last of the guests.

Nervously she watched the quick efficient movements of the caterers as they began cleaning up, but her mind was on Brandon. His black mood had persisted through the rest of the evening, and he'd come close to being openly discourteous to both Louis and Hamlin when they'd left. Toward herself, Brandon's tongue had been unusually cutting, as though he were angry with her and deliberately wanted to hurt her.

The purposeful tread of approaching footsteps told her Brandon was returning. She shivered, almost dreading their time alone together not only because of her own doubts about resuming her relationship with him but also because of his uncertain mood.

The footsteps paused, and Lannie sensed Brandon was watching her. The familiar tingle of awareness spread through her as she turned to face him.

In the darkness he loomed tall and broad-shouldered, overpoweringly masculine. Her eyes met the hot intensity of his black electric gaze. There was an odd, yet strangely alert expression on his lean features, and she realized she was deeply affecting him in some perplexing way that he didn't fully understand and didn't like. The minute her eyes met his, he smiled casually, as though he deliberately sought to dispel whatever emotion she evoked in him.

For no reason at all she felt strangely shy and even more apprehensive. She shivered. This time it had nothing to do with chill and little to do with her dread. In spite of his hostility, it was a delicious feeling, a purely female flutter of excitement caused by knowing that in spite of his anger Brandon found her attractive. She held the same power over him that he held over her, and he didn't like it any better than she.

"I suppose it's time for you to drive me home," she said uncertainly.

"Not quite." His eyes still held hers. "You may be tired of me, but I'm not taking you home yet." There was the faintest trace of anger in his low voice.

"Brandon, I'm not tired of you," she replied softly, hoping to ease the tension between them.

"Good, then you won't mind spending more time with me."

"Where could we go?" she reasoned gently. "We're miles from the nearest city, and we can't stay here."

"Why not?"

"It's your house."

"You make that sound like a den of iniquity." He laughed brittlely. "Which is hardly the case. It's filled to the brim with servants, not to mention Genevieve and John. But, don't worry. I have no intention of staying here. We'd be much too well-chaperoned. I'm taking you to *Calypso*."

At her gasp, he smiled. There was the beginning of a devilish twinkle in his eye, as though the thought of having her completely to himself partially restored his good humor. *Calypso* was his luxurious hundred-foot motor yacht that he kept tied up at a very secluded dock between Brandon Chemicals and his home. It had five staterooms, each complete with a private bath and each lavishly decorated.

"That's even worse," she retorted wryly.

"Or better." Again there was a gleam in his eyes. "It depends on your point of view." He smiled, as though he were purposefully attempting to improve the atmosphere between them. "We'll have complete privacy, something we both want." He paused. "You probably remember the entire area leading to the dock and boathouse where I keep *Calypso* is fenced-off. But what you don't know is that recently I installed a sophisticated alarm system that protects both the grounds and the boat."

He stared down into the exquisite, upturned face, its delicate beauty only slightly marred by her frown. "We'll be totally alone." His black eyes gleamed.

Her frown disappeared. A warm flush flowed through her, staining her cheeks with embarrassment. Why was she even arguing when she really wanted to go, probably more than he did?

"Brandon . . ."

"No more attempts to talk me out of it," he stated firmly. "You and I made a bargain—half the night, so half the night it is. Besides, I didn't fly halfway around the world to spend tonight with my grandmother. You and I haven't had a chance to talk yet."

There was a suppressed passionate element in his tone that made her think talking wasn't all he had in mind.

"Halfway around the world?" she questioned, her curiosity getting the better of her.

"I had to make a quick trip to Kuwait unexpectedly. In fact I left in the middle of the night, or I would have called you. A rather delicate negotiation had been mishandled so I decided I'd better take care of the matter myself."

"I thought you were in New York."

"I was, briefly." His arm slid beneath her elbow as he led her along the brick path to his car. Softly, he asked, "Do you think I would have left Louisiana so suddenly without knowing whether or not you were going to break up with John if an emergency of the most severe nature hadn't come up?"

Was he saying that she mattered to him? She hadn't realized he'd left before John had broken their engagement, and his explanation cast his abrupt departure in a new light.

"I didn't know why you left," she said quietly.

"Because I had to."

They paused for a moment, their eyes meeting.

"When you didn't call I couldn't help wondering." She hoped she revealed none of the desolation his leaving had caused her.

They reached his car.

"There's that suspicious note in your voice you always get when you don't quite trust me," he said knowingly, opening the door of his Mercedes and helping her inside. Nervously she tucked the flowing organza skirt into the car and tried not to look at him, but at last she couldn't stop herself.

He was staring down at her, his bold black eyes so assessing that she couldn't hold his gaze and, therefore, she veiled her emotions and looked quickly away.

Not finding what he wanted to by studying her beautiful features that she so carefully arranged in an artificially cool expression, he slammed the door more forcefully than was his custom and strode rapidly around to his own side of the car.

The tension between them as they sped silently through a thick stand of aromatic pines was almost a tangible thing, and Lannie was still at a loss to understand its cause.

Brandon was certainly not his usual cool and unruffled self. Something that he tried to hide was bothering him.

In casual possession Brandon had draped his arm over the back of the seat around Lannie's shoulders, and pulled her to him so that her body was snugly fitted against his.

She was keenly aware of her thigh resting against the corded length of his upper leg and of his hand that lightly caressed her shoulder. How could he make her ache just by holding her close?

When he pressed an electronic device on his car, the heavy gates leading to *Calypso*'s dock opened soundlessly and he maneuvered the car through them, his fingers pressing the same button a second time and thereby closing them.

He drove to the dock and, turning the ring of keys, switched off the ignition and headlights.

The boathouse and pilings were black shadowy forms, silhouetted eerily in the pale moonlight. Around them crushed the dense overgrowth of semitropical shrubs interspersed with towering pine and oak trees.

He twisted his lean hard body so that he was facing her, and she felt his intent gaze upon her like a burning caress. For a long moment neither spoke. She sensed his coiled tension, just as she was aware of her own excited nervousness. What was it about just being with him that made her feel so totally alive? And yet her attraction for him was so powerful it seemed vaguely frightening. She felt that he was as vividly aware of her as she was of him.

In the silent vast darkness of the forest she had never felt so dangerously alone with any man. It was as if they were the only two people in the whole world.

Organza rustled as his hands moved expertly over her body, drawing her against himself so that she felt every hard muscle of his body imprint its shape against her own feminine form. Her arms slipped eagerly around him, longing to touch him and explore his muscular frame, hoping that her touch would lighten the dark mood that gripped him. For a long time he just held her to him, savoring the intimate feel of her.

A wild warm madness pounded through her veins, and she could not resist the impulse to trail her mouth lightly across his cheek. Beneath her lips the texture of his skin and slight masculine growth of beard felt as rough as sandpaper.

He groaned aloud at the delicate nibbling of her lips against his flesh. Then in the enveloping black softness his lips sought hers, claiming them hungrily, his moist tongue entering her mouth to mate with hers in the most searingly intimate of kisses.

A deep hunger drove them and their lips clung in a warm fluid kiss that went on and on until Lannie was quite breathless and withdrew her lips so that they hovered a scant inch from his.

"Oh, Brandon," Lannie lightly sighed at last against his mouth, her warm breath touching his flesh like a gently fanned ray of heat. "No woman is safe with you." She felt dazed and all shivery and yet hot with a radiant emotion.

His palm caressed the tip of her breast, causing a delicious ripple of sensation to flame through her, and she sighed blissfully again, arching her body to his touch. His other hand gently trailed a path downward over her satiny cheek and moved beneath the thick masses of her hair to lingeringly caress the sensitive flesh at the nape of her neck.

"You're safe with me, and as for other women, they don't matter at all," he muttered passionately. There was a ragged edge to his low tone.

"Not at the moment, anyway," she persisted, jealously testing, planting a light teasing kiss on his hard male mouth.

He drew back, tensing. "What are you trying to make me say, Lannie?"

"Nothing," she murmured, pausing and then recklessly continuing. "Only—" She broke off.

"Only what?" She detected exasperation in his deep voice.

"Only I wish things were different between us."

He drew a deep impatient breath. "I do too," he said almost bitterly, "but they never will be. The sooner we accept our relationship for what it is, the happier we'll both be."

He bent his mouth to hers again and brushed her lips lightly at first with the intent of deepening the kiss. But before he could do so, she pulled away, ignoring the electric shock waves stirring through her. Beneath her fingertips that pushed against the taut muscles of his chest she felt his pounding heart.

"And what is our relationship exactly?" she persisted, the demon of insecurity in her heart demanding her to ask.

She was aware of him staring down at her in the darkness, of the deliberate effort he had to make to control his desire.

He sighed heavily, drawing away from her and thrusting the door open so that the cool damp night air invaded the car. "It looks like this is going to turn into a heavy conversation," he said. "Let's get out of the car and go on board *Calypso*."

As he led her up the gangplank and aboard she was dimly aware of oiled teak railings against shiny white fiberglass, of gleaming brightwork, of brass fittings polished to perfection. He escorted her through the lavish main saloon of the yacht and then below and through a passageway that led to an elaborate stateroom that was obviously his. Everything about the stateroom was masculine from the navy bedspread and nautical drapes to the thick brown carpet that softened the room's austerity. Paintings of sailboats hung against the cherry paneling.

He went to the built-in wet bar at one end of the room and poured himself a brandy and offered her one, which she refused.

"You never did tell me what you feel about our relationship," she said at last, going to him and standing at his side.

"It's very simple," he replied coolly, his voice masking his emotions as he slid an arm around her slim shoulders caressingly. "We need each other in a very basic way, and in spite of our differences we enjoy each other when we're together." He paused, lifting his crystal glass to his lips and draining it. "However, sometimes I'm not sure we like each other. But I've come to terms with myself on this matter, and I'm through denying my feelings, Lannie. Why should I? I want you back, and I intend to have you."

His words were a shaft of disappointment piercing her heart. "And that's that?" she asked, trying to conceal the ache his words produced.

"Why shouldn't it be?" he asked, still in the deliberately casual tone she hated.

For a moment she was at a loss for an answer. "I . . ."

"Even if I thought a permanent arrangement between you and me could work, you know I'm not the marrying kind, Lannie. And neither are you. We'd be divorced in six months."

"Why do you always say that?" she demanded, trying not to let her hurt show.

"Well, for one thing, I've never stayed in one place long enough to settle down. I've gotten into the habit of constantly being on the move, and I'd feel chained if a woman tried to tie me down."

"You grew up in one place—Louisiana." There was a faint tremor in her voice.

"That was a long time ago," he replied evenly.

It was painfully obvious he had no intention of ever changing, not for her or anyone else.

"While I was gone," he continued, "I thought about everything you said, and I'm willing to compromise. You can go on living here at Belle Rose teaching school if your independence really is as important to you as you said it was. We can see each other when we can get away from our careers. The important thing is that we see each other."

He was offering her an affair, his time when it was convenient for him. The proud tilt of her head concealed how deeply hurt she felt.

"That isn't enough," she said slowly, feeling so wretched the rest of what she would have said remained clogged in her throat. Dismally she realized he couldn't begin to understand how deeply she felt that a man and a woman who cared about each other should be willing inevitably to commit themselves to one another. It wasn't that she wanted to chain her husband to her; it was that without even the hope of an eventual marriage, a couple could not build a stable relationship that would nurture not only each other but their future children.

"It isn't enough for me either, my darling," he replied more gently, misunderstanding her completely. "Compromises rarely make either party happy. I've told you I want you with me all the time, but you said you wouldn't give up your career and that you wanted to be independent financially. As much as I hate to see you struggling over money when I could so easily help you, I'm willing to go along with that if that's what you really want. I decided that it was damned unfair and selfish of me to expect you to give up priorities in your life because of me that I would never give up for you."

His hand had moved beneath her hair and continued its slow stroking motion. Her sensitive flesh was tingling in response. In desperation she pushed him away. She could scarcely think when he touched her.

His low reasonable tone had rolled over her in the semidarkness with the smothering violence of a rolling surf. She thought of Denise and the money that was needed for her operation. It would be so easy to ask him for it. But she couldn't ever take money from him again and thereby slip back into the old patterns that had nearly destroyed her.

If she allowed herself to enter into the kind of relationship he was outlining, wouldn't she be constantly tempted every time a financial emergency came up in her life to go to him for help? Wouldn't he be tempted to force her to let him help her? Was she crazy to feel that if she let herself get close to Brandon she would gradually begin to rely on him financially, and, thus, her independence and self-esteem would be slowly eroded and all his old accusations about her character would be proven true?

She felt like a drowning swimmer in an emotional sea fighting for her survival. Her brown eyes glistened, and then hot tears spilled over her long lashes. She felt confused. She wanted to be with him always. She loved him, and yet basically he considered her an enjoyable plaything he couldn't trust or commit himself to. But was that really so bad? If she would only let him, he would be generous to a fault.

He wanted her body, and she wanted him to claim her heart. Were her convictions and pride foolish?

She'd already given her body to him countless times and reveled in the glories of his lovemaking. Why not go on doing so?

But he didn't care for her. He didn't love her, and he made it patently clear that he never would. He wanted her passion, not her love. And without his love she would be desolate. She wouldn't have the only thing that mattered to her—a secure future with the man she loved. Wistfully she thought of children.

She loved Denise, and she longed for a child of her own. Brandon's child. But that could never be.

And yet, in spite of what he said there was a new tenderness in him. She sensed it, and she loved him so much that maybe if she gave him what he wanted, he would learn to love her.

Did she expect the impossible from him right now? She couldn't expect him to change overnight, and she knew he was willing to give her more than he had ever given any other woman.

No! She had to say no to both himself and her! A tiny anguished cry escaped her lips. The thought of giving him up was so devastating that she was plunged into utter despair.

"How can you sound so noble and sincere," she cried, knowing that she had to drive him away permanently. Her voice shrill and quivering, she lashed out at him in fury and despair because of her acute frustration and pain. "When you're so completely ruthless and selfish?"

One of his cheek muscles spasmed violently and he slammed his empty glass down on the bar. Her outburst took him completely by surprise, and he couldn't control the anger that had been eating at him for the past several hours.

"Ruthless and selfish?" he exploded, his own volatile temper ignited by her violent and unexpected accusations that he considered totally unfounded. "I've been too damned generous where you're concerned!" Because of his anger his own distrust of her surfaced. "Who are you to label me in the light of your own past? You've used me and Genevieve and probably everyone else you've ever known. You were ready to marry my brother when you didn't care about him! And you call me ruthless!"

She was too upset herself to back down. "It wasn't like that!" she cried. "I never used Genevieve, and I thought I was in love with John!"

"Like hell!"

"I did think I loved John. But then when you came back I felt—"

"I had more money. And not only that, you knew that I was going to make your life damned unpleasant if you didn't do as I said."

Everything he said tore at her heart, and when she spoke her voice was soft with despair.

"Brandon, if you really believe that about me I want you to take me home—right now. There's no point in our continuing to see each other."

"I suppose you plan to take up with Louis, or someone like him," he said furiously. "When I saw you tonight with Louis, I wondered if any man as long as he has enough money would do? Are they all the same in your book? And if that's so, why shouldn't I be that man?" His icy drawl sliced through her.

Lannie winced at the painful thrust and edged away from him closer to the door. Tears sprang into her eyes, but she fought them back. Her fingers clasped the brass handle to the door. She knew only one thing—she had to get away from him and the terrible hurt his attitude toward her inflicted.

"I want you now," he said in the coldest of tones as he reached for her even as she shrank from him.

"No, Brandon. Don't," she begged tremulously. "Not like this."

"You don't really want to fight with me any more than I want to fight with you," he muttered hoarsely. "You came out here for the same reason I did—to go to bed with me." He paused, his words hanging in the silence. "There's only one language you and I can speak without getting into an argument and that one has no words."

She choked back a sob, feeling hurt. She backed away, realizing his intent.

Easily, in spite of her attempt to escape him, he drew her inside the iron circle of his arms, mashing her breasts against the hard wall of his chest so that his body fitted tightly against hers. A fierce, determined anger drove him.

His hand moved over her, molding her every curve against himself. In spite of everything the feel of his hard body was sensually arousing, and her pulse was fluttering crazily. She struggled in his arms, fighting against the violent tidal wave of desire that was swamping her.

The warmth of his breath fanned through her hair; she smelled his masculine scent. Everything he did stirred powerful erotic memories only he could awaken. Desperation, that he could compel her female awareness of him as a man when she felt wounded and should despise him, flared through her.

"Oooooh . . ." She emitted the inaudible sound that was a mixture of anger, pain and frustration, because she was unable to put her chaotic thoughts into words. Only he could do this to her—enrage her and inflame her and humiliate her in the same moment. She twisted wildly, but he, aware only of his own torment, only drew her closer against his lean body.

As his lips sought her mouth, she twisted her face away, crying out, "Don't do this! I don't want you to." But even as she protested, he was lifting her into his arms and carrying her easily across the thick carpet toward his king-sized bed. As she felt the soft mattress beneath her hips, an aching fire coursed through her veins, the sweetly savage fire of betrayal.

He ripped the bedspread aside. "You will, with a little persuasion," he murmured, his deep voice softly mocking as he followed her down.

"I won't! I hate you!" But her silky voice only sounded weak and ineffectual.

"No you don't," he ground out. "No more than I could ever hate you, no matter how much I might want to."

Expertly his hand pulled at the zipper at the back of her dress. It gave, the soft red material sliding apart so that his hard warm hands could easily explore every part of her creamy exposed flesh. When he encountered the gauzy material of her bra he loosened it, and her breasts swung free.

He pushed her dress down to her waist, and bent his black head to nibble at her lush breasts, tasting them hungrily as though they were ripe melons and he starved for their sweet fruit.

She felt on fire as he continued to ravage her thus, his hands moving over her gently even though she knew if she offered the slightest resistance they could tense into bands of steel, imprisoning her. Every kiss, every velvet touch devoured her strength to fight him.

She twisted her hands into fists and swung at him, but it was like hitting a rock wall and her feeble blows had no effect.

"You have absolutely no respect for me as a person!" she murmured weakly. "And you never will."

"You're wrong," he muttered, smothering her mouth with his own, drowning out her protests with a long, drugging kiss.

How could she have even considered for a minute that he and she could ever have a chance, just because she'd made the terrible mistake of falling in love with him. Her love wasn't nearly strong enough to combat the forces that were driving them apart.

She was no more to him than any woman he was determined to use for his pleasure. The only difference was his attraction for her was more intense than usual and had been more enduring. He believed she only wanted to use him. But if that was all their relationship meant, it would never be enough.

A dizzying weakness flooded her as his skillful love-making slowly eroded the last remnants of her will to fight him. His bruising kisses gentled as her own arms wrapped around his back and caressed him. Vaguely she was aware of his hoarsely muttered apologies against her ear, of his heated love words as his hands stripped away her clothes and then his own.

He stretched back upon the bed. Tenderly he pulled her down on top of him into his lap, and she gazed down at his broad, powerful shoulders, his hard muscular chest. She felt his naked hips thrust against her soft body. All the rigidity drained out of her, and she flowed against him in rhythmic unison with his movements, their passion building in intensity.

There was a raging wildness in him that night, and an answering consuming response in herself. Their hot emotions drew them out of themselves, and they became one in a fiercely blinding blur of ecstasy. But as soon as the waves of shattering release had washed over them, they lay back, their passions ebbing, each feeling lost in a separate, silent world like a forlorn sea creature cast violently from the ocean upon an alien beach.

With every jerky beat, her heart ached with a strange piercing pain. Lannie felt as though now that he no longer held her and made love to her, she'd lost him forever.

Trembling in spite of Brandon's warm body pressing close, Lannie slid away from him and pulled the sheets and navy quilted spread about herself. She shivered violently again; even the thick spread could not warm her inner chill. She felt cold and empty inside as she stared out a porthole and forced herself to concentrate on the sparkle of the river and the blackened shapes of the trees against the starry sky.

The crushing realization that he didn't love her and never would had changed everything, and she had found no peace in his embrace—only a wild soaring passion that was now spent. Until tonight she'd held onto a small fragile hope that he might someday love her. But no longer. Now she felt utterly drained, her physical need satiated, and yet strangely incomplete and alone. For the first time his lovemaking produced no radiant afterglow. She felt used, and glancing in his direction, she wondered if he did too.

He was certainly silent, unusually so. Her heart lurched hesitantly at the masculine perfection of his noble profile etched against the dimly lit background. Oh, she loved him, and so hopelessly.

His magnificent body was slumped against the thick pillows in a posture that in any other man would have signified defeat. For a moment a wave of tenderness washed over her. But no matter how he might appear, he was not a man with whom she could associate defeat. Thus, she was at a loss to understand his mood.

A terrible yearning that things could be different between them assailed her, intensifying the painful thudding of her pulse. As she continued to observe him, she saw the faint sheen of perspiration covering his swarthy skin. His neck was tilted back, the muscles of his throat stretched like tight bands, his tousled black head lying against the massive headboard as he stared broodingly upward. He did not seem relaxed. There was a suppressed stillness about him that was tense and unnatural. The sensual line of his mouth was grim.

If only he would pull her against his broad shoulders

and soothe away her hurt. Maybe then the aching place in her heart would heal. But he didn't touch her, and even though she longed to, she was afraid to reach out to him. What was the use? He didn't care if she felt hurt. He didn't care . . . period. And in that moment her pride overruled her love for she felt too vulnerable. She would not beg for what he would not willingly give, and a terrible depression settled upon her.

When he felt her anguished gaze, Brandon turned toward her reluctantly as though she were the last vision he wanted to look upon. His black eyes met hers and held them for a long, tense moment as he studied the solemn, soul-wrenching loveliness of her face.

A pang of guilt stabbed him at the sight of her, so fragile and stricken. And he was the cause. He'd been a brute and bully to overpower her resistance, feeble though it had been. Silently he cursed himself for his part in their quarrel, but ever since he'd seen her with Louis a madness had driven him. Then later her nearness had aroused him. Why had she started that damned conversation anyway? The fire in his loins and his foul humor had combined into a dangerous force and when she'd so rashly goaded him, he'd lost control.

She'd said she hated him more than once. He drew a deep breath. There was that odd twisting feeling in his guts that came every time he thought of her hating him. But in spite of it, no emotion showed in the proud, implacable planes of his handsome face. After this night, he couldn't blame her for feeling that way, he thought grimly.

This painful wrenching of his conscience was an unfamiliar experience; he was used to viewing women like Lannie as delightful conveniences necessary for his pleasure but not indispensable. Suddenly, this one with the velvet eyes that were darkly glowing was bewitchingly different. Every time he looked upon her delicate innocence, her exquisite beauty inflamed him, and he felt an intense raw urgency such as he'd never known before. Damn it—it both baffled and angered him. He had no place in his life for this weak dependency on a woman he knew he couldn't trust.

Still, looking into her beautiful luminous dark eyes, he felt like a heel. He thought back over his actions and felt nothing but contempt for his behavior. Seven years ago he'd blackmailed her into a relationship with him until finally she'd summoned the nerve to escape him. Then two weeks ago he'd come back to Louisiana and forced her to break up with John. And because she was such a temptingly luscious piece, he'd coerced her into his bed even when she'd begged him not to and taken her for himself.

The Kuwait crisis had been the perfect excuse to leave her after he'd talked her into breaking up with John, but she'd haunted him all through the days at odd moments and hours. When he should have been studying contract and lease agreements, she'd dominated his thoughts. In the nights his dreams had been filled with visions of her dark beauty. Thus, he'd cut short his business trip because he had to see her again.

And now, this forced mating was the result. He'd let his physical need and anger overpower everything else. Once again he'd behaved contemptibly toward her, taking her without gentleness, without the slightest regard for her feelings. He'd used her. He grimaced at this novel unpleasant image of himself.

In that instant he made up his mind. He was through with force and coercion where she was concerned. Unless she came to him of her own accord, they were finished. It was the most terrible risk he'd ever taken, and he hated the thought of losing her. But he had no choice, for if he followed the same path as before, she would only run away from him again. It wasn't enough anymore just to have her; he wanted her to be happy with him.

Though he didn't stop to analyze this decision, for the first time in his life, Brandon was considering the feelings of a woman and finding that they mattered more to him than his own needs.

In the darkness he was aware of her shivering even more violently than before, and it took all his willpower not to fold her into his arms. But he knew she didn't want him. He longed to comfort her so much he scarcely trusted himself to speak.

But he heard his low voice ask in an abnormally clipped tone, "Cold?" When she nodded mutely, he commanded in the same flat, hopeless voice, "Get dressed, and I'll drive you home."

She started to say something but the throbbing pain in her throat prevented it. She couldn't know that he was hanging on her next words, that his consuming gaze hungered for any sign of affection from her.

She only thought that never had he sounded more coldly indifferent to her, and she wondered if she was no more than a body that could satisfy his physical needs. She flushed scarlet with shame at this horrible thought. Tears sprang to her eyes, but she blinked them back so that they hung in frozen anguish.

Her movements were stiff and self-conscious as she rose from the bed. She searched for her clothes and slipped into them. As she neatened the bedcovers, she was aware of him shrugging into his own clothes.

Once when she moved around to his side of the bed to pull the spread over his pillow, she bumped into him accidentally. His touch sent an electric shiver quaking through her. And she jumped quickly away like a startled doe.

He growled a terse, "Sorry."

"I-it's okay, Brandon," she murmured miserably, thinking silently that nothing would ever be okay again.

"You don't have to cringe when I touch you," he said

caustically, glowering at her, his mood blackening by the minute. "You act like you're afraid of me."

A tense moment of silence lapsed. She shuddered convulsively not from fear but from the tight band of pain encircling her heart. He misunderstood her action, and thought that it was her fear of him that caused her trembling and brought that haunted expression of pain to her beautiful features.

A savage emotion that was a mixture of pain and fury rose up in him. "Don't worry," he said, his exasperated voice biting in the darkness. "This won't happen again. I didn't think it mattered to me how you thought or felt about me, but it does. You said you hated me, and I'm beginning to believe you."

"Brandon . . . I didn't mean—"

His harsh voice overrode her attempt to explain. "I thought sex was all I wanted, but I was wrong. It's not enough anymore. Apparently I'm not the same man I was seven years ago."

Her own intense hurt welled up inside her as she realized that he must mean he was through with her.

A tear spilled down her cheek and then another as she bit into the soft fullness of her bottom lip for control. His darkly handsome face was swimming in a haze of tears. But the emotions surging through her were too powerful to curb, and she could not stop herself from hurling back a reply.

"Don't think you're the only one who's feeling rotten and disillusioned right now, Mark Brandon." Broken-hearted was a more accurate description of her feelings, but pride kept this admission silent. "You took what you wanted, and now that you don't want me any more, you blame me, as if what happened tonight was my fault! I tried to stop you. Animal lust can't give emotional satisfaction, even to someone like you."

Even in the darkness she saw him whiten. She heard

his low curse. "Lannie, don't push me too far," he muttered, warning her.

"You are ruthless," she stubbornly cried, ignoring the pull of muscle along his jawline. "You take what you want, any way you can. Whether it's people, or what they have . . . money . . . land. . . . You took my father's land, even The Shadows."

The Shadows was the real name for the Sugar Castle.

"I bought The Shadows for a very stiff price," he said tightly. "There are some people who think I was taken by your father in that deal."

"That's a lie! You've taken everything I ever had worth giving—my self-respect . . ." She would have said her heart and her love, but she didn't get the chance, for her harsh words drove Brandon blind with rage.

"Then I've taken the last thing from you," he said in an odd, low tone. "In the past I took what you were only too willing to give to me. Once you set a very high price tag on yourself, and I paid dearly for my pleasure." *Dearly*—in more ways than money, he thought painfully. He remembered that terrible time right after she'd left him when he'd been wild to find her. With an effort he suppressed the bitter memory. "If that included your precious self-respect, then that's your problem."

Lannie stared at him in speechless pain and horror as his black eyes raked her with hungry appraisal as though she were a slave on an auction block and he a bidder considering such female merchandise. He was remembering his old feelings for her. His hot intense look was devouring. But when she jerked away, his tanned hand reached toward her in the darkness, and his fingers cupped her chin, turning her face back again so that he could view it better.

Warily she held herself still. Then slowly he traced a path down her throat to the soft swell of her breasts.

Her blood ran hot and cold, and she began to tremble. Why was he doing this to her?

"Lady, your price is too high for me now," he said darkly, thinking that her price now included something he valued much more highly than money—his prized independence and his very soul. He removed his hand. "But I've no doubt there'll be others willing to pay—"

That again. She didn't let him finish. "I do hate you," she whispered in a breath.

A muscle jerked along his jawline as though he were suffering from a sharp hurt he was attempting to ignore.

"No more than I hate myself at this moment," he countered thickly.

"And I don't ever want to see you again," she cried, "because you make me feel so terrible."

"For the first time tonight we agree on something," he said wearily, tossing his coat over his shoulder as he moved toward the door. "Let's get out of here."

It was over between them! The impact of this realization felt as blackly horrible as death. In frustration and a desperate attempt to focus on something mundane Lannie eyed herself in the mirror one last time to make sure she looked all right. She saw that her zipper had snagged on a piece of organza beneath her shoulder blades. She tugged helplessly at the back of her dress, but the zipper remained stuck.

"Brandon . . ."

In the darkness her voice was a velvet sound, and he hated the hope that sprang up in him.

"What?" he demanded gruffly.

"I-I can't zip my dress. Would you mind . . . helping me?"

Disappointment that this was her only reason for speaking shot through him as he automatically moved over to help her.

Beneath his fingers he felt the warmth of her satiny

flesh. At his touch, she trembled slightly, and he flinched, wondering if she hated him that much. The delicate perfumed scent of her that rose to his nostrils was sharply painful; it reminded him that he might never have her again.

In the hushed stillness he was aware of her uneven breathing. When his hand accidentally brushed her cheek he felt its dampness and realized that she was weeping in silent despair. And he was the cause of it.

He fought back the powerful impulse to take her into his arms and kiss away the pain. He would have done so if she'd given him the faintest sign. But instead she squared her shoulders and stood in rigid misery.

Tonight he'd hurt her, and he vowed that even if it meant losing her he would never intentionally hurt her again.

Later, after he'd driven her to Belle Rose and left her standing on the veranda shivering and hugging her transparent organza wrap about her slim bare shoulders, she stared after his car until it completely disappeared in the thick enveloping darkness.

As he drove away, his black gaze was riveted to his rearview mirror and he could not stop himself from watching the tiny scarlet figure grow smaller and smaller until the distance and blackness snuffed her out completely as though she were no more than a breath of flame.

Each, feeling numb with pain, faced a future that without the other seemed desolate and empty.

Chapter Thirteen

*L*annie thrashed wildly as though a demon chased her, her nightgown tangling about her legs and then edging upward over the curve of her olive thighs. Then she kicked again so violently that her sheets and blankets were thrown onto her bedroom floor that gleamed softly in the pale moonlight.

Her pulse was racing with terror as she struggled to escape the smothering blackness that was suffocating her. She opened her eyes but the crushing blackness remained. She couldn't see no matter what she did! She was blind again!

Desperately like a trapped animal she lashed about. A wordless scream spasmed in her throat, the harsh guttural sound awakening her.

For a long moment she lay gasping in relief, sinking into her pillows and concentrating on the pale strip of moonlight gleaming on the yellow flowered wallpaper across the room. The ribbon of light was the most blessed of sights for it was proof that she could see.

Her terror had as usual only been caused by a nightmare. When she'd regained her sight, the nightmares had begun. In her sleep she relived those first startling moments when she'd realized she was blind.

Her brow still damp with perspiration, she sat up in bed and switched on the lamp. Brilliance flooded the room. But as always her terror was slow to drain away. She had to fight back the desire to run through the house and turn on every light. Then she thought of Denise who could never switch on a light, who would never know this sweet relief.

After several minutes when she felt calmer she forced herself to turn the light back off, but she lay awake, not wanting to shut her eyes again. This was the second time in the week since the barbeque and her quarrel with Brandon that her old dream had recurred. Before that it had been six months, and she'd thought she was past that period in her life. It was an indication of how deeply disturbed she was.

As she lay thinking of Brandon her beautiful mouth twisted in pain. Not once had he called, and she now knew for certain that she'd lost him. Sadly she remembered the one time four days ago she'd happened to see him in the village grocery store with Genevieve.

When she'd caught sight of his tall broad-shouldered form towering over his tiny grandmother, an intense bittersweet excitement had coursed through her. He'd looked up, his bold black gaze meeting her gentle dark one. An involuntary smile had fluttered the edges of her lips, but he'd only nodded curtly in her direction, the expression on his handsomely dark features a grimace of pain. Something inside of her had crumpled at his coldness, but somehow she'd managed a brave smile.

She'd even chatted pleasantly with Genevieve while Brandon, standing nearby, attempting to ignore her, had begun fidgeting restlessly through an assortment of canned goods. Lannie had then realized miserably how deeply her mere presence upset him, while she'd felt almost mesmerized by his male charisma.

Genevieve, sensing his lack of ease, had tried unsuccessfully to draw him into their conversation, telling Lannie that going to the grocery store was a special treat for her these days with her arthritis so painful, and how kindly Brandon had offered to take her. Brandon's scowl had only deepened, making it painfully obvious he did not want his grandmother even discussing him with Lannie.

But when Genevieve had reminded Lannie that she'd promised to visit her at Brandon House the next day, Brandon had shoved the can of soup he was indifferently fingering back on the shelf, and had stomped toward them, his black eyes seeming even blacker than usual as they swept Lannie.

"But, Genevieve," he began harshly before he deliberately gentled his voice, "tomorrow I planned to take you to New Orleans to show you my new offices. With construction starting at Brandon Chemicals, I won't have any other free time for quite a while."

Lannie lowered her lashes, refusing to meet the painful encounter of his furious gaze. But the vision of his rough-cut masculinity was stamped in her mind's eye. Jet-black hair waved across his bronzed brow. Long ago she'd memorized the gleam in his dark eyes that could stir every sense in her body.

Her downward gaze ran over the perfect cut of his navy business suit that outlined his broad shoulders and lean muscular torso. She couldn't stop herself from remembering the feel of his hard body pressing closely against hers.

He was magnificent, and she was so terribly aware of his physical magnetism that she felt slightly breathless.

"Well . . ." Genevieve's voice quavered with uncertainty.

Lannie knew that a day with her grandson was a rare treat. Gently Lannie said, "Genevieve, you go along with Brandon tomorrow. I'm really pretty tied up with school right now anyway. I'll call you some time."

Four days had passed since that encounter and Lannie hadn't called Genevieve because the idea of going to Brandon House and possibly running into Brandon when she knew he didn't want her there was too upsetting.

Pulling the sheets about her, Lannie thought again of her nightmare. In its own way this past week had been as devastating as that time when she'd first lost her sight. Perhaps that was why the dream had started to recur. The awful feeling of aloneness, the horrible sense of being cut off from everything that mattered, from life itself, was every bit as strong right now as it had been at that time. As she lay awake in the darkness pondering her heartbreak, no easy solution occurred.

Another week passed, a week of sleepless nights punctuated by two more nightmares. Each day without Brandon seemed more difficult than the one before. In a vain attempt to put him out of her mind, Lannie threw herself into her work with a vengeance, volunteering to sponsor several events in an annual school contest. She left for work early every morning, and stayed late coaching her students. By Friday she was so exhausted she collapsed in her bed before nine.

The next morning, clad in jeans and a T-shirt, Lannie sat stiffly in the kitchen against her highbacked wooden chair munching into a piece of Hilary's homemade bread that was buttered and toasted. The delicious aroma of eggs and bacon and brewing coffee filled the kitchen. Ralph and Sherry were teasing Denise about her new pet gerbil, while Hilary devotedly watched John scrape the last bit of egg onto his toast and devour his breakfast with his usual enthusiasm. Lannie sat silently, wrapped in her own private pain. The toast which was delicious seemed as tasteless as paper, and she set it down on the corner of the plate with the rest of her untouched breakfast.

The phone rang and Hilary dashed to answer it. In a moment she returned. "Lannie, it's for you. . . ." There was an odd speculative inflection in her voice.

Lannie's heart seemed to stop beating, and then to make up for lost time it began pounding in a rush of excitement.

"I'll take it in the parlor," she said, hoping her voice sounded calmer than she felt.

"Hello," she answered breathlessly, lifting the phone to her ear.

"Lannie . . ." The deep masculine voice was familiar but it belonged to the wrong man.

"Hello, Louis." She slumped against the couch.

"I'm calling about Sugar. This is the first time since I saw you at the barbeque that I've had a minute to spare. I've got my truck and trailer and could come over in an hour and pick her up and write you a check."

Ever since the barbeque Brandon had been the center of her thoughts, and she'd pushed the problem of selling Sugar into the back of her mind.

"Oh, I . . ." she stammered. "So soon?"

"I told you I'd come by ten days ago. Are you still willing to sell her?"

Dully, she replied, "Yes."

They talked a few minutes longer about the details of the sale and then hung up. Slowly Lannie returned to the kitchen and sat down again before her breakfast that seemed even more unappetizing than before. She poured herself a cup of very black Louisiana coffee and sipped it.

With an air of importance Ralph pushed his chair back from the table. As always his wire-rimmed spectacles were perched upon the narrow bridge of his nose at a cockeyed angle so that he looked quite like an eccentric intellectual. This morning for some reason the gray eyes behind his glasses sparkled with excitement.

"I was waiting for you to come back, Lannie," he said momentously. "I have an announcement." He glanced toward Denise.

For an instant everyone was so still that there was no sound other than that of the second batch of coffee bubbling in the percolator.

"Don't keep us all in suspense, Ralph," Hilary said, dispelling the tension with one of her quick giggles.

Ralph smiled proudly. "Well, I've been asked to play the concerto I wrote with the symphony in Baton Rouge next month."

"Oh, Ralph!" Sherry was radiant. "That's wonderful."

Denise clapped her hands in glee and looked toward his voice, a gentle smile curving her lips.

"I'm going to play some Liszt, too, at the end of the program," he continued. Again he looked fondly down at Denise, and then reached out and touched her affectionately. "And Denise has promised to help me."

Sherry's brow knit in puzzlement. "I don't understand, Ralph," she said, her dark gaze wandering uncertainly from her daughter's beaming upturned face to Ralph's. "How can Denise help you?"

"I want her to turn pages for me. I've decided to use my score with Liszt. She knows the music by heart because she's been turning the pages ever since I started working with the piece."

"Why, Ralph, that's a wonderful idea," Lannie

began. "You couldn't have chosen anyone better quali-
fied."

Everyone was laughing and congratulating Ralph
and Denise, when Sherry's voice, usually so soft and
gentle, slashed them. She was very pale, but her eyes
blazed with a fierce protective mother-love. "Don't any
of you understand that Denise can't do that! Ralph, I
know you meant well, but there'll be thousands of
people out there in the audience. Your career will be on
the line! If Denise makes a mistake, the consequences
for you . . ."

All the joy went out of Denise's lovely features and
she averted her face so that the others could not see her
quivering lips.

"You should be worrying about me chopping Liszt
up like a hatchet-man, and not about Denise," Ralph
said smiling, circling Denise's trembling shoulders with
his arm and pulling her to him as though he instinctively
knew how desperately she needed his supportive comfort.

"It's easy for you to say that!" Sherry cried, unde-
terred. "You and Lannie are always so sure she can do
anything! But what if she gets out there and stumbles
on the stage or turns the page at the wrong moment.
The concert will be ruined and Denise will be humili-
ated."

Suddenly Ralph, whose nature was as gentle as
Sherry's, was angry too. "What if she does, Sherry?"
he asked quietly. "It won't be the end of the world like
you seem to think."

"Denise is blind, Ralph! How many times do I have
to tell you that before it sinks in?"

In the deadliest of hushed tones he replied, "It sank
in the first minute I set eyes on Denise. You didn't have
to say a word! Sherry, I hope you change your mind
about the concert, but the concert doesn't really matter! What matters is your stupidity in handling this

gifted and very sensitive child. If you keep on, you're going to ruin her."

"You can't tell me how to raise my own child."

Wearily he shoved his chair from the table and stood up, his lean, angular frame slightly stooped in defeat. "Unfortunately, that's true. I only wish there was someone who could." With that he stalked from the kitchen.

Sherry stared after him looking stricken, but stubbornly she poured herself another cup of coffee and stirred in a lump of sugar, her spoon clattering rather too loudly against the sides of her china cup as she did so.

Everyone else had sat listening, appalled, and with Ralph's departure, Hilary rose from the table and began bustling furiously about the kitchen in her slapdash manner, washing dishes, sweeping and mopping, starting one task before she'd completed the other. John excused himself hastily, saying he needed to call the hospital.

Only Denise, Sherry and Lannie remained, an uncomfortable threesome seated at the table. Lannie was feeling heartsick over the quarrel. Denise was as white as the lace ruffle at her throat. Her glossy black pigtails bobbed as she wept gently. Lannie realized how keen the child's disappointment was and she ached to comfort her.

If only Denise would cry out with her usual defiance —but to watch her sobbing like that was almost more than Lannie could bear. Yet she dared not interfere between mother and daughter at such a strained moment.

Finally Denise lifted her face that was streaked with tears. She didn't look toward her mother when she spoke but instead stared unseeingly at the wall, a blind person's gesture that she knew infuriated Sherry. Denise's voice was so low it was scarcely audible as she mumbled her excuses to leave the table. Shuffling away, knowing full that this was another annoying gesture Sherry hated, Denise's slender shoulders drooped in defeat.

Watching her, Lannie could almost read Denise's mind. *All right, Mother, I'm blind, and you think that makes me a zombie. From now on I'll act and look blind.*

Suddenly from the doorway the zombie came to life, and Denise cried out in surprise as she stumbled over the mop and broom that Hilary had carelessly left propped against the open pantry door.

Denise lay sprawled on the wet linoleum for a long tense moment before she began groping to pick herself up.

"Denise, baby," Hilary soothed, reaching her at once, but resisting the urge to lift her to her feet as though she were no more than a child. "The counter's by your right hand and you can grab onto it and pull yourself up."

"Thanks, Hilary," Denise mumbled.

"Don't thank me. You ought'a sock me, kid. I'm the dope who put the mop there."

"Denise," Sherry cried in panic, racing to her daughter and placing her hands on her to help her up.

"Leave me alone, Mother," Denise said, shrugging away from her touch.

"But your arm is bleeding."

Desperately, she cried, "I don't care! All I want is to get away from you!"

Sherry's outstretched hands fell to her sides and she stared helplessly as Denise pulled herself to her feet and shuffled clumsily out of the room.

"Hilary," Sherry began, taking out her frustration on the nearest available person. "How many times do we have to tell you to put things where they belong. There's no way Denise can get around if she can't memorize where everything is."

Hilary looked so chagrined that Sherry relented.

"I'm sorry, Hilary. I know you try," Sherry apologized softly before she, too, fled the room.

An hour later the atmosphere at Belle Rose was still unbearably tense. Outside Ralph had thrown open all the windows of the *garçonnière* and loud piano music thundered as he banged furiously up and down the keyboard. Upstairs, Denise's bedroom door had remained shut ever since she'd slammed it an hour earlier. Sherry's door was also closed. John had left, and Hilary was nowhere to be seen.

Normally Belle Rose was not a house of closed doors and locked-up emotions, and Lannie did not like the feeling. But try as she might, she could think of no instant resolution for the conflicts between Ralph, Sherry and Denise. Lannie wanted desperately to help them, but she decided that for the moment she'd best let their heated feelings cool down before she tried to talk to Sherry again.

Lannie was on the veranda sweeping as she thought about how to best try to approach Sherry when Louis drove up, his trailer bouncing behind his pickup along the deeply rutted road. Setting her broom aside to watch his trailer, she was sharply reminded that her road was badly in need of repairs like so many other things at Belle Rose. As soon as he stopped his truck, he sprang out of it, moving gracefully toward her with long easy strides.

This morning he wore jeans and a yellow checkered cowboy shirt stretched across his muscular frame. Sunlight shone in his golden hair, and if she hadn't been so painfully in love with Brandon she might have succumbed to his hot masculine gaze that swept her in flattering appraisal, noting the ripe curve of her full breasts jutting beneath the thin fabric of her shirt, her slender waist and the swell of her hips and thighs encased in tight denim.

"You look even prettier in broad daylight, Lannie," he said, smiling.

Her lips curved gently. "Flatterer," she whispered, well aware of her old jeans and blouse and flyaway hair. "No wonder everybody says you're a ladies' man."

"Then how come I can't have the lady of my choice?" He eyed her thoughtfully, his eyes sliding to the swaying movement of her hips as she glided down the stairs to lead him to Sugar's stall.

From the doorway came the softest of voices calling after her, "Lannie . . ."

Lannie recognized the faint whisper instantly as Denise's. Lannie turned, feeling relieved, for the way Louis continued to look at her was beginning to make her uncomfortable.

"Yes, honey."

"Can I talk to you?"

"Sure. But Louis Trajan's here right now and we were just on our way to the stables. Why don't you come with us?"

Louis sighed impatiently as though he didn't welcome a third party.

"I don't want to bother you," Denise said.

"You won't," Lannie assured her, feeling quite relieved that Denise would be joining them because suddenly she had no desire to go to the stables alone with Louis.

As soon as Denise reached the bottom of the stairs, Lannie clasped her tiny hand warmly in her own and led her toward Sugar's stable.

Sugar stomped and neighed loudly in greeting. Then seeing Louis, the mare snorted and raced to the furthermost edge of her paddock and only with the greatest effort did Lannie woo her back. It was the sight of a juicy carrot in Lannie's upturned palm that finally induced Sugar to return within reach of the halter.

"This is clearly a case of love at first sight," Louis mocked as Lannie slipped the halter over Sugar's ears and buckled it. The mare rolled her eyes suspiciously at the sound of his voice and warily observed him.

"You're sure you still want to buy her?" Lannie asked.

"A lady that's hard to get only turns me on more," he said, his eyes meeting hers meaningfully.

Denise had stood quietly beside Lannie up until this point, but suddenly she burst out, "Lannie, are you selling Sugar?"

"Well . . ." Lannie hesitated, not knowing what to say.

"I talked her into it," Louis explained, "the other night at the barbeque. It wasn't easy."

"But you love Sugar," Denise cried.

"Louis will take good care of her," Lannie replied softly, trying to keep her voice steady. "And he's offered me a very good price that I don't feel I can afford to pass up."

"Is it because of me?" Denise persisted.

Lannie hesitated a fraction of a second too long, and Denise cried out.

"It is! It's because of that operation Mother wants! You're going to loan her the money, aren't you?" When Lannie made no denial, she pressed for an answer. "Aren't you?"

"If she needs it, yes."

"Even when I told you that I didn't want that operation, that it wouldn't do any good?"

"Denise, your mother said . . ."

"Mother's wrong about the operation, about everything! And if you sell Sugar I won't ever forgive her. I mean it!"

Louis shifted uncomfortably, bringing Lannie's attention back to him.

"Lannie, if you need more time before you make a final decision about selling Sugar to me, you've got it," Louis offered kindly.

Casting an anxious glance at Denise's distraught face, Lannie said, "I'm afraid I will, Louis. I'll let you know, one way or the other, soon."

Louis inspected Sugar with the thoroughness of a man who knew horses well, and then all three of them returned to Belle Rose. Parked in the drive was Brandon's silver Mercedes.

At the sight of the gleaming car Lannie felt the blood pump through her arteries in a rush of excitement. A radiance tinted her olive skin.

Seeing the car himself, Louis whispered into Lannie's ear, "I'm beginning to understand why you resist my advances, little one. You're out for bigger fish. But that one can be a shark—which means I'd better be going before he comes out and gobbles us both up."

"Coward," she teased.

"Where Brandon's concerned—yes," he replied lightly, waving goodbye as he climbed into his truck. "Let me know about Sugar."

When Lannie and Denise stepped into the parlor they discovered that it wasn't Brandon who'd driven over but Genevieve. Genevieve was dressed in a shimmery amber dress with a narrow golden chain ornamenting it. Her bright black eyes snapped with love as her gaze met Lannie's, and Lannie thought her regal and lovely in her elegant outfit. Hilary was pouring Genevieve a cup of steaming herbal tea.

"Genevieve, I'm so glad you came by," Lannie welcomed her, suppressing the keen disappointment she felt that Brandon was not seated beside his grandmother.

"I was feeling better than usual this morning, and the mood just struck me. Brandon was at the plant and I didn't even ask his permission to drive his car."

"Well, I'm glad you did, and I want you to meet Denise, a very special friend of mine."

Genevieve half rose and took the child's hand in hers as though she intuitively understood how much a kindly touch could mean to a blind child. Genevieve drew her closer. "I can see that," she said gently.

Genevieve had a way with children and soon, beneath her gentle questioning, Denise had forgotten her unhappiness and was chattering happily about Sugar and her new gerbil. Only when Sherry called down for her did she become solemn once more, saying goodbye to Genevieve and Lannie and going to her mother.

The next hour passed rapidly as Genevieve and Lannie talked animatedly, enjoying one another as much as ever.

Their conversation turned to Denise and Lannie found herself confiding all her fears about Denise's relationship with Sherry, including their recent quarrel and Denise's reaction to the prospect of Lannie selling Sugar.

"But, Lannie, you shouldn't have considered selling Sugar, as much as you and Denise love that animal, when you know I would have been glad to help you."

"I couldn't ask you. . . ."

"You're not," Genevieve said briskly. "I'm offering. I'll give you the money for the operation, and if Sherry decides against it, you can give it back to me."

"Genevieve, I can't accept the offer. It's much too much for you to do."

"But you were going to do the same thing yourself at a much greater personal sacrifice. All it is is a gift from one of your friends for another of your friends."

Suddenly Lannie was thinking of Brandon. He would

not approve of Genevieve giving money to her, whatever the reason. "I can't," she murmured.

"Really, child, why not," Genevieve persisted with gentle determination. "It would give me so much pleasure to think that I might have helped you and that little girl and her mother."

"When you put it like that, how can I refuse?"

Genevieve withdrew her checkbook from her amber leather purse and hastily scribbled a check. "I make this gift with only one condition," Genevieve warned, holding the completed check in her bony fingers.

"What's that?"

"That you don't tell anyone. It will be our secret."

"But why not?"

"Because it makes me feel awkward when people feel too beholden to me. I have a great deal of money and although I like to help where I can, I feel shy and . . . uncomfortable about it."

"You have the tenderest, most generous heart and you deserve credit for the good that—" Lannie began.

"Child, just knowing that you have the money if you need it, is all the credit I want."

Lannie's eyes slid to the check and gasped. It was three times the amount that the operation would cost. Involuntarily the fear foremost on her mind slipped out. "What will Brandon think if he finds out?"

"Brandon . . ." Genevieve looked perplexed. "I don't see why he would care one way or the other. Our monies are entirely separate."

He would care. Lannie knew that for sure, but she made no argument.

"How is he, Genevieve?" Lannie asked softly, unable to resist the question.

Genevieve's brow puckered. "I'm worried about him. He hasn't been himself lately. He's throwing himself into his work even more than usual, and he never sleeps. He skips meals. Something's bothering him, but he's too considerate to confide his problems in me. I've wished for years that he would meet the right woman and marry, but it's never happened. I suppose it all goes back to something that happened even before you were born."

"What was that?" Lannie asked, curious.

"It's not something any of us ever talk about, but I feel safe in telling you since I've always felt you were practically family. When Brandon was only nine years old, Celia, his mother, left my son Daniel for another man. That poor little boy. I never felt so sorry for anyone in my whole life! He loved Celia so. She was one of those charming but rather shallow people who knew how to endear herself with pretty smiles and gestures without really doing much else. I know I sound harsh, but after what she did to Brandon and to Daniel, I find it hard to forgive her."

"I don't blame you," Lannie murmured.

"Brandon couldn't understand why his mother left him. If you ask me, he never got over her. I think that's why he's afraid of marriage or seriously committing himself to a woman. He remembers that time before his father met Rosalind. Daniel was so bereft he turned to drink, and we all thought it would be the end of him. He completely ignored Brandon. Poor mite—had neither father nor mother. So I took him over until Daniel married Rosalind."

"I always thought Rosalind was his mother."

"That's because Daniel forbade any of us to ever mention Celia. All her pictures, clothes—anything she'd bought for the house—were destroyed. Rosalind tried to be a mother to Brandon, and he liked her and I think he grew to appreciate her efforts. But there was no real closeness there. I think he was afraid she might leave too."

A short time later Lannie helped Genevieve down

the stairs and into the Mercedes. When Genevieve had gone, Lannie headed to the stables.

For the first time Lannie was beginning to understand why Brandon was the way he was, and with understanding dawned a deep compassion.

She still missed him so much she actually ached at times. But how could she win his trust and get him back?

Chapter Fourteen

*I*n the weeks that passed Lannie exhausted herself trying to talk Sherry into relenting about the concert. She enlisted John's help and that of Dr. Ludkee, but Sherry wouldn't listen to anyone. She steadfastly clung to her dream that the right operation and the right doctor would eventually restore normalcy to Denise's life, and that until that time Denise would have to settle for the things that she could do competently.

Denise reacted by withdrawing into a shell. Her once glossy hair fell in black tangles about her shoulders, and she refused to wash it or brush it. She took no time with her clothes, and more often than not they didn't match. Sometimes her shoes were from two different pairs. But not even Sherry dared to point out that a certain orange plaid blouse looked hideous with a red striped pair of slacks. Lannie knew that Denise was deliberately defying her mother by dressing poorly. She was silently crying out, "You want me to act blind! So okay! I will!"

Denise would sit silently during meals, no longer participating in the conversation. Nor did she go out to Ralph's to help him with his music. Instead she spent long hours upstairs inside her room with her door closed, lying on her bed, staring vacantly upward, shutting everyone and everything out. Lannie was at a loss to cheer her.

The Thanksgiving holidays were soon approaching and the weather was crisp and coolly delightful, but with every passing day Lannie felt more exhausted than the day before. Her appetite was nonexistent, and she was losing weight.

The hours when she was at school dragged by, and she found herself losing her temper much more often when her students were mischievous than she usually did. She was looking forward to the four-day Thanksgiving holiday more than she ever had in any previous year. Usually she wasn't this ready for school vacations until the spring.

It was the hopelessness of her feelings about Brandon that was making her so listless, she told herself. She loved him, and he didn't return her love. She kept hoping that with time, the hurt would lessen, but as the days passed she felt no better. It seemed he was impossible to forget.

Finally one Monday morning she was feeling so wretched that she called in sick. She didn't quite feel nauseated, but the thought of eating was even more repugnant than usual. Feeling vaguely queasy, she lay in bed until ten, too lethargic to make the slightest effort to do anything.

Really, she scolded herself, she was carrying her pining-away act too far. But no matter how she talked to herself, she still felt too rotten to get out of bed.

Denise had also stayed home from school that morning, saying she was sick, and she came in to visit Lannie. Denise was dressed in the wildest ensemble thus far—a purple polka-dot blouse and maroon culottes. On her left foot she wore a sneaker and on her right a scuffed loafer.

Denise sat down on the far corner of Lannie's bed and they chatted for a while, or rather Lannie talked and Denise did a poor job of feigning enthusiasm for their conversation, making automatic responses at all the right moments. But to Lannie she seemed more withdrawn than ever.

It was practically noon before Lannie finally dragged herself out of bed and took a long hot soak in her tub. Then she could scarcely force herself from the bath. When she managed to, she slipped into a flowing red caftan, and descended the stairs, going to the kitchen.

Even though she didn't feel hungry she opened the refrigerator door and reached for a package of cheddar cheese and a bottle of milk. Her queasiness was practically gone, and she had to eat something.

The cheese toast was grilling in the toaster when she heard a car in the drive. The brass knocker resounded throughout the house, and she cut off the burner under her sandwich. Her red velvet slippers were silent as she crossed the slick wood floors to the front door.

At the sight of the tall, broad-shouldered form outlined in the beveled glass window, Lannie's heart caught in her throat. Brandon! A dizzying sensation made the foyer spin, and for a long moment before she opened the door, Lannie clung to the brass doorknob for support. Then with his help, she managed to open the door, and her imploring dark eyes met his angry black gaze.

"Come in," she murmured shakily, wondering at the reason behind his visit. Her emotions were in such turmoil she couldn't think.

He was leaner, his loss of weight sharpening the harsh planes of his rugged face. Lannie understood why

Genevieve had been worried about him, for he looked deeply troubled.

For a timeless moment his gaze held hers, and he stared deeply into her eyes as though to search out her soul and read it. Or did she only imagine the intensity of his interest because of the passionate yearnings of her own heart?

Of course she did.

She barely managed to resist the overpowering urge to throw herself into his arms and tell him how terrible these past weeks without him had been for her. She backed rigidly against the wall.

His expression darkened at her apparent lack of welcome. Brandon stepped inside and closed the door, his black gaze sweeping her fragile loveliness, taking in every detail of her changed appearance from her wan complexion to her delicate figure, her thinness evident even in the loosely flowing caftan. He frowned as though he didn't like what he saw, and her heart began to beat painfully.

"Brandon, are you all right?" she asked anxiously, equally worried about him and yet upset that he gazed at her so critically.

"Thriving, like yourself," came his brittle retort. "You're as skinny as a toothpick. When I talked to your principal he said you were home sick. I hope it's nothing serious."

"I think it's just a virus I haven't been able to shake," she said offhandedly, lowering her gaze. "I haven't had much of an appetite lately, especially at breakfast."

"And breakfast used to be your favorite meal," he mused thoughtfully.

She flushed. She wished he would get off the subject of her health and stop inspecting her figure. His intense examination was making her feel self-conscious.

"Would you like some coffee?" she asked finally, trying to distract him.

"All right."

He followed her into the kitchen and sat down at the kitchen table, stretching out his long legs and crossing them, filling the kitchen with his male presence. His darkly elegant pressed business suit was in sharp variance with the homey atmosphere of the room, but she was glad of him being there.

Lannie felt a warm prickly sensation spreading through her. She was acutely aware that his eyes followed her movements as she set a pot of coffee on to perk and she felt vaguely nervous.

"Have you seen a doctor about this . . . er . . . virus?" he persisted.

"No, it's nothing. I'm fine. It's just . . ."

"It's damned peculiar if you ask me! And you're a long way from being fine. I've never seen you like this—so scrawny-looking. Have you eaten anything today?"

His deep voice was gruff with emotion as though he cared, and she spun around to face him, a look of surprise on her delicate features. But his harsh expression belied his concern, and she thought she must have imagined the odd inflection in his voice.

"Well, no. Not yet. I was toasting a grilled-cheese sandwich before you came," she admitted.

"Eat it," he commanded.

"Would you like a sandwich too?" she asked, lighting the burner under her sandwich again to warm it.

"I've eaten lunch and breakfast, and you'd better start doing the same before you waste away to nothing."

Again she wondered that he seemed to care. Slowly she ate her sandwich while he sat silently watching her as he drank his coffee, a look of intense satisfaction stamped on his handsome face. When she finished her first glass of milk, he poured her a second and insisted she drink it.

When she'd finished, she cleared away the dishes, leaving them in the sink and pouring herself a cup of coffee before she returned to sit beside him.

For a long moment they sat in silence, and then she asked very softly, "Why did you come by, Brandon?"

At her question his expression hardened, and his black gaze slashed across her lovely face. "I've no doubt you could guess." He spoke in such a low voice she knew he was trying to suppress his anger.

"I have no idea," she replied innocently, growing slightly alarmed.

"Damn you, Lannie, you drive me crazy, the way you look and act . . . and lie."

She felt the harsh intensity of his dark gaze upon her face as he searched for something, for what she didn't know. Just the way he looked at her rocked her deepest emotions and left her feeling as bewildered as he felt when he forced himself to look away.

"I'm not lying," she said quietly.

His gaze riveted sharply back to her. "Did you take money from Genevieve?" His cold stare made her tremble. "Tell me the truth!"

"No, not the way you mean," she said tremulously.

"I've seen her checkbook, and the money has been withdrawn from her account."

"Brandon, let me explain. I didn't *take* anything from her! She gave it to me!"

"Same difference!" His black eyes smoldered with fury. "She's an old woman, and you've taken advantage of the fact that she loves you and you used her again."

"Genevieve knew exactly what she was doing. I didn't take advantage of her. I wouldn't do that! Brandon, if you won't believe me why don't you ask her?"

"I don't have to ask her," he said bitterly. "What

kind of fool do you take me for? It isn't as if this is the first time you've done something like this!"

Her lovely face was very pale, and she sat deathly still, her darkly glowing eyes luminous with pain. She wanted to say something to defend herself but faced with his passionate hostility the words wouldn't come. "I-I . . ."

She pushed back her chair and attempted to rise, longing to escape his accusations. But as she started to stand up, her old queasiness assailed her. Her breath seemed caught in her lungs. The room started to spin, blackening. Suddenly before she could cry out or do anything to save herself she was crumpling and falling into a pit of swirling blackness. As she fell the last thing she saw was Brandon rushing toward her, his dark face grave with alarm as she murmured his name helplessly.

Lannie regained consciousness almost at once. She was in Brandon's arms, her ink-black hair streaming toward the floor as he carried her purposefully through high-ceilinged rooms, coming at last to the parlor where he placed her gently on the upholstered settee.

He was smoothing her hair back when her lashes fluttered open and she looked up into his dark, anxious face.

"W-what happened?" she asked in confusion.

"You blacked out." The feel of his warm hand against her cheek was feather-soft and very comforting.

"I what?"

"You fainted."

"But nothing like this has ever happened to me before."

"That's why just as soon as you're feeling better, I'm driving you into John's office myself—today."

"Brandon, just because of a little virus . . ."

"I have a feeling this is more than a little virus."

"I can drive myself," she stated, remembering his

recent hostility toward her and trying to sit up, feeling that she had to assert her independence.

"You're obviously in no condition to drive. What if you blacked out at the wheel?"

The logic of this statement was undeniable, so weakly she acquiesced and let him drive her into town.

An hour later Brandon brought her home, since he'd insisted that John rush her before all his other patients. John had performed several routine tests in his office, advising her that if the results were negative and she didn't get better, he would hospitalize her and perform a more extensive evaluation later. However, he assured her that he was not in the least alarmed, and that he was almost certain she was not seriously ill.

"But what's the matter with me?" she'd demanded at last, feeling frustrated by his medical evasive answers.

"I think we'll have your answer very soon," John stated cryptically, staring first at Brandon as though he were a patient too and then at herself, and yet revealing nothing.

Once they were back at Belle Rose Brandon did not bring up the subject of Genevieve again. Instead he was solicitous of Lannie's every need, extracting a promise from her that she would stay in bed until she heard from John later in the day. Brandon even prepared her a cup of hot tea and brought it to her in bed. Their mood was almost congenial when Brandon Chemicals called looking for Brandon, and although he seemed reluctant to leave her, he did so, saying he had to and promising to check back with her later to see how she was.

Though he wouldn't hear of her coming down to see him off Lannie got out of bed and went outside on the balcony to watch him drive away. As his car disappeared beneath the spreading green foliage he noticed for the first time how dark the sky was. Thunder rumbled faintly in the distance.

When Lannie stepped back inside she bolted the long doors. Bemused, she thought of Brandon, marveling at the way he'd behaved toward her. He'd been furious over the money, and yet anxious about her health. He must care . . . he must. If only he could believe in her.

Lannie was asleep two hours later when Sherry burst into her bedroom without even knocking. Sherry's brown eyes were wide with alarm. A sob caught in her voice as she began talking.

"Lannie, Denise . . . Denise . . ."

Even though she was incoherent the terror in Sherry's voice brought Lannie instantly awake. "What about Denise?" Her own pulse was suddenly racing with fear.

"She's run away!"

"What?"

"And she left this! I found it in her room!"

Sherry pressed a crumpled note into Lannie's trembling fingers. The note was badly jumbled and several words had been written over with other words, but Lannie managed to make out, "Not going to have operation even if Lannie gives Mother the money." This was followed by illegible scribble and then at the bottom of the page, ". . . run away where they'll never find me. Never."

It was not obvious whether or not Denise had deliberately left the note for her mother to find, but Lannie surmised that she had. The note was handwritten instead of having been typed on her special typewriter.

"Oh, Lannie, if anything happens to her, I'll never forgive myself."

"Blaming yourself won't find Denise," Lannie comforted gently. "We've got to search everywhere. She could still be in the house."

"I don't think so. . . ."

"We'll need to search the grounds, of course. I'll get Ralph and Hilary, while you call the police."

"The police! Oh, my God!"

"Don't panic," Lannie advised softly.

"Just look at the weather," Sherry moaned. "The sky is almost black, and she's out there all by herself—blind. There's no telling what might happen to her. . . ."

"It won't do any good to dwell on every horrible possibility at this point, Sherry. What we need to do is start looking for her. I'm going out to find Ralph."

An hour passed before the immediate grounds and the entire house had been thoroughly searched without revealing a trace of Denise although it was discovered that Sugar's paddock gate had been unlocked and the horse had wandered off.

The police came and jotted a few notes, trying to comfort Sherry by saying that most juvenile runaways returned within twenty-four hours. The sergeant advised Sherry to stay near a phone at all times, because it was likely Denise would call.

When the officers left, Ralph went out to his car, saying he was going to drive around and search all the roads and the village for Denise. Sherry was still sitting anxiously by the phone, knotting and unknotting her fingers while Hilary had gone to the kitchen to brew Sherry one of her pots of soothing herbal tea.

"I think I'll go mad, just sitting here waiting," Sherry cried out. "What if she doesn't call? You know how she's been lately, and to run away when she's blind! Oh, how she must hate me!"

"She loves you very much. But I do think she ran away so you'd listen to her and pay attention to what she's fighting for so desperately—her independence."

"Why couldn't she understand I just didn't want her to do things that would hurt her. I never thought she'd . . ."

Hilary returned with the herbal tea, and now that Sherry was no longer alone, Lannie decided to leave her and go in search of Sugar. She was beginning to suspect, although she didn't want to mention this to Sherry for fear of further terrifying her friend, that Denise had ridden Sugar off somewhere.

Lannie stepped outside into the deep shadows of the veranda. A lightning bolt sizzled across the blackening sky against the horizon. The air was damp and smelled sweetly of rain as Lannie raced down the stairs and across the thick lawn. Overhead branches swayed as an ominous wind stirred roughly through them.

Lannie whistled and called for Sugar as she walked toward the mare's stable. A wild neigh followed by a gentle whinny greeted her as Sugar galloped out of her stable. A bridle that had been clumsily fastened hung lopsided over the mare's ears, the reins trailing in the tall grasses.

Fear quaked through Lannie, and her heart sped at an uneven pace. Her own illness and all the promises to Brandon to remain inside and take care of herself were forgotten. All she could think of was Denise. Had she tried to ride Sugar and been thrown? Was she lying somewhere hurt?

Another bolt of lightning streaked the sky, and Sugar rolled her eyes back and reared, pawing the air and causing Lannie to remember how much Sugar hated storms.

The mare had come back to get out of the weather, but what had happened to Denise? She had to find out. There seemed to be only one way—she had to saddle Sugar and ride out looking for Denise. And Sugar didn't like storms. . . . For a moment Lannie thought again of Brandon and how adamant both John and he'd been about her taking it easy. But then the thought of Denise being lost and afraid overpowered everything else, and she knew that she had no choice.

Lannie rebuckled the bridle and looped the reins around a post so that Sugar couldn't run away. Then she went inside the stable and brought out the saddle. With much coaxing she managed to get it on Sugar. Swinging herself up into the saddle, Lannie dug her heels into Sugar, so that Sugar sprinted across the pasture.

The wind was cold, and shivering, Lannie wished she'd worn a heavier blouse. Her hair whipped behind her like a darkly flickering flame. Sugar's hooves pounded into the soft earth, jarring Lannie's weakened body and reminding her that she wasn't feeling nearly as strong as she usually did.

She drew in on the reins, thinking that it would serve no purpose to exhaust both herself and Sugar. She guided Sugar to the levee and as they plodded along she was able to see the fields of flat black earth with their yellowed cane stubble on one side and the flat brown expanse of the Mississippi on the other. But there was no sign of Denise. She passed Gallier Landing. Beneath the gnarled live oaks the dock stood empty and forlorn.

Lannie twisted in her saddle and through the pines she glimpsed the Sugar Castle standing as proudly as a regal pink princess against a purple sky.

Lannie shivered violently. The storm was about to break, and Sugar shied as a tree limb crashed to the forest floor some distance away. With gentle comforting words and a fierce will Lannie brought the mare back under control.

As they neared the Sugar Castle Lannie saw new lumber stacked in front of the mansion. It was evident that major reconstructive work was being done on the old house. Sagging beams were being replaced. The porch had been repaired. The windows and doors had been changed. In spite of her anxiety about Denise Lannie felt gladdened that Brandon had decided at last to renovate The Shadows.

Icy raindrops pattered slowly down, and Lannie realized that she wasn't making any progress in her search for Denise. Suddenly Lannie was overwhelmed with the urge to go to Brandon House and see if Brandon was home. She longed to tell him about Denise, for she was beginning to despair of finding the child herself. Perhaps he would know what to do.

Leaving the Sugar Castle behind her, Lannie urged Sugar onto the winding road that led to Brandon House. The ten-minute ride between the two mansions took half an hour because of the storm. Gusts of wind pelted the horse and rider with a battery of fat raindrops.

The rain was driving down in a blinding fury by the time Lannie trotted up to the steps of Brandon House. Lights blazed a warm welcome from every window of Brandon's home. Lannie was vaguely aware of a drape being whipped back for an instant in an upstairs room and of the tall dark man silhouetted against the brilliant square of light. Then the curtain fell back into place. Suddenly lightning flashed nearby and an angry clap of thunder resounded, causing Sugar to rear wildly.

Caught off guard, Lannie screamed in terror as Sugar pranced backward on her two hind legs.

"Easy girl. Easy . . ." Lannie remembered to soothe, her own fears ebbing as she regained her balance.

Sugar neighed frantically, but she was gentling. All four hooves were dancing on the road once more.

Brandon raced out of the house and leaped down the graceful spiral of stairs, taking the steps two at a time. His tanned face had gone white with shock at the sight of Lannie on the terrified horse. He jumped heedlessly out into the thickly falling rain. His black corduroy shirt was at once plastered to his skin, as were his black slacks so that his clothes molded his lean muscular frame.

As he approached Sugar he slowed his long strides so as not to frighten Sugar into bolting. Brandon came toward the mare and woman warily, his low tone soothing. Then with one expert motion he seized Sugar's reins and steadied the horse so that Lannie could dismount.

Still holding Sugar, Brandon's deep voice was calling for a servant who came instantly and led Sugar away to a dry stable. Lannie was sinking into Brandon's arms, suddenly as aware of her own exhaustion as she was of the exquisite sensation of being wrapped against his hard protective strength.

She was trembling all over with cold, and her face was pale, her shaking lips blue.

"Damn you," he muttered gently, lifting her into his arms and striding toward the stairs. "I can't trust you for a minute. I thought you were going to spend the day in bed. What were you doing, trying to kill yourself and the—"

His words were lost as another shaft of lightning was both blinding brilliance and deafening sound. The entire world seemed to shudder.

They were in the house when he set her down. Its magnificent opulence was like a snug cocoon after the violence of the storm. Water dripped from their clothes and shoes onto the Aubusson rugs and polished oak floors, but Brandon seemed careless of the damage they were inflicting on his home.

Instead he carried her up the gleaming stairs to his suite of rooms, his wet boots treading uncaringly into the plush royal-blue runner that partially covered the staircase and wide hall. Lannie knew that beneath the carpet the famous scars a Union Cavalry officer's horse

233

had made when he'd ridden upstairs during the Civil War still marred the oak steps.

When Brandon deposited her in a sumptuous chair in his bedroom, she protested because of the upholstery. But he ignored her, ordering his servant who seemed to appear as if by magic to fetch dry clothes for his guest.

His bedroom was as utterly masculine as the man itself. Everything in it was of vast proportions. Browns and golds and delicate ambers dominated the color scheme. The antique furniture shone in the soft light. Guns and an assortment of other weaponry hung against one wall while oil paintings of hunting scenes adorned another.

Brandon stripped a blanket from a nearby chaise lounge and wrapped it around her trembling shoulders.

"Brandon, I have to talk to you—" Her soft eyes met his intent black gaze.

He cut her off. "Did John reach you?"

"No, but that's not important. Denise—"

"Not important!" his deep voice rumbled. For an instant he had the oddest expression on his face, harsh and yet protectively tender at the same time. "Then you . . ."

She was so concerned about Denise that she paid no attention to what he said.

"Denise has run away," she blurted, "and in this terrible storm. We can't find her anywhere! And, you know, she's blind!" Lannie shook convulsively as a chill gripped her.

"And you came out in this weather . . . because of Denise?" He was staring at her oddly, as if her obvious selfless concern for Denise's plight confused him.

"Yes. Oh, we just have to find her. I . . ."

The servant had returned with the clothes that, doubtless, belonged to Genevieve.

"Your catching pneumonia won't help Denise," he said practically. "So I want you to take a quick hot shower and get dressed in dry clothes. My bathroom is through that door."

"B-but Denise . . ."

"If you do as I say, I'll help you any way I can," he said more gently, as he realized how truly desperate she felt.

Nodding mutely, she stood up and reached for the clothes. The blanket fell away, and as his gaze flickered downward over the luscious outline of her very feminine figure that her wet clothes clinging immodestly to every curve revealed to him, his gaze burned her like a hot caress. Then deliberately he turned away, banking the fires he'd lit, and she knew he was deliberately suppressing his attraction for her.

"Well, what are you waiting for?" he asked gruffly, his harsh tone prodding her into action.

"N-nothing," she said, scampering away and closing and locking the bathroom door behind her.

Ten minutes later she emerged clad in apricot slacks and a matching silk blouse that were a size too small for her. Her bra had been discarded because it was wet, and as she moved across the room toward Brandon, toweling her long hair as she walked, her thrusting damp breasts bounced lightly against the soft fabric of her blouse.

Brandon sighed deeply, forcing himself to look away. "You were going to tell me about Denise," his low tone reminded her. He too had changed into dry clothes and he now wore a long-sleeved navy shirt open at the throat. Jeans tightly molded his muscular thighs.

Just for a moment she felt slightly breathless as she succumbed to the sexual magnetism his male virility exuded. Tremulously she replied, "Yes, I was."

She poured out the story, omitting no relevant detail. When she'd finished he was silent for a long time. Then he said, evidently surprised, "It's obvious you love this little girl very much."

"Oh, Brandon, she means everything to me. You see, I was in a car accident several years ago, and I was temporarily blinded. . . ."

"My God! When?"

"Six years ago, not long after I left you. I was blind for nearly a year, and Denise helped me through that difficult time. Without her I don't know if I could have ever adjusted. She's a very special person. Someday I'll tell you all about it, but now we simply have to find her."

"We'll find her. I agree with you about her taking Sugar, which probably means she isn't too far from Belle Rose—a radius of two or three miles, I'd say. Before we do anything why don't you call Belle Rose and see if they've heard anything yet."

Sherry answered the call on the first ring, and the minute Lannie heard Sherry's quivering voice, Lannie knew the answers to the questions she was going to ask: Denise hadn't called and the police hadn't made any progress toward finding her.

When she hung up Brandon made a call to his plant manager at Brandon Chemicals. Lannie caught only snatches of what he said.

"Yes, Gifford, she's blind! Pull every man off the job that can be spared. Reach every off duty man you can at home. I want you to head up a search party. . . . The area surrounding Brandon Chemicals . . . about two miles south of the plant to . . . about three miles north. . . . Concentrate in the vicinity nearest Belle Rose. I don't think she got very far because the horse came back. I'll hang up now so you can get on with it before we run out of daylight."

When Brandon hung up the phone Lannie flashed him a warm grateful smile. "Oh Brandon, thank you."

"We haven't found her yet."

"But at least you're doing something. I-I don't know

how to say how much this means to me. I just knew you would help me." Her love for him was shining so fiercely in her eyes that surely he must see it.

His dark gaze held hers for a long moment, and something in his look stirred every emotion in her heart. Then abruptly he rose and went to a nearby closet, removing two raincoats and a large flashlight. He helped her into a shiny black coat that fell to her ankles, swallowing her.

"I must look ridiculous," she smiled up at him as she buttoned the coat.

"Not to me," he replied warmly, looking down at her, his gentle gaze a caress. "I didn't want to take any chances on your getting wet again." This time she noted the odd protective quality in his voice. He was slipping his arms into his own coat.

When he led her to the front door and opened it, a blast of wind hurled rain onto the wide gallery, splattering them. The storm raged as wildly as ever, reducing the visibility to practically zero. Lannie knew it wasn't going to be easy to find Denise in this weather.

Nevertheless, Brandon and she ran toward the garage and got into his car. He backed out slowly, and then inched along the road, both of them leaning forward and straining against the windshield to see through the liquid curtain for any sign of Denise.

Brandon knew all the twisting back roads, and every secluded farmhouse. They must have stopped at fifty such houses, asking the people who lived in them to be on the lookout for Denise and giving them instructions to call if they found her.

Last of all Brandon searched the swamp, talking to the rough bayou people who were as wild and savagely proud as their land. They lived in crude tumble-down houses perched on stilts or in listing houseboats tied up alongside the bayou. These people made their livings picking moss, trapping and fishing, but all were willing to help a lost little blind girl, especially if the owner of Brandon Chemicals offered a handsome reward.

When it grew dark Brandon and Lannie drove wearily back to Brandon House. The storm had slackened into a gentle rain.

As soon as Brandon stepped inside the house Genevieve came down with a message for him.

"Hello, Lannie dear," she welcomed her young friend gravely, and as she did so, Lannie was rawly aware of an involuntary tightening in Brandon's expression as he witnessed his grandmother's trusting affection for Lannie. "Brandon, a Mr. DeBlanc who lives near the plant has been trying to reach you for more than an hour."

Mr. DeBlanc owned the first house that Lannie and Brandon had stopped at when they'd begun their search.

"Lannie, there's an extension in the hall if you want to listen," Brandon said, his faint hostility softening as his eyes met her fearful and yet hopeful gaze.

When Brandon nodded toward her that he'd finished dialing she lifted the phone to her ear and listened to the short conversation that followed.

"This is Brandon returning your call."

"This might be nothing," the man said.

"Go on with it."

"After you left, Mr. Brandon, my littlest kid told me something that might interest you. He said he saw lightning strike earlier this afternoon and a horse throw someone near The Shadows, you know that old place on your property right across from mine. Looked to him liked the person stumbled up onto the porch of the old house. Might not be anything but I just thought I ought to let you know after what you said about the little girl. . . ."

"Thank you so much, Mr. DeBlanc," Lannie breathed.

She turned toward Brandon. Never had she loved him so much. "It might be . . . Denise," she murmured.

Somehow because it seemed so right she was in his arms. "If it isn't, I don't want you to be too disappointed," he warned gently, his fingers stirring through her damp hair. "We'll find her."

His attention shifted to Genevieve who had been momentarily forgotten by both of them. She was watching the intimate moment between them, and the loveliest of smiles lit her ancient face.

Immediately Brandon stiffened as he remembered the money that Genevieve had given Lannie and all of his old doubts surfaced. Lannie edged silently away from him.

Even though the actual distance that separated them could be measured in inches, Lannie felt as though an invisible barrier had been erected between them that was invincible.

Brandon believed the worst of her. He always had; he always would.

As the two of them headed out to his car, Lannie's heart ached with defeat.

The beam of Brandon's flashlight illuminated the vast ruined ballroom as its steady beam darted to each shadowed corner.

"Denise . . ." The eerie sound of the wind moaning as it swept around the Sugar Castle drowned out Lannie's fragile voice. "Oh, Brandon, she's not here!"

"I'm not so sure about that." He held his light on a stack of lumber that had been overturned, and a box of nails that had been scattered across the new floor. "Looks like someone fell against this wood and cut himself, or herself." A small patch of blood stained the edge of a piece of lumber. "And I don't think it was a construction worker or he'd probably have picked up after himself."

On the way over Brandon had told Lannie that he was remodeling The Shadows to serve as the new offices of Brandon Chemicals, and she'd been delighted.

"I'm going to take a look upstairs," he said at last. "Denise!" he yelled loudly, his voice rising above the noise of the storm.

There was the faintest answering sound, and both Lannie and Brandon moved eagerly toward the stairs.

"Be careful, Lannie, and don't fall," Brandon warned protectively, reaching toward her to help her up the stairs.

Above them a board creaked, and Lannie cried out as loudly as she could, "Denise!"

"I'm up here, Lannie. . . ."

The fragile sound was the dearest Lannie had ever heard.

When Lannie and Brandon reached the top of the stairs they found Denise huddled in a shadowy dark space, her hair falling in wet tangles, her garish polka-dot blouse grimy with dirt. Her sneaker was missing, and she wore only the scuffed loafer. She was shaking, and yet Lannie thought her skin felt as if she were burning.

"Denise, honey . . . ." Lannie threw her arms around the child and held her close, tenderly brushing damp hair out of Denise's face as she helped the child to rise. "Are you hurt?"

"No, but I'm c-cold." Her teeth were chattering. "S-sugar threw me."

"I was afraid of that. Oh, honey, we've been so worried. You mustn't ever run away again!"

"I've b-been so scared. This house makes such

f-funny sounds. I started remembering all the ghost stories about it."

Lannie held her more closely to reassure her. "I can well imagine."

Suddenly Lannie looked up and was aware of Brandon staring deeply into her eyes, and she flushed. His expression was gentle, even tender, as though he at last understood how much Denise really meant to her, as if he understood that she could genuinely care about someone other than herself.

Lannie reached out and clasped his hand tightly in her own and held onto it for a long moment, including him deliberately in the wonderful reunion. Very softly she murmured to him, "Thank you, Brandon . . . so much for helping me find her." Gratitude and love shone in her velvet brown eyes. Overwhelmed by an emotion all his own, Brandon's fingers tightened around hers and they held onto each other for a timeless moment. Then Denise broke the spell by wailing, "I want to go home, to Mother." She collapsed against Brandon as he lifted her easily into his arms.

"That's exactly where we're going," he said very gently. "I'll carry you downstairs."

Lannie was glad of Brandon's arms circling her in a light embrace while she'd sat beside Denise's bed in the shadowed bedroom. His touch had been like a rock of strength she'd held onto through the difficult hours while they'd waited together to make sure that the little girl would be all right. Sherry and Ralph were holding hands as they hovered over Denise who lay snugly tucked into her bed. John had examined her and given her some medicine because she was suffering from a fever and chills due to exposure.

"You were right about Denise, Ralph," Sherry was saying, as Lannie and Brandon tiptoed out of Denise's bedroom. "I'm going to try to listen to you in the future when it comes to Denise. It won't always be easy because it's in my nature to try to keep her from being hurt any more than she already has been."

"No more operations?" he asked gently.

"Not unless you think it's for the best."

"I should hope so," he replied lovingly, "for I intend to be her new father, if her very beautiful mother doesn't have any objections."

"Oh, Ralph," Sherry returned passionately. "I never thought I could love anyone as much as I love you."

The time for words had come to an end, and as Lannie moved down the hall with Brandon at her side she knew that Ralph and Sherry were in each other's arms.

When Brandon and Lannie reached the dimly lit foyer the old tension was back between them. Lannie watched, feeling the awkwardness of their silence as he removed his raincoat from the coatrack and tossed it over his arm. From the kitchen Hilary's high-pitched giggle sounded as she laughed at something John was saying. In that moment Lannie had never envied Hilary or Sherry more, for she longed for the sort of easiness between herself and Brandon that they had with their men.

Brandon turned toward Lannie, his black gaze sliding over her. He said gently in goodbye, "It's late and I guess I'd better be going. . . ." Yet he seemed reluctant to leave her, just as she was reluctant for him to. Somehow, briefly Denise had drawn them together.

"You don't have to. . . ." There was an expectant note in her soft voice, but it didn't quite bridge the invisible barrier that separated them. "I could fix coffee." Oh, how much she wanted to.

He rejected her offer. "I think you've had enough excitement for one day, a day you promised me you'd spend in bed. I don't want to keep you up."

Was he as indifferent as he sounded? She scarcely heard her own mechanical reply. "There's no need for you to worry about me, Brandon. I'm fine, and you've just reminded me that I was only supposed to stay in bed until John called with the results of those tests. He's in the kitchen. I can ask him now, and then if he gives me a clean bill of health you can—"

"There's no need for you to bother," Brandon said coolly, his expression altering subtly.

"What do you mean?" she questioned uncertainly.

"It's quite a common problem." There was a new element in his voice, and he shifted as though he felt very uncomfortable in her presence, as though he somehow felt uncertain about something. Still, because he felt he had to, he forced himself to pursue the topic. "It's hard for me to believe you haven't guessed before now." His black compelling gaze that held her own was steady and intense. He was watching her in the unnerving way he had where she knew he could read her every emotion, her every private thought.

The tension between them was like a throbbing wound. Suddenly she knew, even before he spoke. It was in the strained lines of his face. In an instant she understood the oddly protective manner he'd adopted toward her all afternoon.

Shock drained her face of color and her dark eyes widened as she shrank away from him back against the wall, a hollow pain gnawing at her. Why hadn't she thought of the inevitable consequences of making love with a man as virile as Brandon? The first night had been so spontaneous that neither of them had given a thought about taking precautions. And now . . .

"You're pregnant," he said tonelessly, her blanched face hammering a nail of pain through him.

There was no place to run or to hide, she thought, because he was watching her with black burning eyes. The line of his jaw was hard, his expression so harsh and unyielding she almost winced in anguish. She yearned for one scrap of tenderness, one sign that he cared, but it didn't come.

Her lungs felt choked as though she couldn't expand them to draw a breath. She was carrying his child! And if only things could have been different between them, if only he wanted this baby as much as she did, this would have been the happiest moment of her life. But instead she was desperately unhappy, for an unwanted pregnancy was a complication that would only drive them further apart.

Never had she seen more clearly that he was lost to her forever. Tears were streaming down her cheeks, and she stumbled blindly away from him toward the stairs.

Suddenly she felt his arms, hard and warm, lifting her against his body.

"Lannie . . ." His voice was strangely rough, not tender like she wanted it to be.

"Don't!" she cried out. "Don't touch me or hold me. You'll only make it that much more unbearable!"

When he released her, through her tears she couldn't see that his dark face was as colorless as a waxen mask, his expression as stricken with despair as her own.

She turned and fled up the stairs toward the darkened upper story. A terrible numbness was closing around her heart, freezing all sensation.

"Lannie . . ." His voice following after her sounded odd, as though it wasn't his at all. She only ran faster. She didn't want to hear anything he might have to say.

Never had she felt so alienated from the only man she'd ever loved.

Chapter Fifteen

$\mathscr{D}$awn colors—oranges, golds and muted lavenders—splashed the sky and swirled in the eddying flow of the eternal great river. Acorns and gumballs crunched into the damp earth beneath Lannie's sneakers as she walked toward the Belle Rose landing. Ralph's large *pirogue* was tied to the dock and rocked gently against the tall green willows that grew close to the bank. After the violence of the previous day's storm a strange, brooding peace had settled upon the lush, semitropical land. This peace did little to lull the wild pain of Lannie's own tumultuous feelings.

Brandon's news had thrown her world into a tailspin. There was no way that she could continue teaching in her rural school as an unwed mother. She would have to leave Belle Rose, sell it eventually perhaps and make a new life for herself and the baby. A life that would never include her baby's father.

A tear pricked her lashes, and idly she wondered if

the baby would be like him. She hoped so. She longed for a son who would grow dark and tall. With her baby she could start fresh and slowly win his trust, that vital ingredient so necessary in all meaningful relationships.

But she had to start thinking practically and not emotionally, she told herself. Where would she go? What would she do?

Something snapped behind her. A twig or a branch had been carelessly stepped upon, and wildlife fluttered in the woods as though caught by surprise.

"Lannie . . ." That deepest, most masculine of voices drawled her name in a thickly slurred musical cadence that made her heart race at an uneven speed. "I know it's early. . . ."

She whirled. "Brandon . . ." she murmured softly in shock, her gentle gaze taking in his disheveled, tortured appearance. He was still wearing the same navy shirt and jeans; he hadn't shaved. His black hair was rumpled, and from the dark shadows beneath his eyes she guessed he hadn't slept any better than she. She caught the faint scent of liquor and realized he must have been drinking.

"I've been out in the car waiting for it to get late enough for me to see you. I must've finally dozed off and when I woke up I thought I saw you heading down this way. . . ."

He'd spent the night in his parked car in front of Belle Rose. "You look terrible," she murmured compassionately.

"Terrible," he mused dryly, his lips curving into what looked like a painful smile. "I couldn't look any worse than I feel. I've got the most damnable hangover." His head felt for the world like it was going to split in two. "But, nevertheless, it doesn't help matters for you to say I look awful. It's about time you learned how to compliment me if you're going to be my wife."

"What?"

"I'm asking you to marry me," he said in a husky tone that sounded far more confident than he felt.

His proposal was followed by a long silence that grew increasingly awkward as it lengthened until each stared uncertainly at the other in frozen anguish.

Was this why he looked so tortured, that he was forcing himself to do what he considered the right thing? The thought of him marrying her and not wanting to was even more painful than his complete rejection. She whitened, and her eyes glazed with pain.

"Not long ago, I would have given anything to hear you ask that question," she said in a quivering voice. "But not like this. I can't marry you, not now. Not because of the baby."

He was folding her into his arms, so that his warmth and vitality flooded her system and caused her to be achingly aware of every corded muscle that insinuated itself against her soft body. Oh, it felt so terribly, so deliciously wonderful to be wrapped in his arms!

"It's my baby, too, Lannie," he murmured into her perfumed hair, drinking in the scent of her as if he were starved for it. "And I want you, not just the baby and not because of the baby." She felt his warm breath against her temple, and it was an exquisite sensation. "I always have, even when I didn't want to," his low voice continued persuasively as he nuzzled her. "I love you, and I can't live without you. You've got to believe me." There was desperation in his deep voice that matched the desperation in her own soul. "I want to marry you. It's been hell these past weeks, wanting you, hoping that you would come to me. But you never did. That night after the barbeque I felt rotten because I'd made you make love to me against your will and it wasn't good for either of us. I made a vow to myself that night in the car that I'd never force you to do anything again.

And I won't. I'm *asking* you to marry me because I don't want to have to live without you. But if you can't, I'll help you with the baby any way I can."

She'd never heard him sound so humble, and she was deeply moved.

"But what about your distrust of me . . . and my relationship with Genevieve?"

"Yesterday when I saw how frantic you were about Denise, how you searched for her even when you were ill, how you stood by her until John came, how you attended to a thousand other little caring details for her—I realized how wrong I've been about you. How could I expect you to want my child or me? I couldn't face myself and how I've treated you. Last night I went out and drank too much, but even then I couldn't forget what I've done to you. When I came home stumbling drunk in the middle of the night and feeling desperate because I'd lost you due to my own stupidity, Genevieve came to my room and told me why she gave you the money." He paused. "We talked about your accident and your temporary blindness and how much you've changed, how wrong I'd been about you. Genevieve's always believed in you, always known you to be the good person that you really are. We talked a long time about my mother, and she told me over and over again that you were nothing like her."

"Genevieve told me about your mother, Brandon, one afternoon when she was here."

"I think secretly I've always been afraid of falling in love, of really caring for a woman for fear I'd lose her. I've thrown myself into my work and chased around the world to escape a kind of pain I was afraid to face a second time."

"That's not hard to understand, Brandon."

"Lannie, I don't know what really happened in the past, and I don't even care any more. But I don't believe you stole that bracelet."

"I didn't."

He was staring deeply into her eyes, his eyes filled with trust and love. "I know that, my love," he said, "and maybe someday you'll trust me enough to tell me what really happened."

"Maybe someday," she agreed softly. Her fingertip reached up and gently outlined the bridge of his nose, hesitating at the sensual line of his mouth.

"You were protecting someone?"

"Yes," she admitted for the first time, tracing her fingers along the edge of his lips.

"I have something for you," he said, removing his hand from her flowing hair and searching the depths of his pocket.

Then very carefully he kissed her left hand that caressed his mouth, and reaching for it with his own hand, he slid an enormous diamond engagement ring onto her finger. Then he brought her hand back to his lips again and kissed her fingers warmly again.

"I bought this weeks ago, before I knew about the baby."

She held out her hand and looked at it. The ring blazed like a brand of diamonds against her olive skin, branding her forever as the one woman he loved.

"Oh, Brandon, it's so beautiful. . . ."

"Not nearly so beautiful as you, my love." His lips were in her hair, and she was shivering at the intensity of emotion they evoked as they moved over her.

"Yesterday you said I was scrawny," she just managed, the words quivering with the passion he evoked.

"And so, my pet, I'm not the only one who likes compliments," he teased, stepping back and smiling jauntily down at her, some of the pain leaving his eyes as he looked into her own that shone brilliantly with her deep love for him.

She felt radiant with happiness, and stretching onto her tiptoes, her soft body shaped to the solid frame of his, her lips met his in a smoldering kiss that deepened until they were both quite breathless, trembling as they held one another in an embrace that symbolized their everlasting love.

"Mark," she whispered, "I love you so. . . ."

"No more than I love you."

If you enjoyed this book...

...you will enjoy a Special Edition Book Club membership even more.

It will bring you each new title, as soon as it is published every month, delivered right to your door.

15-Day Free Trial Offer

We will send you 6 new Silhouette Special Editions to keep for 15 days absolutely free! If you decide not to keep them, send them back to us, you pay nothing. But if you enjoy them as much as we think you will, keep them and pay the invoice enclosed with your trial shipment. You will then automatically become a member of the Special Edition Book Club and receive 6 more romances every month. There is no minimum number of books to buy and you can cancel at any time.

Silhouette Special Edition

MORE ROMANCE FOR
A SPECIAL WAY TO RELAX

$1.95 each

1 ☐ TERMS OF SURRENDER Dailey
2 ☐ INTIMATE STRANGERS Hastings
3 ☐ MEXICAN RHAPSODY Dixon
4 ☐ VALAQUEZ BRIDE Vitek
5 ☐ PARADISE POSTPONED Converse
6 ☐ SEARCH FOR A NEW DAWN Douglass
7 ☐ SILVER MIST Stanford
8 ☐ KEYS TO DANIEL'S HOUSE Halston
9 ☐ ALL OUR TOMORROWS Baxter
10 ☐ TEXAS ROSE Thiels
11 ☐ LOVE IS SURRENDER Thornton
12 ☐ NEVER GIVE YOUR HEART Sinclair
13 ☐ BITTER VICTORY Beckman
14 ☐ EYE OF THE HURRICANE Keene
15 ☐ DANGEROUS MAGIC James
16 ☐ MAYAN MOON Carr
17 ☐ SO MANY TOMORROWS John
18 ☐ A WOMAN'S PLACE Hamilton
19 ☐ DECEMBER'S WINE Shaw
20 ☐ NORTHERN LIGHTS Musgrave
21 ☐ ROUGH DIAMOND Hastings
22 ☐ ALL THAT GLITTERS Howard
23 ☐ LOVE'S GOLDEN SHADOW Charles
24 ☐ GAMBLE OF DESIRE Dixon
25 ☐ TEARS AND RED ROSES Hardy
26 ☐ A FLIGHT OF SWALLOWS Scott
27 ☐ A MAN WITH DOUBTS Wisdom

28 ☐ THE FLAMING TREE Ripy
29 ☐ YEARNING OF ANGELS Bergen
30 ☐ BRIDE IN BARBADOS Stephens
31 ☐ TEARS OF YESTERDAY Baxter
32 ☐ A TIME TO LOVE Douglass
33 ☐ HEATHER'S SONG Palmer
34 ☐ MIXED BLESSING Sinclair
35 ☐ STORMY CHALLENGE James
36 ☐ FOXFIRE LIGHT Dailey
37 ☐ MAGNOLIA MOON Stanford
38 ☐ WEB OF PASSION John
39 ☐ AUTUMN HARVEST Milan
40 ☐ HEARTSTORM Converse
41 ☐ COLLISION COURSE Halston
42 ☐ PROUD VINTAGE Drummond
43 ☐ ALL SHE EVER WANTED Shaw
44 ☐ SUMMER MAGIC Eden
45 ☐ LOVE'S TENDER TRIAL Charles
46 ☐ AN INDEPENDENT WIFE Howard
47 ☐ PRIDE'S POSSESSION Stephens
48 ☐ LOVE HAS ITS REASONS Ferrell
49 ☐ A MATTER OF TIME Hastings
50 ☐ FINDERS KEEPERS Browning
51 ☐ STORMY AFFAIR Trent
52 ☐ DESIGNED FOR LOVE Sinclair
53 ☐ GODDESS OF THE MOON Thomas
54 ☐ THORNE'S WAY Hohl

Silhouette Special Edition

MORE ROMANCE FOR
A SPECIAL WAY TO RELAX

55 ☐ SUN LOVER Stanford

56 ☐ SILVER FIRE Wallace

57 ☐ PRIDE'S RECKONING Thornton

58 ☐ KNIGHTLY LOVE Douglass

59 ☐ THE HEART'S VICTORY Roberts

60 ☐ ONCE AND FOREVER Thorne

61 ☐ TENDER DECEPTION Beckman

62 ☐ DEEP WATERS Bright

63 ☐ LOVE WITH A PERFECT STRANGER Wallace

64 ☐ MIST OF BLOSSOMS Converse

65 ☐ HANDFUL OF SKY Cates

66 ☐ A SPORTING AFFAIR Mikels

67 ☐ AFTER THE RAIN Shaw

68 ☐ CASTLES IN THE AIR Sinclair

69 ☐ SORREL SUNSET Dalton

70 ☐ TRACES OF DREAMS Clare

71 ☐ MOONSTRUCK Skillern

72 ☐ NIGHT MUSIC Belmont

73 ☐ SEASON OF SEDUCTION Taylor

74 ☐ UNSPOKEN PAST Wisdom

75 ☐ SUMMER RHAPSODY John

76 ☐ TOMORROW'S MEMORY Ripy

77 ☐ PRELUDE TO PASSION Bergen

78 ☐ FORTUNE'S PLAY Gladstone

$2.25 each

79 ☐ AN ACT OF LOVE Hastings

80 ☐ FAST COURTING Douglass

81 ☐ LOOKING GLASS LOVE Thornton

82 ☐ CAPTIVE OF FATE McKenna

83 ☐ BRAND OF DIAMONDS Major

84 ☐ THE SPLENDORED SKY Stephens

LOOK FOR LOVE'S GENTLE CHAINS
BY SONDRA STANFORD AVAILABLE IN MAY

SILHOUETTE SPECIAL EDITION, Department SE/2
1230 Avenue of the Americas
New York, NY 10020

Please send me the books I have checked above. I am enclosing $_____
(please add 50¢ to cover postage and handling. NYS and NYC residents
please add appropriate sales tax). Send check or money order—no cash or
C.O.D.'s please. Allow six weeks for delivery.

NAME _____

ADDRESS _____

CITY _____ STATE/ZIP _____

Silhouette Special Edition

Coming Next Month

Enchanted Surrender by Patti Beckman

Haunted by her past, Sandy Carver worked to build a new life—one with no room for love. But Carl Van Helmut insisted that she find a place for love—and for him.

The Marriage Bonus by Carole Halston

An unhappy stint as a "country club wife" had left Charlene longing for real love and a real man and in Burt, her high school sweetheart, she found both.

Jessica: Take Two by Diana Dixon

As if redoing a scene for one of her films, actress Jessica Steele had a chance to try again with the one man who had mattered: her ex-husband, Grahme Foreman.

Paradiso by Antonia Saxon

Pat Jessup thought she had found her own private paradise in Mexico. But it was a paradise without passion—until she met local mayor Santos Ribera.

Sweet Adversity by Kate Meriwether

Probation officer Meredith Jennings gave her whole heart to her job, until it led her into the chambers of Judge Warren Baxter, where a whole new challenge awaited her.

Passion's Victory by Jennifer Justin

Five years had passed since Alexandra O'Neill had been in the arms of Matt Farraday, but nothing—not time, not space—could diminish their passion for each other.

READERS' COMMENTS ON SILHOUETTE SPECIAL EDITIONS:

"I just finished reading the first six Silhouette Special Edition Books and I had to take the opportunity to write you and tell you how much I enjoyed them. I enjoyed all the authors in this series. Best wishes on your Silhouette Special Editions line and many thanks."

—B.H.*, Jackson, OH

"The Special Editions are really special and I enjoyed them very much! I am looking forward to next month's books."

—R.M.W.*, Melbourne, FL

"I've just finished reading four of your first six Special Editions and I enjoyed them very much. I like the more sensual detail and longer stories. I will look forward each month to your new Special Editions."

—L.S.*, Visalia, CA

"Silhouette Special Editions are — 1.) Superb! 2.) Great! 3.) Delicious! 4.) Fantastic! . . . Did I leave anything out? These are books that an adult woman can read . . . I love them!"

—H.C.*, Monterey Park, CA

*names available on request